Praise for *The Clairvoyant of Calle Ocho*

"Bad decisions, they say, make great stories, and Mariela, our shortsighted clairvoyant, has made a disastrous romantic decision, to date her married tenant, Hector. What could go wrong? Everything can. *The Clairvoyant of Calle Ocho* reminds me of why I started reading in the first place—to be enchanted, to be carried away from my world and dropped into a world more vivid and incandescent. Anjanette Delgado loves her characters, even the miscreants, and makes us love them too. Here is a literary mystery novel that carries the news of Miami's Cuban community to a larger world. You're going to thank me for telling you about *The Clairvoyant of Calle Ocho*. Go buy it now!"

—John Dufresne, author of *No Regrets, Coyote*

"Through an unforgettable cast of characters, Delgado captures the passions that pulse through a vibrant Miami neighborhood, and gives us a thrilling, hilarious, and mysterious romp that will captivate and charm you to the end. I devoured *The Clairvoyant of Calle Ocho*—or rather, it devoured me."

—Patricia Engel, author of *It's Not Love, It's Just Paris*

The Clairvoyant
of Calle Ocho

ANJANETTE DELGADO

KENSINGTON BOOKS
www.kensingtonbooks.com

KENSINGTON BOOKS are published by

Kensington Publishing Corp.
119 West 40th Street
New York, NY 10018

All Kensington titles, imprints, and distributed lines are available at special quantity discounts for bulk purchases for sales promotion, premiums, fund-raising, educational, or institutional use.

Special book excerpts or customized printings can also be created to fit specific needs. For details, write or phone the office of the Kensington Special Sales Manager: Attn. Special Sales Department. Kensington Publishing Corp., 119 West 40th Street, New York, NY 10018. Phone: 1-800-221-2647.

Kensington and the K logo Reg. U.S. Pat. & TM Off.

eISBN-13: 978-1-61773-391-8
eISBN-10: 1-61773-391-1
First Kensington Electronic Edition: September 2014

ISBN-13: 978-1-61773-390-1
ISBN-10: 1-61773-390-3
First Kensington Trade Paperback Printing: September 2014

10 9 8 7 6 5 4 3 2 1

Printed in the United States of America

For my daughters, Lyan and Anjie, because
they never give up on being happy

Acknowledgments

This book owes its biggest debt to Lynne Barrett, who nurtured it, and me, for close to two years. I also want to thank John Dufresne for his incredible heart and for being such an inspiration to me over the years.

To Patricia Engel, for her friendship and support.

To the Bread Loaf Writers' Conference team in Vermont for two of the best weeks of my life.

To all of my students at the Florida Literary Arts Center and to Mitch Kaplan and Cristina Nosti of Books and Books for their warm embrace and support. To Mitch for letting me make a character out of him, and to Cristina for giving me a reason to like the cover of this book. :)

To my "kids" at Telemundo NBC's digital unit who share my days and, for the most part, leave me alone to write at night.

To my fabulous agent and editors, Andy Ross, Mercedes Fernandez, Margaret Guerra Rogers, Silvia Matute, and Casandra Badillo.

To my best friend, Migdalia, and to the other three Ms who read horrible, early versions of this book: Maria Cristina, Melba and Marisa, and to my other moms, Berta and Helga.

But most of all to my family: Vanessa, Veronica, Dany, Chloe, Lucy, Yadira, and Solange.

I love you all.

Chapter 1

No hay peor ciego que el que no quiere ver. There is none more blind than he who doesn't want to see.

In my life, I've found that this is most true of women married to unfaithful men. As for the mistress in the equation, the truth is that being the other woman is a decision. A conscious one. Don't believe any woman who tells you she didn't know what she was doing when the penis belonging to your husband just happened to land inside her vagina. Walk away if she starts with "I didn't know," "We started out as friends," or "By the time I realized what was happening, it was too late and we were in love." Because this woman isn't stupid, innocent, or deluded. She's lying.

I can assert this with such conviction because I've been both: the blind woman married to a man who likes to spread it around and the other woman with no excuse.

Or at least that's who I was that afternoon, casually checking into the Hotel St. Michel in Coral Gables. Me, walking into the freshly cleaned room with its French hay-yellow walls, blue-and-white chinoiserie-patterned linens, and dark wood furniture. Me lighting tea lights inside the whiskey glasses I'd lugged here in my environmentally conscious, recycled cotton "Feed" tote, before slipping into the sheer, navy blue, boatneck baby-doll I'd picked up at a Ross Dress for Less discount store for a quarter of its Victoria's Secret price. And none other than *moi,* waiting for my married lover, Hector Ferro, to walk through the door.

Yep. All me.

A new me. An unmarried me. A me without an owner. Where before I'd wasted life hours straightening my long, wavy black hair because "my husband likes it this way," I now sported honey-colored, neck-length curls around my too-pale face and wide-set brown eyes. Where I used to wear A-line skirts to hide my protruding backside, I now sported snug-enough jeans all the time (high-waisted, low-waisted, skinny, or destroyed to a literal inch of their useful lives), like a symbolic uniform, to show I belonged with the strong, the sexy, and the free.

As I walked around the cozy little room making myself at home, early afternoon sun shafts of light seemed to slip in through the shutters, igniting the yellow walls and making it seem as if the whole room were aglow. In that light, it was easy to imagine I was in Paris instead of Miami, to accept the role of mistress, to allow myself its perks. I was glowing too, more so at thirty-nine than I ever had at twenty-nine, and looked as radiant as if I'd just had a facial, thanks to the green vegetable shakes my neighbor Iris swore by and had taught me to make. That, and a recipe for Dr. Etti's fruity rooibos tea drink, had helped me eliminate almost thirty pounds from my five-foot-five-inch frame in mere months. (Place pineapple and apple peels and a handful of goji berries in a pot of hot water. Allow to boil. Add a few tea bags of African red bush, also called rooibos, set aside to cool, and then refrigerate. Drink with a squirt of raw blue agave nectar for a delicious diuretic.)

Of course, there was more to my glow than tea. I was now, for the first time in my life, enjoying being the object of a man's reckless desire and nothing more. I'd played the role of the betrayed wife twice before. Wasn't I entitled to be on the other side of the broken vows for a change?

A single rap on the hotel room door told me he was here, and I rushed to open it, loving that he jumped all these hoops for no other reason than to make love to me, while resting in the complacent knowledge that the unfaithful ways of the man now slowly and knowingly taking me in with his eyes were someone else's problem.

Hector was in his late forties and attractive in a sophisticated, sexy, citizen-of-the-world kind of way: strong jaw, dark blue eyes that crinkled at the slightest smile, ash-brown hair parted on the side like a newscaster's, and the lean, lanky build of those who can eat what they want without putting on weight.

He'd been a college professor in Argentina and still dressed like one: tan slacks, slightly rumpled cotton shirts always open to reveal crisp, white undershirts, and the same careless khaki trench coat that he must have worn around his Buenos Aires campus, because even in Miami, he never took it off, rain or shine. I could imagine him walking to classes, absorbed in his thoughts, never imagining his country's economy would get so bad he'd have to emigrate to the United States with his wife, a nutritionist of some sort, and use what savings he'd protected to buy a small bookstore in Miami's far-from-gentrified Little Havana.

He was one of those men whose thinning hair did nothing to diminish the power of his charm and undeniable masculinity. I could almost see how his unruly brows coupled with the smile I'd come to know so well, always somewhere between properly friendly and slightly mischievous, might have been hard to resist for even the most emotionally stable of his students.

He was smiling that smile now, as his eyes took in my feet and then my hips, lingering for a moment on my breasts. Next: the outlining of my mouth, and finally a full stop right into my eyes, before grinning with feigned modesty, as if the evil of his thoughts were too much even for him.

"Hey," I said.

"Ey," he returned my greeting, forgetting the *h,* stepping into the room, and kicking the door shut with his foot before wrapping his arms around me and walking forward, all the while holding me tight, so that I was forced to walk backward in a jumbled tango two-step past the suite's little salon and into the bedroom area, where I heard him toss what I knew would be a book onto the bed behind me.

"I brought you *somesing,*" he said into my ear, the thick Argentinean accent that seemed to underline every sound before it came out of his mouth seeming, to me, even more sexy than usual that day.

I scurried away to see what message might be hidden in the book he'd chosen to bring me this time. It was the pocket version of *Chiquita,* a novel about a real-life Cuban burlesque dancer who drove men crazy in the late 1800s despite being little more than two feet tall. I smiled. Hector had placed a piece of cigarette box foil on page 405, marking the beginning of a paragraph that I proceeded to read out loud while fighting his efforts to liberate my body from the baby-doll.

"A scandal like that was in no one's best interest so, with all the pain of their souls, the lovers had to separate," I read, then closed the book, confused.

"What's wrong, *flaca?*" he asked, using his favorite endearment for me, which means "slim" and is common in Argentina.

"Trying to tell me something, mister?"

"What? No! Of course not. The marker, eh, how you say? It must've slipped. You can see how sophisticated it is." He smiled, taking off the trench and slipping off his shoes. "Nah, I just love the author. And, you know, he's local, comes into the store a lot, so, if you like it, I can introduce you to him one of these days."

"Oh."

"Why? Were you scared I was telling you *somesing?*"

"Pu-leeze," I said, pursing my lips to the side like a good Cuban.

"You do look a little scared," he said, coming closer with pretend concern.

"Nope. I don't do scared, and, frankly, my dear, you think too damn much of yourself," I finished, making my voice deep and husky, my best imitation of Rhett Butler.

He gave me the puzzled look he saved for trying to figure out what movie I was quoting or referring to.

"*Gone with the Wind*? 'Frankly, my dear, I don't give a damn'?" I said.

"Aaaaah, my God, why don't you quote books? Books make good quotes."

"It *is* a book. A book with over a thousand pages I'll never read when there's a perfectly good movie to tell me the story."

"But if you read the book, you'd know the quote is 'My dear, I don't give a damn.' None of this 'frankly' business. Simple. As it should be. That's why you should quote, and read, books."

"Yes, Professor Ferro," I mocked him, making a mental note to buy the book and read at least the first few chapters, see what I'd been missing.

That was one of the great things about my affair with Hector. Though I never went to college, I wanted to learn and had long before decided to make up for the formal education I'd denied myself by reading everything I could get my hands on. I'd spent countless hours learning all kinds of things: art history, math, philosophy, politics, biology, and enjoying nothing as much as I enjoyed fiction. Literary or trashy, it didn't matter. I craved stories and felt frustrated when my limited education prevented me from fully understanding the old English expressions in a great love story like *Wuthering Heights*. (I'm sure I'm still missing a lot of it, though I've read it twice.) But now, with Hector, it was like having a private tutor who could unlock any book's secrets. He called it providing context. I called it finally connecting the dots I'd been accumulating for years and loved the thrill of "getting it" when he explained something I'd missed.

"Oooh, forget what I'm saying. A beautiful woman in my hotel room and me a terrrrible, terrrrrible bore," he was saying now. "Why should I tell you what to quote? We're different people with different lives. If you want to watch the movie, you watch the movie, and I'll read the book. Perfect, eh? We'll complement each other."

"Exactly," I said, unsure I liked this interpretation of us.

"Too bad I'll never know what you're quoting," he said, kissing me, his hands searching my willing hips, the keys to my common sense relinquished so many months ago.

"We're not that different," I said, eyes closed, trying to fix what was bothering me. "You're the one who says we have the story chemistry, and—"

"Wait! What is this?" he asked suddenly, focusing the tips of his fingers on a particular spot along my outer thigh.

"What's what?"

"This," he said seriously, lowering himself until he was sitting on his haunches, pretending to examine my thigh with his hands, dragging the tip of his index finger softly over my upper leg, as if outlining something.

"What?"

"This, eh, like a circle, right here."

"Oh. That. It's a birthmark," I said. Then trying to give the smooth, round, cinnamon-colored stain a positive spin, I added, "My mother had it too," as if that settled that and made it a family heirloom.

"A birthmark. Interesting," he said, closing his eyes and kissing the fleshy top part of my leg where he'd been "tracing."

Then, "Hey! Where did it go?"

I shrugged my shoulders innocently, holding my arms straight and close to my body in order to help the baby-doll fall to the floor, then putting my hands on my hips and looking directly into his eyes.

"A vast improvement," he said, eyes slowly traveling up my body, reaching and meeting my gaze.

"I thought I'd show you I have nothing to hide," I said.

"Clever," he responded, imitating my pure business tone. "Maybe now we'll be able to find it."

"Maybe," I said, thinking men can be endearing when they're being ridiculous and preferring this Hector to the one who lived to argue and to lecture, but could never admit to being wrong.

"Unless you're hiding it," he said, kissing a line across my pelvis. "You do understand, I must be thorough in my search?" he continued, effortlessly coming up to my belly button, kissing it, then my right rib cage. Then, "Wait! I think it may have hidden under here," he said, slipping his palm under the slight curving of my breast as if to cup it. "Um-huh. Yes. Right here."

"I . . . I don't think so," I managed.

"Yes, the, eh, wadduyucallit? The birthmark. It is hiding, like a spy. Unfortunately, she leaves us no choice but to coax her out. It can get very warm under there. Very dangerous for her. May I?"

I wanted to laugh, but humor had always been my downfall, and I was too excited, despite myself.

"All right. If you must, then do what you will, but my birthmark and I have principles and will not reveal a word no matter what you do," I said, giving up.

"Ah. A defiant one, are you?"

"Yes, sir. Yes, I am."

"Very well. Then I have no choice but to teach you both a little compliance," he said.

"Compliance?"

"Um-huh," he mumbled, his tongue already doing a deft reconnaissance of the sensitive hollows within my mouth, his hands moving down my back like a pair of hikers carefully descending a dangerous peak.

"Hector," I began when his palms reached my buttocks, steadying them only to press himself against me, his scent seeping into me like the ink of a henna tattoo, his mouth kissing my words away, stopping to peer at me only once it was clear I had nothing intelligible to say.

"You do understand I must examine the area if we're going to find this, eh, cunning birthmark," he said then, smiling knowingly, teasingly.

"Well. Like I said. If you must," I responded, trying to take off his shirt despite my shaky hands and buckling knees.

But he leaned in, steadying me at the waist with one hand and interrupting my progress by bringing my left breast to his mouth with the other, kissing and rubbing his lips softly against it, as if outlining the pink-brown edge of my nipple with his breath, until we both fell back onto the bed, I as convinced into "compliance" by the clever approach of his seductive imagination as by the skill of his hands and the warmth of his breath.

When a loud sigh escaped me, he whispered, "Shhhhhhh. Please! I'm supposed to be stealthy, surprising my enemy. You will scare her away!"

Which made me burst out laughing.

"I resent that," he said then. "Especially in the middle of a tactic mission."

"You mean tactile mission?" I asked, aware of his breath

slowly traveling toward the foot of the bed, south of my heart, along the length of my body.

"Yes, very good. I always, eh, wondered how . . . you say . . . that word . . . correctly."

"Tac—"

"Shhhhhh, *flaca,* quiet," he whispered. "I believe I have found her."

Chapter 2

I wish I could say it was being the other woman that got me into all the trouble that followed. But it wasn't. What really got me into trouble was being a lousy clairvoyant.

It started with the bad marriages. They were my first overt signs of blindness.

This is what happened: at twenty-four, and then at thirty-five, I married two apparently different men who turned out to be exactly the same. Both cheated on me, and both must have studied from the same user's manual (as in manual for using others), because when I divorced them, both fought me for alimony and half of all I owned despite the fact that *they* were the ones who left *me* for other women. Why didn't I know they were cheaters? Wouldn't even a bad clairvoyant have had a clue at some point?

Well, that depends. It's true that understanding men has nothing to do with predicting the future and everything to do with being able to see clearly what is already right in front of you. In other words, if you listen to what he's actually saying, you'll never have to wonder what he's "really trying to tell" you. You'll know what's going to happen between you because very often what's going to happen is the direct result of what is happening now. (Best clairvoyance lesson I ever learned.)

But here's the thing: Psychics use feelings to see. What this means is that when our emotions are involved, our sight goes to hell. And how can your emotions not be involved when what is happening, is happening to you? Which explains how we can see *your* future, while being blinder than a severely myopic bat about our own screwed-up lives.

But I didn't know any of this back then. In fact, not knowing this little tidbit was exactly what had made me renounce clairvoyance after my mother was diagnosed with breast cancer during my senior year of high school. I thought, *What kind of a clairvoyant am I? How could I not have known?* To the eighteen-year-old me, I'd as good as killed my mother, or at least failed to save her, and was no better than an incompetent security guard asleep on the job and drooling on that guest sign-in pad. If my psychic power had seen it sooner, she might have lived. But it didn't, and in my great guilt, and shame, I decided right then and there to kill my so-called gift by ignoring it forever.

And do you know what happens to a woman who goes through life refusing to see beyond the tip of her nose? She loses her "trouble radar" when it comes to men, that's what. How else could I have been so dense as to marry the wrong man twice, and then decide that the only way to protect myself from loss was to become the other woman. To stick to married men. Wonderful, short-term men with no long-term expectations swirling about them. Men incapable of causing me further loss of free and clear Miami real estate or of my own estate of real being. Men I'd have to be crazy to grow attached to.

Or so I thought.

Because it was just this fearful, over-self-protective thinking that resulted in the very thing I was trying to avoid: I fell in love with one of them.

His name was Jorge, and he was, oh, so wrong. A free spirit, childlike, light, and impulsive, despite being in his mid-thirties then and only three years younger than I. He missed the family he'd left behind in Cuba and worked as a chef, while saving to bring the wife he'd married during a visit to his homeland. He was fun and kind and foolish, and very, very sexy. And he knew food. It was his religion and his native language, and he knew how to use it to fill you up until you cried with relief, or until what ailed you became loose, or until you loved him and became crazy with fear, with knowing that he could just as easily use this language of his to conquer your heart, as to demolish it.

So what did I do? I ran. Straight into the arms of the first "less dangerous" married man I found, which happened to be my married tenant of several years, Hector.

Yep, it must have been the fear of heartbreak that made me stupid, convincing me that I could get away with using Hector to protect myself from my own heart, that I could have an affair with him, right under the nose of his wife, Olivia. It was also this thinking that made me unable to see the terrible thing that would happen *after* he broke up with me, when it was too late for anything, really.

That's when I had one of my dreams, the first in years. It was a strange dream and in it, all I knew was that something very bad was about to happen and that *I* was somehow responsible. It was just a dream, so I ignored it. I mean, when was the last time my instincts had pointed me in the right direction?

Unfortunately for me, for the first time in years, this time they turned out to be absolutely right.

Chapter 3

Yes, it was good for me too, thank you very much. Sex with Hector at the Hotel St. Michel always was.

But.

For the first time in eight months, the moment it was over, he went into the bathroom to wash instead of lounging in bed talking about a million silly things with me. Which is probably the only reason his earlier comment came back to haunt me, loud as an ambulance siren, as I lay in bed covered only with a sheet: "We are different people with different lives." And then there was the line in the book. What was that about?

Despite the fabulous foreplay, *"somesing"* was not right. How did I know? Because the one infallible thing men have taught me is that if a man is in a big rush to get to another area of his life right after sex—for whatever reason, no matter how reasonable, and even if only mentally—something's wrong, and you don't need to be clairvoyant to know it. No exceptions.

"Everything all right?" I asked when he came out of the bathroom.

"Yes. Sure. Why?"

"Yes-sure-why—because you seem anxious and rushed. That's yes-sure-why."

"I'm not rushed."

But he didn't step out onto the suite's narrow balcony in his boxers to smoke his cigar or try to scare me into thinking he'd pee right onto some unsuspecting doorman standing solicitously by the St. Michel's entrance.

"Should we order coffee? Maybe one of those little lava chocolate soufflés you like so much?" I asked.

"Sorry. I can't. I have this bookstore thing, this meeting. It's very important. You stay and rest if you want to."

I looked at the digital clock on the nightstand.

"A meeting at almost five in the afternoon?"

"Yes."

"On a Wednesday?"

"Yes, on a Wednesday, and, Mariela, please. Whatever you do, don't do that, okay?"

I knew what he meant: Don't break the sacred mistress oath and start acting like a wife.

"You're right. I'm being silly," I said, jumping up and grabbing the underwear, T-shirt, and jeans I'd worn to the hotel and heading to the bathroom. "I have things to do too. Landlord things. In fact, you should give me a ride back to the building."

"Now?"

"Yes, now," I said, mimicking his tone. "What's wrong? You not headed down there?"

He sighed, looking more than a little displeased. "Yes, of course. Go take a shower then, so we can leave."

"I need to deal with a few things," I said, as if I had to justify myself.

He was silent. Didn't even give me an absentminded nod. Something was definitely up. This was the opposite of the detail-oriented, experience-motivated Hector I knew prided himself on "taking care" of a woman "before, during, and after."

"I can always just get a cab," I called out before closing the bathroom door.

"No, no. I'll just, eh, drop you off a few blocks away," he said, doing his usual pause when using American colloquialisms.

They fascinated him, always making him think about their literal meaning.

"Nothing we haven't done before, right?" I said.

In fact, we'd done it plenty of times in the eight months since our affair began because, as I might have told you before, Hector, and his wife, happened to be my tenants.

I own a small fourplex building the size and shape of a big house, with two floors, and two apartments per floor. I lived in *apartamento uno*, while Hector and Olivia had lived in *apartamento cuatro* for almost three years now. I didn't plan such an inconvenient arrangement, but you can see why it wouldn't have done to carry on anywhere near his home or mine, which were as close to the same thing as they could be without being exactly so.

My other tenants were Gustavo and Ellie. Gustavo's *apartamento dos* was located directly across from mine on the first floor, both our homes having the entryway on one side and the stairway to the second floor on the other. He was a single guy in his early thirties who worked at a neighborhood hardware store by day and sculpted kinetic metal works of art by night.

Upstairs in *apartamento tres,* directly above mine, and across from Hector and Olivia's *apartamento cuatro,* was Ellie, who was in her mid-twenties, worked as a cashier at the McDonald's on Calle Ocho and Fifteenth Avenue, and had begun to make a habit of not paying rent until the month was close to over and I'd threatened her with eviction.

"All right, *flaca,* just hurry up, please," he said, resigned, heading for the balcony, cigar in hand. "You know, you should really buy a car. It doesn't have to be new. Just something to get around."

"You know I'm scared of driving, and don't say, 'Get over it.' I've already tried."

"I know, but this is Miami. Who lives in Miami without a car?"

"I do," I said. (Where was this coming from? Hector knew I

worked from home and did most of my errands and shopping online.) "And why do I suddenly need a car, exactly?"

He looked at me as if the exact reason were entirely obvious, then said, "You should think about a car," and stepped out onto the balcony.

I got into the shower wondering what was suddenly so wrong.

As I lathered up, a distantly familiar fog began to envelop me so subtly that, at first, I thought it was just all that steaming hot water this side of the closed bathroom door. Then the fog spoke. Somewhere inside of me, it said, "This is the beginning of the end." And that was all it said. But before you go saying, "Well, duh," let me tell you that this is *exactly* how we all deceive ourselves when trying to figure out our love affairs. In fact, I said the same thing to myself that afternoon. I thought, *What's so special about thinking that it's ending with my lover, when he's so suddenly, and for the first time in our history, in a rush to leave my side after sex?*

Having ignored my instincts for so long, I'd lost the ability to appreciate the difference between my own conscious mind and a message given to me with a certainty and force that I could physically feel. The fog had not said, "Maybe he's getting tired of you. Maybe it's over," as my own insecurity would've said, and did. It read, "This is the beginning of the end." I say "read" because the effect was one of seeing words in a foreign language that slowly became clear and understandable when translated.

I should've listened, but it had been a very long time since I'd been clairvoyant. I was sure my inner sight was dead, buried alive, or lost somewhere inside me, and never even considered the possibility that my gift might be making a half-assed appearance in a last-ditch effort to save me from myself before it was too late. This is why, instead of paying attention to the unusual strength of that "doom and gloom" mist spraying its troubled essence over me, I chose to "use my head." I told myself that his behavior was just reminding me of all those other unhappy endings. Then I rationalized: Maybe he was worried. Maybe something was wrong with his bookstore. Maybe he was just having an off day. All I needed to do was stop worrying, and if I should be right and this was the "beginning of over," so be it. Hector was my lover, not the love of my life, I reminded myself.

Fifteen minutes later, we were in his restored to perfection, black 1993 Saab 900 Turbo, silently heading toward Little Havana.

"Have I done something wrong?"

"No," he answered in a tone I'd never heard him use before.

I stared at him until he sighed, turned on NPR's *All Things Considered,* and without taking his eyes off the road, put his right hand on my knee before saying, "Look, sorry about being such a *boludo.* How you say in English? The one with the *j?*"

"Jerk?"

"Yes, but, no, eh—"

"Jackass."

"That one. Look, I'm sorry, eh? I just have a lot of *estress.* You understand, right? It's okay?" he asked, smiling at me now.

"Of course. Of course, it's okay," I said, pulling his earlobe playfully and noticing, with a sinking feeling, how relieved I felt the instant he chose to speak to me as if nothing were wrong. So relieved as to believe that maybe nothing was, and going so far as to marvel over my own ability to *"estress"* myself out over absolutely nothing.

Chapter 4

So now I'm going to have to tell you about the list.

I believe every woman (except virgins and, maybe, nuns) has a list, be it written out on actual paper or on the multicolored Post-its of her memory.

No, not the list of every quality she wants in a man (which only works if you work on being all the things on the list first, by the way). The list I'm talking about is the one with the names of every man she's ever slept with. Or every man she ever slept with whom she really loved. Or every man she ever slept with who was truly fabulous in bed, or whatever else is important for her to keep track of about the men she's slept with.

And no matter what that is, or whether your list is made up of men or women for that matter, the parameters you've chosen to impose on that list of who you've let inside you, and what has happened afterward, say more about your past, present, and future than any tarot card reading ever will.

Mine listed every man I'd ever slept with who had given me a long-lasting reason to wish I hadn't.

But, to be fair, you do choose them, these men, for a reason, and my reasons could always be traced back to my mother.

And since there's no easy way to, say, slip in this bit of information, I'm just going to say it: My mother was a prostitute.

A smart, terribly beautiful, devastatingly voluptuous one.

And unlike the dollar-store sluts who sometimes pollute the stoop of my Coffee Park fourplex walking around like hens without heads, she had a business strategy, a niche she liked to call "womanly kindness." She knew there was a good possibility that a powerful man willing to pay for it was a man whose self-esteem was on vacation. She also knew that such a man craved a belly laugh when he made a joke and an admiring glance when he dropped his pants, more than he craved the bursting, raging, cataclysmic orgasms he was, purportedly, risking his marriage and reputation for. The reason my mother knew, or thought she knew, so much about men with power is that they were the only kind she'd "date"—powerful (and possibly corrupt) power brokers, bankers, and politicians, that was the rule. Good thing it was the late seventies and there were plenty of those to go around in Miami.

"Be nice to your men when you grow up, Mariela," she'd say while braiding my hair on lazy Sunday afternoons. "Pick 'em up when they're feeling down and they'll never be able to forget you."

But forget me they did, which goes to show that one woman's fortune-making niche can be another's losing streak.

And if my mother's illness was the reason I was never much of a butterfly as a young woman, her lifestyle was the reason I grew up yearning for love, for a community, for a simple life, the opposite of what she'd had.

After she died, I sold our house and filled my hours with renting and managing the properties she had left me: a mid-century bungalow in the southeastern neighborhood of Pinecrest, a Mediterranean cottage in central Coral Gables, and the Coffee Park fourplex. I also worked part time at Lion Video, a small, artsy store specializing in foreign and hard-to-find films, and spent all my free time and money watching movies at the mall, missing her terribly and trying to go on with life all by myself.

Then I met my first husband, Alejandro.

He was forty-one years old to my twenty-five when we married. An avid reader who taught children with special needs, he had absolutely no money and was as different from my mother's "boyfriends" as I could possibly find.

At first, we were happy, probably because I didn't know any better. I was young and welcomed his guidance and his stable routines. I liked being the wife and playing house and dreaming of the children we'd have. Six years later, I'd grown up and begun to enjoy him less, to feel stifled by his stability and bored by the sameness and the arbitrary nature of our, or rather his, routines.

It didn't help that he seemed to save all his patience for his students. He was from Spain, where it's considered slightly vulgar, but not uncommon, to tell people to go take it in the ass as a slang way of sending someone to hell. *"A tomar por el saco, tío"* he'd say in the middle of the slightest altercation. Incidentally, I had discovered that it was also the only way he liked to have sex, and I was seriously rethinking our marriage when he surprised me by leaving me for a local TV weather girl. Said he wanted a woman with a real career, not someone who "played" at being a real estate investor but spent all her time at the movies, talking to her tenants and neighbors, or on her computer.

Since, thanks to my mother's real estate investments, I had a "level of solvency" that he had become "accustomed" to and a lifestyle his teacher's salary could not maintain, and since he had no assets besides his Kia, while I had three very desirable, free and clear properties in then home-value-rich Miami, the judge gave him the Pinecrest seventies-style bungalow we lived in based on the value acquired by the property while we'd been married.

Oh, how I loved that house, so surrounded by trees in the middle of a neighborhood full of sixties-inspired slanted roofs. I could have fought for it, but by the time Alejandro and his lawyer were done with me, my will to speak, much less negotiate anything, had died, and my only hope was that he'd take it easy on the weather girl, she who had to stand to do her job.

I moved back to Coffee Park, my refuge after every failure, until a few years later, in a society-induced panic over turning thirty-five and not having children, I married Manuel and moved into the Coral Gables house with him.

Manuel was the opposite of Alejandro. Puerto Rican, sexy, good in bed, really funny, and really irresponsible. Two years later, I had begun to tire of lying to people about his whereabouts when they called threatening to sue us if he didn't finish the roof they'd already paid him to fix, when he managed to meet a yoga teacher who felt that supporting him was the least she could do in exchange for the "sheer joy" he brought into her life.

"You know what your problem is, Mariela? You don't really see people. And you know why? 'Cause you're just not spiritual. You don't see people for who they can be. Do you even appreciate all I've done for you?" he'd said to me one of the many times I'd had to call to tell him that a very angry client was on my doorstep and that I'd give him his mistress's address if he didn't come and take care of it right away.

I remember taking some time after he said that to me to sift through my memories of our marriage, trying hard to think of what part of him I'd neglected to see, and though plenty of things came up, none were positive, so I guessed he was right. There must have been some good—there always is—and if I hadn't seen it, it's because I hadn't been looking. He never truly saw me either, but I didn't blame him for that. I'd never told him, or Alejandro, or anyone, about my mother, or about my stillborn clairvoyance. So how could I expect him to see what I hadn't been willing to show?

This was almost three years ago and it had taken all this time to get the divorce finalized. In the end, I agreed to have him keep the Coral Gables house in exchange for a release of liability from his lawsuit-prone construction business on which I'd been an enthusiastic cosigner, stupid woman that I was.

It was a beautiful house in a great location right smack in the middle of Coral Gables, which is right smack in the middle of Miami. It had a big yard, a coral rock-rimmed pool, an all-around wooden fence, and rested on the quiet, tree-laden side of Aragon Avenue. Perhaps best of all, it was walking distance from Books and Books, an old-style independent bookstore and café that is, to this day, my very favorite place in all of Miami, not just for the books, but for the place itself, all wooden bookcases, Spanish-style iron railings, and a cozy courtyard with orange patio umbrellas and dangling garden lights on breezy autumn nights.

But I couldn't afford the upkeep, there was no way to turn the house into a multifamily home, and at the time, the rent I could have gotten for it would barely have covered the taxes and landscaping. So I let him have it. Something told me that when the "joy" he'd be able to provide his new wife after paying Coral Gables's obscenely high property taxes got too sheer for her taste, she'd promptly throw him out on his lazy ass.

I read somewhere that actress Zsa Zsa Gabor once said, "I am a marvelous housekeeper. Every time I leave a man I keep his house." Well, you can think of Dumb and Dumber as the Zsa Zsa Gabors of my life and list.

After those two, I thought the problem might be marriage, the absurd need to complicate everything with the blatantly false promise (since the person making the promise cannot be absolutely sure he'll be able to keep it) of security and exclusivity.

No longer did I wonder if my mother wouldn't have been happier with an honest man willing to devote his life to her, instead of hurrying to live, and work, and save for her sunny horizon only to die from Olympic-speed cancer instead. No, my mother had had it right all along. It was my strategy of "normal" relationships based on "true love" that was wrong. And it wasn't just marriage. It was the hope of "ever after" and the attachment that surely followed that had caused my poverty of both finances and faith.

I realized something had to change, so I changed it.

First, I moved back into my fourplex's *apartamento uno,* hung a vintage, Chinese-red tin sign proclaiming me "The Landlord" on the door, and a hand-painted, cursive one on the window that read GESTIONES Y DILIGENCIAS, offering my services for odd jobs of a clerical nature. I knew a thing or two about lawyers, courts, and divorce, and how to find information using a computer. I could fill out forms and use a phone, and I *was* bilingual. So I bought a desk, a computer, a printer, and a fax and "opened" for business.

Second, I had to figure out a way to protect myself from my marrying heart. I couldn't allow love to once again deliver me into the hands of a man who'd take what I had left and leave me asking what about me made me so easy to leave for another. Since all I had was real estate, it seemed to me that as long as I didn't make the mistake of marrying, I was safe. Which is why, with the ink on divorce decree number two still wet, I made the very conscious decision to sleep with married men and only married men.

And who should come along but lucky number three.

I met Jorge through my tenant in *apartamento dos,* Gustavo, who brought him over one day and asked me if I'd help his friend with a small business loan application. Jorge wanted to make sure it was correctly filled out and didn't trust his English as a second language skills. He also wanted to hire me to find a place where he could practice what he did know on the cheap, as he was saving to open a small café of his own.

He told me he'd been a chef and worked at some of the best Varadero hotels in Cuba before making his way out to sea, officially becoming a *balsero* (a rafter) and spending almost two years at the Guantánamo Bay prison camp for refugees during the 1994 exodus, before coming to Miami.

He was six feet tall, all bony muscle and energetic, fast-moving limbs. He walked fast, and it was a while before I noticed he slumped a bit from the habit of bending over the counter to be almost eye level with whatever he was cutting, chopping, or seeding. Instead, what I noticed the first time I saw him, was the wavy brown hair that looked good even though it seemed to go every which way, and his eyes, big and dark, giving him an air of mournful thoughtfulness. Until he smiled. Then they brought out his true nature: friendly and flirty, earnest, like a shy boy who has learned how to be daring, and I hadn't been able to resist him.

He'd taught me how to dance salsa casino, how to cook, and how to tell a good joke using my body and all of my face. He also taught me how to play dominoes like an expert and the correct way to kiss the sides of fingers and ankles, the inner wrists, and the backs of the knees. (Open your mouth a little, push your lips out, and then softly drag the warm, fleshy, moist part of your lips over the chosen body part until your lower and upper lips meet on the skin. Stay there for a second. Breathe into the skin. Now kiss.)

How could he do all this with me while being married? *Ay,* my friend, I should tell you, if you don't already know it, that when it comes to Cuba and Cubans, it's always complicated.

After being in Miami for a while, he'd been allowed to go back to visit his mother. During the visit, he met Yuleidys, a nurse. They'd married sometime after that, but she couldn't leave and he couldn't go back there to live. After almost two years of visits and paperwork, she got her release papers from the Cuban government just before I met him, and for months had been supposed to arrive "any day now." Theirs, I thought, was the most romantic relationship, made perfect by the ninety miles of sea between them, romanticized with letters, pictures, home videos, and long $1.29 per minute phone calls even in the post-Skype era of free international calling.

He had a kind heart and often stayed the entire night if he was off from the restaurant. He'd bring me *café con leche* in bed and always treated me as if what we had was real, as if he loved me, even though I knew I was just his temporary medicine against the loneliness and frustration with the politics of politics.

Not that I was his only remedy. He often dealt with his nostalgia by partying with his chef friends after he got off work, drinking wine and smoking pot until the wee hours of the morning, sleeping 'til all hours, and living his "promised land" life during the few hours before he had to be back for his shift.

"You're so talented. . . . I don't know why you treat your life like a light version of a *Miami Vice* episode," I told him once.

It was a variation of something I'd say more and more frequently over the six months we were together. He'd always answer the same thing:

"Mi vicio eres tú," which meant that I was his vice, and sounded just as corny in Spanish as it does in English. But he'd say it in the softest voice while looking at me with the look you give the people you know you could never say no to.

One day, after a bowl of heavenly seafood soup, too much homemade *tinto de verano* (Place the following ingredients into a big glass jug: two cups of cheap Spanish rioja wine, one quarter cup of grenadine, a squirt of fresh lime juice, half a cup of fresh orange juice, half a cup of club soda, and four heaping tablespoons of brown sugar. Chill. Serve with a sprig of mint.) and sex, I made a mistake. I told him my secret: that I used to have to cover my ears to avoid the whispering and the calling of people I couldn't always see, that I'd known what it was like to feel the dark weight of strangers' secrets when they walked past me, and how I'd murdered it all the same way he'd be able to someday murder his nostalgia for the friends, the streets, and the little rituals of poverty he thought he'd left behind. I told him this to give him faith that his sadness too would pass. To give him something to hang on to. To keep him from partying his life away.

The next day, he begged me to go with him to see his godmother. She was Dominican but had fallen in love with a Cuban man and had lived in Cuba until the day he died. Now she lived in the Miami neighborhood of Allapattah, in a little blue frame house that was almost completely obscured by shrubs and fruit trees, and I had only to lay eyes on her to be scared out of my freckles.

She had brown skin and freaky green eyes, so intense they seemed fluorescent. But what scared me was her voice. The moment she spoke, it's as if her voice's shadow went off on its own to tell stories of women who threw themselves at the coffins of men they'd loved, of the trembling palms of young men about to pull triggers while looking into the eyes of other boys, and of the hearts of mothers, lurching and shaking in the knowledge that their daughters would not be coming home that night, or any night. It was a bit like a double sound track. One song is saying hello and asking Jorge how he knows me, and the other is performing a spoken poem made up of the world's saddest headlines.

I think I scared her too, because two minutes after first taking my hands in hers, she opened her eyes wide as if urgently displeased with whatever I had "brought in with me." Then both her voices became one, and this section of the poem was composed of the events of my entire life. She told me I could've had children but that it was too late now, and that I'd be tragically unhappy until I started respecting Yemayá's will for my life, and started to see again like I was supposed to. Then she told her godson to stay away from me if he knew what was good for him because I'd have nothing to give him but problems, and proceeded to pretty much shoo and push us out of her house.

"Mariela, pero no le hagas caso a la vieja, por tu vida, tatica," he said over and over again on the drive home, one hand on the wheel, the other holding my hands to his face, asking me to please forgive the crazy old woman, and to forgive him for bringing me, and even stopping the car on the side of the road to hug me until I'd stopped trembling, promising it would be a long time before he'd go see the dratted witch (*bruja de mierda esa*) again, even if she *was* his godmother. He'd only wanted to help. To show me I had nothing to be ashamed of. He'd wanted his godmother to figure out the perfectly logical reason I hadn't seen my mother's illness so I could understand it. But the experience had shaken me up so much that I continued to cry all the way home, and when a week later, he got notice of his wife's release date two months hence, I convinced him it was a good idea to start preparing for his new life with fidelity and made him promise not to call me again, no matter what. I also promised myself I'd forget him and never again make the mistake of telling anyone about my truncated gift.

But my clairvoyance was not the only reason I ran away from him. I also did it because there'd been something there. Maybe not enough of a something to survive his crazy lifestyle, his even crazier godmother, and my own crazy habit of being drawn only to those relationships most bereft of possibility, but still . . . something. And that something made me want him to have a chance at what I thought I'd never have: a happy marriage, a real life.

I don't say this now because time has passed. I knew what I felt then but figured his godmother was probably right about my having nothing for him. So I renounced him and worked on quickly filling the space he'd left empty before he came back for me, ignoring what I'd said about never contacting me because he realized he loved me so much (my secret fantasy) or I realized he'd never intended to.

Chapter 5

"You'll be okay walking?" Hector asked, slowing down when we neared the corner of Twentieth Avenue and Eighth Street that afternoon. Fifteen minutes ago, we'd left the St. Michel, and already his mind was many worlds away.

" 'Course. Not even dark yet."

"Okay, *flaca. Ciao* then," he said, forgetting to ask me to text him when I was within the safe confines of my apartment.

As I opened the car door, I hesitated, waiting for him to say that he'd call me later to wish me a good night, as usual. But he didn't, so I got out, slowly walking away, my mind caught up in wondering what on earth could be preoccupying him to make him so abruptly distant.

I remember thinking that Hector was acting like a man about to embark on that wonderful time in the life of most affairs called "the beginning." Only, I felt more like the wife than the mistress because if Hector was beginning something, it was certainly not with me.

I heard him drive away in the opposite direction and picked up my pace along the portion of Eighth Street that leads toward the Coffee Park section where I live, remembering to turn my head and cross the street when I passed the corner of Fifteenth, the street where Jorge lived, or maybe, used to live. I did this every time, even though I'd never once run into him in the year or so since we stopped seeing each other.

From that corner, it was a ten-to-fifteen-minute walk to my apartment and, since this is where all the madness was about to unfold, I might as well give you a quick history tour of the area: Little Havana, Coffee Park, and the civil war of sorts that made it a less than ordinary place to live in.

In the late 1990s, there was a movement to more broadly promote Little Havana as a tourist destination, the premier enclave of Cuban culture in the United States and site of the world's largest outdoor Hispanic festival, Calle Ocho's Carnaval Miami.

But tensions mounted when some of the more liberal residents began to feel that the nostalgic earthiness of Little Havana that had brought them there in the first place was being threatened by the city's push to "clean up" and rebrand the area as a sanitized, commercialized, tourist-attracting destination.

"Look, Mariela, if I wanted to live in the suburbs of Disney World, I'd live in the fucking suburbs of Disney World," Iris, who owned the fourplex next to mine, said to me at the time.

The result was that many of the "rebels" ended up moving to our side of Little Havana: Coffee Park, then really just a large square block of greenery and mature trees, but now surrounded by little coffee shops, independent "boutiques," apartments that doubled as yoga studios, art co-ops, and holistic pharmacies attended by young bearded guys high on medicinal marijuana. Coffee Park became the symbol of neighborhood defiance, collectively and consciously turning up its nose at the bureaucrats, deciding that it was going to be as bohemian, progressive, and liberal as it got.

Of course, even as the little businesses sprouted all around, you still had the big Spanish-style houses turned rental duplexes, triplexes, and fourplexes, most dating from the 1920s, '30s, and '40s, proudly holding their ground, alongside the storefronts.

This made for a pretty self-contained community, whose people answered "Coffee Park" when asked where they lived, even though Coffee Park was, officially, and for most practical purposes, part of Little Havana.

My own fourplex was built in 1935, a big Spanish-style square of a building blessed with high ceilings, ornate moldings and arches, and big windows. Manuel, my second husband, had painted it a deep papaya color that I'd hated at the time, but had grown to love for the contrast of its orange-red hues against the green leaves and brown bark of the trees on the square across the street, all somehow fitting right in with the vintage awnings of the boho-chic storefronts.

Inside, it was a charming Spanish-style building with one-bedroom apartments, original hardwood floors, a nonworking fireplace in every unit, and fire escapes off each second-floor kitchen doubling as urban jungle gardens. There was also a small backyard taken over by a big avocado tree, its huge, shady limbs presiding over always-moist green grass.

But charming as my little building was, it was also a money drain. It needed the big roof and plumbing repairs that buildings require every fifteen to twenty years, and I often asked myself why I didn't just sell the damn thing, knowing as soon as the idea crossed my mind that I simply couldn't. It was all I had left from my mother, and, despite the real estate bubble's recent noisy burst, it was the safest investment in the world. I mean, the area just had to take off, surrounded as it was by chic metro neighborhoods like Brickell, Downtown Miami, the Design District, and Wynwood.

I could see it becoming the next Greenwich Village before Greenwich Village realized it was cool, just as my mom had predicted. She bought the little fourplex at precisely the right time, in the middle of a housing slump and a few months before all the feuding about redeveloping Little Havana started. Back then, the square was just an improbable patch of green, located at the easternmost end of Calle Ocho and ridiculously close to Interstate 95. Still, she'd been determined to buy it, as if she'd somehow known that one day businesses, artists, and activists would begin moving into the houses and apartment buildings surrounding the park, turning the square into their own little bohemian enclave.

"This place," she'd say, "has potential. I may not have inherited the gift of seeing the future like you, Mariela, but I have the vision of instinct and experience, and I tell you Coffee Park has nowhere to go but up."

On the Wednesday I returned from my afternoon with Hector, the area was clean, the trees still green, and there were no signs of the loud music sometimes heard on weeknights, of the couple of harmless pseudo-homeless people, or of the few prostitutes who sometimes brightened my afternoons with their sequined tops, hot pants, and high heels. Not that I judged them for being sluts. (How could I?) I judged them for failing to realize they'd attract more customers if they'd just invest $2.69 in a tube of ultra-whitening, tartar control toothpaste once in a while. But, all of that said, Coffee Park was still, for the most part, a great little neighborhood.

It was also the place where I reinvented myself after my divorces. You'll remember that when I couldn't afford to continue living in my Coral Gables home (post husband number two), I'd decided (was forced) to get entrepreneurial, taking my post-divorce, highly sharpened computer skills and my knack for finding information and resources on the Internet and going right back to Coffee Park to hang my shingle.

At first, my clients had been people who had some disposable income, but no patience to wait all day for their turn at the Kiwanis Club of Little Havana, the only truly active community nonprofit offering immigrant services at the time. So they'd come to me instead, and I'd correct a billing mistake, negotiate a deferment on a loan, find an address on MapQuest, or download a bus route schedule. I'd do basic tax returns and fill out college financial aid or loan forms, as I had for Jorge. I wrote letters for every purpose and, once or twice, I'd even been hired to call a boss and say "my husband" was sick and would not be in to work that day.

And then, little by little, a certain kind of clientele began streaming in with more frequency than the rest: women. Confused, heartbroken, pissed-as-hell women getting divorced and who, having heard of "my history," figured I'd have an extra lesson or two to share with them. This was perfectly normal. Living in Coffee Park one heard about everyone's everything, and the fact that I'd twice had to return to the neighborhood after yet another man had cheated on me was the kind of history people tended to remember. Oh, let me tell you, that's when I felt the tug of a new calling grabbing hold of my heart.

Take Silvia, for example.

"Did you already ask for a divorce?" I asked her when she came to see me.

"Of course!"

"Take it back."

"What? Didn't you hear what I said? He's sleeping with my cousin! My cou-cou-couuuuuuuu-sin!" She sobbed for a few minutes before shaking her head and thundering *"My cousin!"* redundantly.

"I know that, Silvia. I know. Trust me. I know how you feel and this is why you need a lawyer: He doesn't have a job. You have two. He's been taking care of the kids while you work—"

"That's the worst of it! Do you know *lo que hizo ese hijo de la gran puta?*"

(Nonliteral translation: son of the mother of all bitches.)

"All right," I said, realizing I'd have to let her vent before she'd let me help her. "What did he do?"

"He'd get movies for the kids, and ice cream, and all kinds of junk food, and sneak that skanky ho in through the back room next to the laundry while the kids were watching TV." She finished on the verge of a thrombosis, her abundant chest heaving like a body of water with tsunami symptoms.

"I know. I know, but—"

"You knew?"

"No, no. I mean that I know what it's like."

"Oh." She nodded, no doubt remembering what she'd heard of "my history."

I tried again: "In court, all they'll know, or want to know, is that you're the breadwinner with the two jobs and no time to take care of the kids, and they'll probably say that keeping it that way would be less disruptive to the children since he's been doing it now for about—"

"Oh, yeah, he's been doing it all right. You want to hear disruptive?"

I sighed, willing myself to avoid joining her over there at the deep, dark end of her rage pool where I wouldn't be able to help her.

"What I'm trying to say is that he could end up with joint custody, the kids living with him, and you having to pay *him* child support."

"No! You think? He wouldn't. He wouldn't dare."

"You say he was sleeping with your cousin, in your house, with your children present, while you were working two jobs?"

"Oh my God. You're right. He would! He *would* dare."

"I'm just saying, be careful. 'Cause let me tell you, that 'equal distribution of assets' in this lousy, no-fault divorce state is Florida's way of charging you for the sunshine."

Silvia nodded, wide-eyed, before saying, "What I need is a badass, motherfucking lawyer."

I was happy she'd gone from "no lawyer" to wanting a "badass" one, but knowing my share of them from the work I did and knowing she didn't have enough money for even five minutes of a Miami "motherfucking" lawyer's time, I said, "Would you settle for a Legal Aid motherfucking lawyer?"

When she nodded urgently, I got the area number for Legal Aid and for the local children and family services office and made appointments for her while printing out every useful document on divorce and family law that I could find online.

It felt so good to help these women. I typically charged a nominal fee of ten dollars per hour, but often reduced my fee or worked extra hours I didn't charge for because, as far as I was concerned, this was now my real gift. I was over clairvoyance and good riddance! If the failure of my marriages had proven something to me, it was that if I'd ever had "sight," it was swimming in shit somewhere else.

On the other hand, with my keyboard I could see farther than any psychic. Sometimes, all I had to do was search the Internet and hand the woman a simple answer (no charge if the search took five minutes or less), and the next thing I knew they'd be looking at my computer and me as if I were magic incarnate and the computer were my crystal ball. I hated that. It reminded me of how my clairvoyance had made me feel special as a teen. You know, before my mother got sick and I realized I was a fraud.

And there I was, Mother-Teresa-with-a-laptop tending to my building, my clients, and my tenants by day, firm believer in my "married men only" rule by night: Both came with no real obligations and no money-loss issues, and had the added benefit of occupying space I might otherwise be tempted to hand over to dangerously unattached men.

I hadn't always been that cynical and distrusting. All my life, I had yearned for a sister or a best friend. Another woman with whom to have an even closer bond than the one I'd had with my mother. But somehow, I didn't know a single female besides Iris whom I could truly call a friend. And probably because so many of them seemed bent on taking my lousy husbands, I had lost the capacity to regret that I might now possibly be taking theirs.

I just went about my life, one day at a time, trying not to think about the fact that I helped women with one hand, while hurting them with the other.

Chapter 6

After Hector drove away, I stopped at Los Pinareños Frutería for a guava milk shake. It was amazing, the perfect mix of tart and sweet, and after just a few sips, I'd convinced myself once again that it was all in my head. There was nothing wrong with Hector. It was just me making a volcano out of an ashtray.

When a woman has been alone for a while, she's like the girl in *The Little Princess,* climbing the stairs of her garret after a horrible dose of forced labor, poverty, and abuse, to find that a rich humanitarian has sent his monkey to leave all kinds of wonderful food, gifts, and comforting treats for her. God was my Humanitarian, Hector was his monkey, and all I had to do was keep my good fortune a secret and stay in the shadow area designated for "other women," and everything would be dandy.

Cars zoomed past me as I walked down Eighth Street sipping my shake, making me wonder why I'd made Hector drive me over instead of staying in the Gables to browse the shops along Miracle Mile before taking the bus back.

That late in the afternoon, traffic was so loud, that by the time I got to Coffee Park, I had a headache and had to stop at the naturopathy pharmacy for some beet drops. Sarah, the owner's girlfriend, was at the counter. She was a youngish-looking thing, all bones and blond, with huge blue eyes in a heart-shaped face where the nose and mouth were the simplest of punctuation marks. She'd come east from California with Pedro, but was from Madison, Wisconsin. The door opened with a clinking of small brass bells tied to a thick red rope, followed immediately by Pedro, hollering at Sarah from somewhere in the back.

"So go. Go back to Madison and raise some cows if that's what you want to do. I don't care!"

"You *wish* Miami had the class and sophistication that's in one Madison, Wisconsin, square block, you hear? Oh . . . hi, Mariela. What can I get for you?"

"I can come back later."

"Don't be silly. No need to mind him."

"Some beet drops, please. If you've got some ready to go."

"Of course," she said with a smile.

Pedro huffed in from the back room, red face on the verge of exploding, about to say something, but saw me, grumbled an embarrassed hello, and went back to whatever he'd been doing in the back.

The moment he was gone, Sarah turned to me and murmured, "I swear I am so sick of that man, I'd go home this minute if I could." She said it with so much hatred, I had no doubt she meant it. In her anger, she hadn't even written down my purchase or bothered ringing it up, putting the money I gave her in her jeans front pocket.

I left thinking there was another benefit to my relationship with Hector: not much time to fight. That was, if I still had a relationship with him.

Rounding the park toward my apartment, I concluded that the tension with Hector had been my fault. I knew the paramount rule of love affairs: always be mysterious, which works just as well for clairvoyants as for regular women trying to hang on to illicit affairs with married men. I also knew that the easiest road to the restoration of lost mystery is absence, which is why, a little rattled by Sarah and Pedro's arguing, I suddenly wished to get home quickly, take a warm bath, find my center, and destroy neediness by cooking my delicious Spanish potato omelet with a side of piquillo peppers cooked in garlic, olive oil, balsamic vinegar, and a pinch of sugar. I'd enjoy a glass of wine, release the drama for one night, be mysterious again, and stop "doing that thing" that Hector had told me not to do. I even felt up to finishing *The Elegance of the Hedgehog*. Set in Paris, it was a novel about the concierge of a Parisian building so in love with art, she'd secretly become as delicate as the most cultured debutante by teaching it to herself. Where I'd left off, it looked like the wise, rich, handsome Japanese widower in her building had guessed her wonderful secret and was falling in love with her. Just thinking about a good story made me excited and hopeful, and I quickened my pace. Life was great again.

Until I got to my building and saw Hector's car parked right there in front of it. What was he doing here instead of at the bookstore? What about his important meeting? I opened the wooden door and stepped into the little foyer that separated my apartment from Gustavo's. It was a small space, about eight by eight feet, housing the electrical closet, the four metal mailboxes, and the staircase that led to the upstairs apartments.

I'd already started to coax my overstuffed mail from the narrow mailbox with *apartamento uno* written on it with nail polish when I heard Hector and Olivia coming down the stairs, laughing about some apparently hilarious thing. It was too late to hurry into my own apartment. In a matter of seconds they were upon me, leaving me no time to recover from the surprise. Her, I hadn't seen in weeks, while he'd been inside me just a couple of hours earlier.

"Well. Hello," I said.

"Hello, Mariela!" Hector said, as if he hadn't seen me in years.

"I was just . . . had things to . . . you know, here," I said, forgetting I lived there and didn't need to explain my presence.

"Well, it's very nice to see you, right, Olivia?"

She took her time answering, and then did so in the same clipped, icy Morticia tone I remembered from the few times we'd exchanged words in the time they'd lived in *apartamento cuatro*: "That's a charming top."

"Oh, yeah . . . yes, well, you look . . . great," I replied, thinking, *If you like that sort of look*. She was in her early fifties and wore her long ash-blond hair curled into ringlets around her pale face, obviously ignorant of the fact that Farrah Fawcett herself retired that look long before she died. She was fashionably stick-thin with an angular face, huge brown eyes, and big lips that seemed to stretch as wide as her face. Her only good features, as far as I was concerned, were her cheekbones, high and pronounced. She'd put some makeup on, all very subdued except for the burgundy red color on her lips, and completed the look with a meant-to-be-snug black cocktail shift that just hung on her and pointy, black kitten-heel pumps. The one thing that didn't match or fit perfectly was a chunky, gold-tone men's watch, glaringly out of place in all its masculinity.

"It's the first present Hector ever gave me," she said, following my eyes. "His father's watch, so I could float around in my little world and still know what time it was," she said with just that drop of sarcasm you can never be completely sure of. Had he said it in that dismissive way back then? Or was she being sarcastic now? The possibilities enclosed within this tidbit of information were fascinating to me. Mistresses always want to know what happens inside the one place that's forbidden to them: their lover's marriage.

"Well, we really have to go," said Hector, pushing her gently down the last few steps and toward the entry door so that they now stood between my apartment's front door and me: Hector, comfortable and relaxed. I, amazed that he could be.

"Your scent," she said.

"Thanks," I said a little too quickly, since she hadn't exactly complimented me on it. "It's lemongrass."

"Yes, I know," she said, freezing my heart. "I grow it in the apartment. Useful for migraines."

That last bit about smells made Hector visibly tense (her intent all along, I suspected), and now I wondered if she knew something because what had there been to be sarcastic about? Lemongrass?

Just when it couldn't get any more awkward, the door to *apartamento dos* opened and Gustavo stepped out with Abril, who rented one of Iris's apartments next door, and Henry, her seven-year-old son. Gustavo and Abril had recently begun dating. They seemed surprised to see us all crowding the rather small foyer, but Henry smiled wide when he saw Olivia.

"You look pretty," he told her, looking up at her with his eyes made as big as hers by the Coke-bottle glasses he had recently begun to wear for his severe myopia, and dragged the heavy, high-top shoes he wore for his flat feet, wobbling over to touch her watch reverently.

"You notice it too, eh, Henry? Good taste!" said Hector, messing up Henry's ash-brown hair, as if delighted to see him.

Since when did Hector like kids? Or maybe he just liked the convenient distraction this particular kid was providing?

Olivia was peering intently into Henry's eyes.

"There's a very good natural eye remedy for children," she said to no one in particular.

"I used a perfectly natural remedy to repair mine: a laser," said Hector, suddenly a comedian.

Olivia ignored him, continuing her intense examination of Henry's face.

"You know, she's always talking about natural this and natural that. Well, what is more natural than light?" continued Hector. Was he finally nervous? Or was he being dismissive of her macrobiotic, environmentally conscious, vegan ways for my benefit?

"You have to buy some licorice root powder," Olivia went

on, without ever looking at Abril, even though it was now obvious that she was talking to her. "Mix a half teaspoon of the root's powder, an equal amount of honey, and about a quarter teaspoon of ghee, and give it to him with a cup of milk on an empty stomach," she finished.

"My stomach's empty now," said Henry, peering right back into her eyes and smiling wide, as if he were playing along.

"Oh, okay, thanks. I'll have to come by your apartment with a notepad, write it all down in detail," said Abril to Olivia as if she were a poor peasant and Olivia were the Pope.

This was something that annoyed me about Abril, the way she was always pushing Henry onto other people and being so thrilled when they liked him back or took him under their wing as if he were an orphan, just because his father was missing in action.

"The doctors say his extreme case of myopia is showing up ahead of time. He's only seven, and it's recently begun to really bother him," continued Abril, oblivious to my bitchy thoughts.

"I got new glasses!" said Henry, smiling his adorable crooked smile at Olivia.

"Yes, well. You should do something about it," said Olivia to Abril, without so much as a glance in either her or Henry's direction, as if the conversation bored her and she was through talking.

I looked at Henry and, just as I thought, he looked hurt.

"Your glasses are really cool, Henry. I like them a lot," I said, falling into Abril's trap, wanting to protect her son from the rude ways of crappy grown-ups.

Henry smiled wide again, nodding at me maniacally.

"See, Henry. I told you they were cool. We picked them out together," said Gustavo, putting his hand on Henry's shoulder protectively.

"We really have to go," Hector said with the same impatience he'd used toward me that afternoon.

"It was nice seeing you both," said Abril in a ridiculously wistful manner. "Henry's always asking me to take him to the bookstore, right, Henry?"

Henry looked at her blankly.

"Yes, well, nice to see you," said Gustavo, coming to her rescue.

Let me tell you, I'd never seen Gustavo so taken with a woman in the five years he'd been my tenant. Don't get me wrong—he was a nice guy and quite good-looking in his "guy's guy" way, but when it came to women, he was a dog. I was pretty sure he'd slept with, or tried to sleep with, almost every beautiful, unattached, adult female under thirty-five in Coffee Park since moving in, quickly moving on without a qualm the minute they began to bore him.

But it was clear that this was different.

Abril was twenty-seven or twenty-eight but looked like a schoolgirl with her long straight hair parted in the middle, her silver hoop earrings and bangles, and her endless assortment of sundresses. And I had to admit she was obviously a good mother who loved her son even if she did annoy me to no end. To further make my point about mystery, she had that air of the unexplained that drove men crazy. After months of acquaintance through Iris, all I knew about her was that she'd lived in Little Havana for a while, moved to New York to be near her Dominican family, and came back with a son. She loved sewing, cooking, Henry, and now, apparently, Gustavo.

"*Buenas noches,*" said Hector again, nodding to Olivia to follow him out, but when he opened the door for her, she turned back to Abril and said, "Myopia that severe is usually hereditary. Are you myopic too?"

"Sorry? Oh. No. No, I'm not, but Henry seems to—"

"So just him then. The licorice."

"Yes. Thanks again," said Abril.

I stood there, noticing that Hector had bathed and changed

into black pants and a dark gray shirt with silver cuff links. This was his important meeting? A date with his wife?

"You okay, Mariela?" asked Gustavo after the door closed behind Hector and Olivia.

"Oh, sure . . . yes, just distracted. A million things. Why?" I answered, rushing to open my own apartment door.

"You looked real strange there for a minute or two."

"You know me, born strange. See you all later. Bye, Henry."

I stepped quickly into *apartamento uno,* locking the door firmly and rushing to the window without so much as turning on the light. I wanted to get a good look at Hector with his damn wife before they got into the car. Would he open the door for her? Smile at her and wink for no reason like he did with me?

But before I could get to the window, I heard Ellie's wooden platform shoes on the stairway, so I rushed to open my door wide and surprise her in the middle of stealing out of her apartment to avoid paying her rent again.

"Just the person I wanted to talk to," I said.

"I was coming down to talk to you myself."

"Who else would, if not 'yourself,' right?" I said, knowing the fact I'd just made fun of her had gone right past the fake designer jean-clad part of her body she used for listening and thinking. I'm not big on grammar, but Ellie's sentences had always been a mystery to me. She'd end them with the word *yeah,* as in "so and so did this and that and then, so . . . yeah."

"Just so you know, I'm moving out sometime next week, so . . . yeah."

"Ellie, we've been through this. Regardless of whether or not you move out, you've already used up your deposit. I need your rent money for this month now, before this month is over, and I need to make sure that the apartment's in good shape before you leave, not after."

"And what are you going to do if I don't have it? Evict me?"

I took a deep belly breath.

"It's not about that. It's about you being responsible and leaving it the way you found it for someone else in this community to enjoy."

"Ooooh mah-god! I'm sooo sick of you Coffee Park people with your 'community honor' and your karma rules. What is *up* with that?"

"Look, Ellie, wherever you go, you're going to have to pay rent. So I don't care how many times you were dropped on your head when you were a baby. You're going to pay your rent, got it?"

"Look, lady, being my landlady doesn't give you the right to threaten me, okay?"

"Ellie, don't be stupid. Nobody's threatening you."

"Who're you calling stupid?"

"I said, 'Don't be . . . stupid.' "

"Look, I don't have to take your bullshit, okay? People here might not know it, but I'm on to you."

"Excuse me?"

"Damn right, excuse you. You're one to talk, but you sure like dipping into 'community resources,' " she said, making quotation marks in the air.

"You have something to say to me, Ellie?"

"Oh, I've said my piece," she said, looking toward the stairs and raising her voice.

"Well, the piece I want to hear is when you're going to pay your rent and hand in your keys."

"When I get to it, got it?" she said, imitating my earlier response.

I was so angry I could've dragged her up and down those stairs, forget I was no longer in middle school tackling girls who made fake scary noises and whispered things when I walked by, just 'cause I'd been stupid enough to believe they were my friends and told them I was clairvoyant. Or in high school, slapping the life out of anyone who dared to whisper anything about my mother. But I didn't.

"Is this the way you want to handle things, Ellie?" I said instead, steadily looking straight into her eyes to let her know I was a lot crazier than she'd ever be and didn't care what she thought she knew, even as I realized that if Ellie knew, and that was a big "if," Olivia might too. (Hence Hector trying to tamp down suspicions by taking her out?)

She must've gotten the message, because she just said, "Screw you," before swinging her bony ass out the door as quickly as she could.

I watched her go with a feeling of doom.

She'd never been a great tenant, but lately it had gotten worse. It was as if she no longer cared about a thing. When she moved in, she'd been a young girl wanting independence from an overbearing mother. I'd wanted to help her, keep an eye out for her. She'd been polite, apologetic even, when I'd talked to her about putting her recycling in the right place and not throwing her cigarette stubs out the window and onto my front garden. But lately she'd become rude, looked a bit dirty, and acquired an expression of unfocused defiance that unsettled me. I wondered if she was doing drugs. I know people think social drugs like marijuana are not "that harmful." But if it makes people be someone they're not and not care about things they'd normally care about, it can't be all that good, can it?

The worst of it was I couldn't afford the expense of a vacancy just then. It was as if God were hitting me on the side of the head: Hector's odd behavior today, Olivia's comments, catching them going out on a date, and Ellie's being "on to me" were all signs that I needed to end the affair. Of course, that would mean running into Hector constantly at the building, while staying away from him for decency's sake. But where was this decency line, really? Wasn't I breaking it now by being with him?

This is what happens when you're the "other woman." You

lose all perspective and spend precious energy thinking about whether being his landlord makes it more or less decent to see a married man who still cares enough about his wife to cut an afternoon with his mistress short in order to take her out for an evening on the town.

That night, I sat at the metal desk in my living room/dining room/office/library, looking out the window at the city that held Hector and Olivia somewhere and trying to write a breakup letter even as I imagined them celebrating their anniversary or some other important thing. I was feeling jealous of them for knowing with a certainty I'd never know for myself that, despite everything and everyone, they'd be together until death did them part. Yes, mistresses are always jealous of the wife, and I was no different.

I was pretty sure I wasn't in love with Hector, at least I didn't think so, but I did know that it was time to stop because whatever I was feeling was obviously defeating the purpose of dating married men as an antidote to heartbreak.

The worst thing was I'd had a hundred opportunities to decide this before, but no. I'd waited until he'd tired of me. Damn it. He was a married man having an affair. What else did I think would happen? Had I subconsciously hoped things with Hector would be different? And if not, then why was I so surprised?

Well, for starters, the abruptness. After putting so much effort into building a connection beyond our bodies and working so hard to get inside my head as a bridge into my pants, he'd just suddenly lost interest. That day. But why? For the first time in years, I considered trying to coax my gift, my clairvoyance, back from the oblivion to which I had condemned it so long ago. I needed to see the future, to know for sure that, Hector or no Hector, loneliness would not be in the cards forever. I realized I was no better than my clients, hanging on to look-alike love in fear the real one would never show up.

It started to rain over Little Havana's Coffee Park, the air going from warm to chilly quickly, as is common in Miami. I put away the letter I'd been writing and made myself a cup of spicy-sweet, milky chai, my omelet and wine fantasy forgotten. It warmed my stomach as I sat on my windowsill, watching the windy rain make dancers in dark green glossy skirts out of tree branches.

Soon, the window became blurry, while the fact that Hector and I were over began to become very, very clear.

Chapter 7

And it's exactly that stupid fear of being over, finished, thrown out, that creates the misery of our mistakes. It's also how notorious number four came to be part of my list.

Well, that, and the bookstore.

And the real estate slump of 2008.

It was during the preceding fall of 2007 that Hector, being an extremely intelligent and strategic man, convinced his wife to sell their home in the character-rich/then value-poor neighborhood of The Roads, which they did just before the bubble burst. This way, he'd explained, they'd be able to save their bookstore and turn their equity into cash otherwise irrecoverable later. The following fall, in October 2008, they moved into my building.

Had I not been in the middle of catching husband number two with the yoga teacher at about the same time, a man who'd sell his house before he closed down a bookstore would have been an aphrodisiac too strong to resist for me.

Now, it's true that Hector first came to see the apartment with his wife, Olivia. But he later returned alone to sign the lease and pay his first month's rent, bringing a book and a chocolate soufflé with him as a "landlord gift."

"Thank you. I thought the landlord's the one who welcomes the tenants with a housewarming gift."

"Oh, you have been more than welcoming. You're obviously

an incredibly warm woman, not to mention a beautiful one, so what else can I do but bring you gifts?"

I'd seen right through him: pompous, oversexed, and with a wife who scared the wits out of me. Always silent, smiling that superior, crazy half-smile. I thanked him for the soufflé, told him he could return the signed lease later, closed the door, and didn't give it another thought beyond, "Fool, please. I am *not* in the mood for people with penises just now."

For a while, all was calm. I had a couple of short affairs, not even worth including in my list. I didn't ask anyone for help, and I didn't encourage any man to ask it of me. I was completely alone: no family, no friends, and no real relationships besides my tenants and the people of Coffee Park.

Time passed. And Manuel passed. And Jorge came and left, and more time passed, and then one day, when I was finally tired of being almost forty and I could feel the loneliness in my bones like mold, he returned.

It wasn't cold that early Miami morning in February when he knocked on my door. Still, he wore a coat and scarf because, as I'd later learn, he always dressed for the season, regardless of where he was.

"Good afternoon, Mariela. So sorry to disturb you," he'd said when I answered, with his precise diction and his thick Argentinian accent.

"It's okay. Something wrong in your apartment?"

"Oh, no, no. I just need a copy of my lease. I seem to have misplaced it."

"Oh, okay. Well, come on in and I'll print you one."

As I looked for the lease on my computer, he strolled casually into my kitchen.

"Where do you keep the coffee? Ah, here it is. I thought we'd share some coffee while I'm here," he explained when he saw I'd followed him into the kitchen with a pen between my lips and a startled look on my face.

"I'm sorry," he said then, looking sheepish. "Am I being too familiar? God, I always do this. I'm such a *boludo*, how you say . . . a jackass? I get the story chemistry and there's no stopping me."

"The story chemistry?"

"You love stories, don't you?" he said, pointing to my large book collection, which took up half the wall space in my small living room/office and could be seen from where he stood in the kitchen.

"Sure," I said, flattered enough to want him to inspect them, to be impressed by my varied choice of authors: John Barth, Carver, Junot Díaz, Doctorow, Vikram Chandra.

"Well, I'm sure you've read this one," he said, handing me a book from the inside pocket of his trench. "But it is an early edition, signed by the author. Very, very valuable. I know you love this book. A woman as beautiful as you has to have this book. Please accept it, as a gift."

It was *Love in the Time of Cholera,* which I'd read, and from which I only remembered that the object of the protagonist's slightly pedophilic affection had red pubic hair.

That's when it happened. And by "happened" I mean that I decided. I decided I liked the sight of this man taking off his coat and scarf and getting ready to make coffee for me in my kitchen. I decided to be open to his possibility, to let him happen, if he wanted to. He wasn't my problem. He was his wife's.

"Do you want to review the lease with your wife, in case you need me to update anything?" I asked later, sipping his coffee and wondering if he understood what I was really asking, wanting to be sure he understood the risks of what he'd come for.

"No, no." He sighed like a father talking about a rebellious child. "Olivia doesn't deal with these things. She . . . doesn't have problems. She's not on earth long enough to have them or to know that she has one when she does," he finished with a tortured, resigned smile that had obviously seen light before this moment.

I nodded, thinking I knew this game. Hell, I might even have invented this game. But I convinced myself his wife either knew and didn't care one bit that she had an obviously unfaithful husband or didn't know and was happy that way. At least with me, she wouldn't have to worry about his divorcing her and taking her assets with him when he left her.

"May I ask . . . how old you are?" he asked.

"No, you may not." I laughed.

"It's just, you remind me of an actress, the mystique of maturity and the smile of youth at the same time, eh, Licia. Licia Maglietta's her name. Italian," he finished in a way that said he felt if something was Italian, it was undeniably superior.

"Well, I'm sure Licia would be mortified, but thank you."

"And sexy," he said.

"Mortified and sexy?"

"No, mature and youthful, sexy and innocent, all at the same time."

I smiled, busying myself with the book he'd given me.

"Wow, your books are expensive," I said. "Thank you for the gift."

I flipped to a page on which he'd placed a cardboard bookmark from his bookstore. There was a handwritten notation on it. I read aloud:

"Sex is in the brain and begins hours, days, months, sometimes years before the actual lovemaking."

"My God, can't believe I forgot that in there," he said, taking it from me with an embarrassed smile. "But, it's true, no? Pleasure is a hunger you feed. If your palate is uneducated in these matters, you lunge hungrily, gulp it like cheap wine. But. If you're someone who really enjoys making love, then you feed it slowly, enjoy each morsel you place inside the mouth of your mind. You'll forgive me for being so forward . . . I feel comfortable in your presence, as if I'd known you a long time."

Priceless, wasn't he? I could clearly see that he was pretentious, chronically unfaithful, unsatisfied, and possibly given to condescension. But I chose to be ignorant. I chose to be ignorant because I was lonely, and bored with life, and hungry for the attention I was afraid I'd never get again.

I chose him because I was empty, and he seemed like just the thing to fill up with for at least a little while. I knew exactly what I was doing, and when he left that afternoon, I knew he'd be back.

Chapter 8

"It was not a date."

"Looked like a date."

"Well, it was not," said Hector.

"A celebration then," I insisted.

"It was not a celebration. It was a dinner. A dinner, okay?" he said, proceeding to sigh loudly into the phone as if I were a misbehaving child requiring more patience than he could muster.

"Okay. A celebration dinner."

"A business dinner, with people from the city's cultural affairs office, Mariela."

"I thought you said it was a bookstore thing."

"It was. They're, eh, putting together a campaign to unite and promote local independent businesses, and for once I had a seat at the table. For once it was me, and not Mitch Kaplan."

Mitchell Kaplan was the owner of Books and Books, the literary landmark I've told you about, and my favorite bookstore in all of Miami. Hector considered him his sworn enemy and flattered himself into thinking his own bookstore, Del Tingo al Tango, which fittingly meant "from here to there," the "and back again" not entirely implied, represented competition for Kaplan.

"So?"

"So it was important to *me*."

"You don't have to raise your voice. And you don't have to give me explanations. I'm just your mistress," I said.

He sighed again.

"Look," he said. "I should not have called you so early and gotten you out of bed, but I knew you'd be upset, and I'm going to be busy later, so—"

"You think I'd be less upset if you'd called at noon instead of at eight a.m. the morning after your date with your wife? Really?"

"What I think is you're trying to start a fight."

"What if I am?"

"You might not like it. I don't care much for them myself."

"I'm already not liking it, so where's the loss?"

"Mariela, I'm trying to give you an explanation. Would it kill you to be nice?"

"You mean play dead? Yes. It would kill me. Mistresses don't do that. Wives do."

Shit. I'd gone too far.

"You know, Mariela, I have, eh, a lot of problems in my life right now. I don't know what I did that is so bad. But I know I don't need this."

"Like what?" I asked.

"Like what?" he repeated.

"Yes. Like what? What problems do you have in your life right now?"

"I wish I could tell you."

"So tell me. Whatever it is. Tell me."

"I may have no choice," he said.

"See? That's a good start. I'll tell you mine, and you tell me yours," I said, trying to bring us both down from the brink.

"I have to go. I'll call you later."

I'd spent Wednesday night after our rendezvous stewing and writing potential breakup letters. This angst over being left was not what I'd signed up for. I couldn't handle it. Not from a married lover. I needed to move on from him before he sucked me in like Jorge had. One minute, I'd been resolved to break it off with him come morning, the next, unsure once more, I'd rip up what I'd written only to begin anew moments later. I'd gone back and forth between the two stances so many times that by the time he called to explain Thursday morning, I hadn't known better than to back him into a fight. And now he'd hung up before I could subtly remind him of my fortieth birthday the day after tomorrow.

There was something else I'd done last night. For the first time in little more than two decades, I'd tried to see. I'd actually closed my eyes with the intention of reaching into the realm of intuition, wanting to see what he was doing, where, and what was going to happen between us. Of course I'd failed. Even if I'd been taking care of my abilities and had remembered what to do, a petty, ego-driven request such as mine would never have been answered.

And now, feeling anxious after he hung up, I did what we all do when we are afraid: rely on whatever seems strong and true from our childhoods, a prayer, a story, a remedy or spell, anything. In my case, it was something I'd often seen my mother do: If she wanted a person to stay away from her, she'd write his or her name on a piece of paper, put it inside a coffee cup filled with water, and place it inside the freezer until it became ice. Then she'd leave it there, among the chicken thighs and frozen vegetables. There were entire families in our freezer for years. From Fidel Castro to the family of a neighbor who'd once screamed at my mother in the middle of the street that her gentleman callers were a bad influence on me, to which my mother answered that at least her callers visited openly, in broad daylight, and not at three in the morning, like hers.

If, on the other hand, she wanted to keep someone close,

she'd write his name on a piece of paper, place it on a saucer, douse it with honey, and leave it on a windowsill for the sun to warm.

I now wrote "Hector Ferro" with a thin-tipped Sharpie on a purple Post-it and placed it on a white ceramic saucer, drenching it with orange blossom honey and putting it in front of the window next to the sink, right next to my Cuban oregano, my mint, and my lavender. We'd see.

I made myself some strong coffee and braced for the day ahead of me. In between bouts of listening for Hector's car and imagining him slow dancing with Olivia at some tango hall, I'd also spent the night thinking about my financial situation. If I could keep all the apartments rented and figure out how to barter for some of the more critical repairs the building needed, I might be able to weather the downturn. This just couldn't be my life, like my mother, having her home in Cuba yanked from under her feet when she'd had to come here as a child, never quite able to get it out of her memory and missing her island so much she used all her money to buy as many homes as she could, somehow trying to make up for the one she could never go back to.

I had to do something and decided to start by fixing the whole Ellie mess. I'd go up there, talk to her, offer some kind of a compromise on what she owed and the chance to stay if she would just make an effort. Defusing the situation made sense financially because fixing up the apartment after she left, advertising, showing, and ultimately renting it would involve more money, skill, and energy than I had at the moment, and certainly more than it would take to get her to stay and pay at least some of her rent.

But when I knocked on her door, the stench coming from her apartment slapped me in the face, telenovela style. It smelled like burning metal, spoiled food, and God knows what kind of dead animal. After knocking several times and getting no answer, I went downstairs for my spare key to her apartment and ran into my neighbor Iris.

She was babysitting Henry while Abril ran some important errand downtown, but had come over with him to bring me a postcard that the mailman left in her mailbox by mistake. It was a happy birthday wish from my dentist.

"Here you go, neighbor. And may I say you look great for any age."

So did she, late into her sixties as she was. She had strawberry-blond hair, and I don't mean people's idealized version of strawberry-blond hair. I mean golden blond hair streaked with thick strawberry-colored highlights. She had bright blue eyes and great cheeks that always seemed to be pulled up into a smile. Most importantly, she had a fabulous sense of style. Like that day: She wore black-and-white-striped leggings, a cut-up, or, as she called it, a "redesigned," deep pink T-shirt, and a silver sequined scarf that showed her to be every bit the joyful soul she was. She'd put that sense of style to good use too, designing summer dresses and T-shirts made from vintage women's slips, lacy affairs she tie-dyed all shades of happy.

"Nice try, Iris. As far as you're concerned, I'm still and always will be in my thirties, okay," I said, motioning her and Henry inside.

"Oh, honey, I used to hide my age. But nobody cares if I'm sixty-eight or one hundred and eight. It's all still old as hell to most." She laughed, following me in. It was sad, but true, like most of the things Iris said.

"All right. It's forty, and it's the day after tomorrow," I said.

"So Saturday, September the twenty-fourth, a Libra, but barely. Well, then I'll say it again: You look great for any age."

"Thanks, Iris," I said, Ellie's key now in hand.

I was about to ask Iris to go upstairs with me when I heard Henry in the kitchen.

"He . . . He . . . Hec—"

"Hey, what are you doing there, my friend?" I said, scooping him up and planting a big sloppy one on his cheek as I brought him back into my living room/office with me.

"Is that my name in the pancake syrup? I can't read it if you cover it up with syrup!"

"It's not syrup. It's honey, and, it's, uh, for the plants," I said.

"Plants eat honey?"

"I've got a bit of a situation upstairs. Will you go up with me?" I said to Iris, trying to change the subject.

"Ellie?" asked Iris, knowing the answer.

I nodded.

"Hey, plants can't read!" said Henry, making a big deal of smoothing his polo shirt now that I'd set him free and he was standing on his own two feet again.

"Well, the ink is good for them," I retorted, heading for the stairs and ignoring Iris's baffled look.

"I can read very good, Mariela, but the syrup made the words blurry," said Henry.

"It's not important, Henry," said Iris. "Come on. We have a scamp to catch. Oh, my Lord, what in hell's name is that smell?"

"What's a scamp?" asked Henry, hurrying to catch up with us despite his heavy shoes.

But the word *scamp* was a gross understatement. Inside, it was as if a suicide bomber had failed on his first attempt and had had to try several times to get it done, and either those were his remains all over the apartment or Ellie had never cleaned a single thing since the day she moved in. In addition to the filth, she'd made deep scratches in the original wooden plank floors in at least a dozen places, burned the kitchen countertop in several areas, and allowed water from a clogged pipe to filter down onto the kitchen cabinets, rotting the woodlike material at the corners. There was a broken windowpane, the intense smell of a cockroach colony all settled in, a broken ceiling fan, about a half-dozen full-to-the-brim ashtrays, and the toilet tank's porcelain top had a deep crack on one of its corners. There were relatively dirt-free sections of flooring where furniture appeared to be missing, and the only clothes I could see were either in piles or strewn on the floor.

There was also some marijuana inside a filthy rice cooker and some sinister-looking black-brown pieces of rock in little plastic Ziploc bags.

Okay, so I cried. I cried remembering the girl who'd first moved in. I remembered telling her she should write stand-up comedy after listening to her tales of working the drive-through window at the McDonald's on Fifteenth, purposely mixing up the orders for rude customers or leaving the thing they'd asked for a dozen times out of their bag. They were immature pranks from a girl playing at being an adult, something I felt I'd never had a chance to do, since I had to grow up the moment my mother got sick. (If you've ever wondered why is it that they can never get the damn order straight, I've got one word for you: Ellie.)

I saw the curtains I'd given her as a moving-in gift still folded neatly in the closet, the only clean thing in the whole apartment, not even worth taking along to wherever she'd begun to move her things to.

"Iris, stay here. I'm going to get some large trash bags to haul all of this stuff out to the Dumpster."

"What about the, um, stuff? Should we call the police?"

"Nope."

"Let's call the police!" chirped Henry.

"We're not calling the police, Henry! And don't touch anything. I'll be right back."

Three hours and eight large, dark green trash bags later, Iris and I had cleared it all out, and Gustavo had changed the lock to Ellie's apartment and left a message on her cell phone telling her that her things would be next to the recycling bins on my side of the building for the next forty-eight hours, after which they'd be thrown in a Dumpster. He also told her that I'd found her drugs and that if she didn't pay back every cent she owed me—eight hundred and fifty dollars in total for the current month's rent—I'd take them to her mother. It was a gamble. I'd flushed it all down the toilet, and calling her mother (whose number she'd listed as her emergency contact) was a weak threat meant more to scare her into not questioning my dubious eviction practices than to get her to pay me the money she owed.

Still, I figured I'd get her out of the unit with a minimum of trouble, and then, once things calmed down a bit, I'd find a way to let her mom know what was going on with her child so she could get her some help. The pot was bad enough, but I was sure those dark, ugly rocks were worse, and I couldn't stand silently by and let whatever Ellie was doing kill her. I just couldn't.

"Gustavo, thank you so much for rushing over on your lunch hour. I couldn't have peace until that lock was changed."

"It's no problem, Mariela. They weren't even expecting me at the hardware store today. I'd asked for the day off to take Abril downtown. Planned to make a day of it, accompany her on her errands, take her to lunch, save her the hassle of coming back on the bus. But it must've been something I said because she changed her mind about having me drive her, got upset, and accused me of wanting to control her," he said, shaking his head, his face contorted in confusion.

Iris and I looked at each other, but Iris lowered her eyes and busied herself taking the Windex from Henry, who didn't understand why he was only allowed to help clean with a wet rag and not given the fun pump with the blue liquid to use, as if he were "a little kid."

We opened all the windows to let a little fresh air circulate through the space and went down to my place.

"So Abril took the bus?" I asked Gustavo, unable to imagine anyone passing up a ride for Miami public transportation.

"I don't know. I'm not going to think about it, and Henry knows why," he said.

"Because nobody can understand women," said Henry very seriously upon hearing his cue.

After Gustavo had swallowed the black coffee I had made for him and gone back to work, Iris told me, "Even I don't understand that girl. You'd think she'd let herself be helped."

"What do you mean?"

Iris gestured toward Henry, who was listening intently, so I turned my TV on to some cartoons for him and followed her into the kitchen so we could continue our shameless gossiping while I made sandwiches and more coffee for us, and some oatmeal for him.

"I think she's found Henry's father," whispered Iris.

"When did she lose him?"

"I'm not sure. You know she used to live down here in Little Havana about eight years ago."

"You mentioned it once."

"She was eighteen or nineteen and living here with an aunt. Then she went to New York City to be near her family. They live in Washington Heights."

"Is that where she met Henry's father?" I said, even as the answer came up from somewhere inside me, surprising me: no.

"That's what I thought. But Henry is seven and change, so you do the math."

"She was pregnant when she left."

"Exactly. And I think she came back because of him. To find him. Or to force him to take care of Henry."

"What makes you think that?"

"Well, first she moves in asking for a month to month lease and a discount because she's just here to resolve 'an important family issue.' Then she begins to ask to use my printer to make copies, and every time I'm able to catch a peek, it's a legal-looking form, an application, or a copy of something official like a birth certificate or a medical record."

"Maybe she's sick," I said quietly, thinking about my mother.

"And she's always asking me to watch Henry or to get him onto the school bus because she has to go downtown at these ungodly early hours. Now, what does all that tell you?"

"Not much, Iris."

"She's going to court!"

"Well, maybe not court, but you may be on to something. She may be going through a child support case process with the state attorney's office. It makes sense. She won't be able to get Medicaid to help with Henry's medical bills unless she has at least made an attempt to locate his father and have him pay child support. Maybe that's all it is."

"Maybe, but get this, yesterday, she asks me to take care of Henry today because it's teacher-planning day and she didn't want to take him where she was going. So I ask her, 'Where are you going?' and she sort of waves me off, saying that if all went well, everything would change, and that Henry was going to be a very happy boy. You know, you're right. I say she's either suing the bastard for child support or she had sued him before and the state just found him."

"Well, I've had a few clients with the same problem, and it can take years for the child support enforcement division at the state attorney's office to locate a father, if that's what she's doing."

Except it was Thursday. Last I'd heard, the child support enforcement division didn't see clients on Thursdays. Still, maybe Abril had found herself a badass Miami motherfucking lawyer, as my client Silvia would say, though I decided not to say so, asking instead: "So you think Henry's father is here in Miami and doesn't want to do the right thing?"

I was starting to get a strange, yet not altogether unfamiliar, feeling about all this, an uneasiness the source of which I couldn't quite locate inside my body.

"I think there's more to it. You know, Henry does have her last name," she said, twisting a strawberry pink lock of hair with her right index finger and a blond one with her left.

"So what? You can give a child any last name you want, and you said yourself she got the money to go to nursing school, so maybe he *is* paying child support."

"Maybe he's married and famous," she said, ignoring me.

"That doesn't mean anything. If he's famous, all the more reason to avoid a scandal."

"Maybe he refuses to give poor Henry his lousy last name and the child support he's entitled to," finished Iris, as if finally articulating a theory she'd been working on for some time.

"Yeah, I can see that," I said, surrendering. "Maybe Henry is Enrique Iglesias's love child. Or Luis Miguel's!"

"Hey, she's pretty enough and smart. Maybe it *is* Luis Miguel."

"He doesn't have a house in Miami."

"That you know of. And you don't need to own a house to run out on your wife, girlfriend, or whatever the guy has," she said.

Well, didn't I know that much to be the truth?

"I'm telling you, Mariela, that girl is going through some big things, but she won't confide in anyone or ask for help beyond having me watch Henry every once in a while. Even poor Gustavo, who's completely gaga over her, she treats like a distant relative."

"Well, he doesn't see her as a distant relative, I'll tell you that. I ran into her coming out of his apartment with Henry yesterday, and they all looked quite chummy, like a little family. It was cute, actually," I said.

Iris remained silent for a moment.

"I miss my husband, Mariela," she said finally.

"Oh, Iris. I'm sorry. Is it still hard?"

"No, no. After ten years, it's easier in a way. But once in a while, I just wish I could see him. Just one more time, you know?"

I lowered my eyes, because the force of Iris's desire was connecting with something deep inside me, and I didn't want to see or hear anything about anyone, not that I thought I still could after my failed experiment the night before.

My silence must've made her feel self-conscious about sharing because she changed the subject.

"Well, anyway, you're right about one thing: Gustavo's in love," she said. "Serves him right. He was such a dog to that cute girl who used to come around looking for him. I forget her name."

"Monica," I said. "Remember that day I had to distract her so he could leave his apartment with that other one, the one with the blue hair."

"That's right! What a crazy boy."

"Who knows? Maybe he was just waiting for the right girl," I said loyally.

"Yeah, sure," said Iris with a smirk. "But enough about him. What're you doing on Saturday for your birthday?"

"Oh, I'll probably throw myself a party cleaning that filthy apartment upstairs," I said, hoping to be at the St. Michel with Hector, getting rid of all the mess between us. Even if I was on my way out as his lover, I wanted to leave him wanting more, not relieved he'd gotten rid of me.

"You should do something fun. Whoever heard of cleaning on one's birthday?" she said, before hollering to Henry that they were leaving.

"Iris, tell Abril I'd be happy to help her find a good lawyer or some free legal aid. I've researched quite a few good programs for women waiting for child support to kick in."

"I'll tell her, but, knowing her, she'll look at me like she doesn't know what I'm talking about. By the way, you know Fridays are Spam All Star nights at Hoy Como Ayer, so if you change your mind and decide to do something special for the eve of your birthday, you're welcome to join my friends and me tomorrow night. You know, start your celebration early with a little Cuban nostalgic funk," she said, dancing a little and making me laugh at the sight of her strawberry-highlighted tresses slashing air to the rhythm of her hips.

"Do we have to leave now?" said Henry, running into the kitchen.

"Yes, sir, we do. Chop, chop."

"But I don't want to chop!"

"Remember, a little dancing, a little fun, wouldn't kill anybody," Iris said to me as she headed out.

"Promise to think about it," I said, sincerely hoping I'd be otherwise engaged. Not that Hoy Como Ayer wasn't fun. The name meant "today as in the past," and it was that perfect mix of nostalgia and hip vanguard that was at the center of its mystique. There was a certain sexy vibe emanating from the raw-gorgeous people singing loudly, laughing gaily, and dancing madly under the club lights and curious-lustful-envious gaze of the cigar-smoking, mojito- or rum-and-Coke-drinking, music-loving nondancers. You could engage with the energy of those around you as much as you wanted (which could lead to very interesting experiences), or retreat, losing yourself inside yourself, alone but not really, until you got your fill of whatever part of you had escaped you.

It was where Miamians went to listen to some of the best underground Cuban music in town, and I hadn't been there in what seemed like ages. Well, actually since just before Hector, during a New Year's Eve celebration, wearing a sweet little blue dress and glittery heels, realizing I was happy, and because of that, breaking up that very night with the one that got away. Except he didn't. I'd thrown Jorge back into the sea myself. Gave him back to his wife because I was afraid of loving him, of losing him, of suffering. That fear alone had been enough to propel me, headfirst instead of heart-first, into Hector's arms. And now, not even a year later, here I was again, on the losing end of . . . something.

After Iris left, I put on an old Julieta Venegas CD and tried to relax. The sound of her silvery voice filled the space with a song about those changes in yourself that you can't see, barely notice, until it hits you that something in you is different. Usually, just a few lines of any of Julieta's songs were enough to lull me into imagined happiness and well-being, but today the topic of this one made things worse. Today, the song seemed to bring the feeling of impending doom I'd had since yesterday to the foreground of my consciousness, troubling me, as if my fear of never knowing what it might have felt like to be truly loved were being confirmed with every verse.

I thought of Hector and our affair, trying to pinpoint what was making it so hard to leave him behind.

At first, it had been exciting, meeting him somewhere different every time. Sometimes we'd meet to talk. And even though I'd loved reading before him, he had taught me how to truly lose myself in the pleasure of a good book, how to peel it like a freshly ripened piece of fruit, releasing its juicy pulp.

"You can learn more about life from a good novel than from all the self-help books ever published put together," he'd tell me.

"Oh, that's not true."

"It's absolutely true."

So he'd read to me. Esmeralda Santiago's *The Turkish Lover* and Julia Alvarez's *Saving the World,* Sandra Cisneros's *Loose Woman,* and Junot Díaz's *This Is How You Lose Her,* emphasizing a thousand and one lessons and seducing me in the process. And he'd hold me, and talk to me, and look at me, and want to know everything about me. So I'd tell him almost everything, and then listen to his voice as it sounded when his lips were warming the vicinity of my ears. And then, I'd choose to forget some more, his words the numbing agent allowing me to remember the man who came before him with a dulled, distant sadness, but without the angst of desperation.

Meanwhile, Olivia, his wife, kept to herself, rarely leaving her apartment except for the organic garden center where she was a volunteer of some sort, seldom answering a greeting, and making it easy for me to convince myself that what I was doing didn't matter, that my affair with Hector was just like the unexpected, fleeting joy of rereading a clever line one wrote long ago, buried among the important things in a diary no one else would ever read.

Of course it was all insanely sexy. Hector was a natural teacher, engaging me in fascinating conversations that mixed the intellectual and the sexual in ways that made me want to stay under his spell forever. He'd analyze me constantly as if I were a complex, rare, and precious firefly, and despite myself, I began to see myself differently through his eyes: light, flowing, sensuous, vibrating, and as alive as I'd ever been.

I didn't exactly forget he was married. The fact just appeared to fade a little more with every month that passed, and I began telling myself that maybe this delicious adventure was the work of one of God's Robin Hood–like helpers deciding that I deserved not to be the one being cheated on, at least this once. I'd settled. And now, here I was. Was it too late? Could I try to really love someone again? To be in a normal relationship capable of growing into something stable?

Where were these questions coming from? It wasn't just the argument I'd had with Hector that morning or the abruptness with which his passion had turned into indifference or thinking of Jorge again. It was these questions that didn't sound like me and couldn't be coming from me. Then again, after so many years of keeping my sixth sense on "off," who the hell knew what the call for help of the real me sounded or felt like?

Most certainly not me.

Chapter 9

"I'm telling you, forty is the new thirty," said the enthusiastic cosmetics counter attendant at the Village of Merrick Park when I told him about my birthday the next day. "Just look at yourself. You should be a model for that magazine—what's it called? The one with all the gorgeous women who are forty, fifty, even sixty? Forget it, I can't remember the name, but this foundation I'm putting on you? It's featured on their latest cover, and you should be on it," he said, opening his eyes wide as much to emphasize his point as to show off the flawless lash work.

"Hmm," I answered, thinking that getting compliments from people who wanted to sell me things would sooner get me into bankruptcy court than on the cover of a national magazine. I'd come for the free makeup application, but now I was trapped inside this glitzy department store, feeling like a criminal for intending to walk away without buying even one of the overpriced things I couldn't afford now being used on my face.

"Now, while I finish, I want you to describe yourself on this contest form," he said, handing me a small notepad with the brand's logo and a pink pen.

I hesitated.

"You could win an all-expense-paid cruise to the *Mediterraneaaaaan*," he cooed.

It was obviously important to him, so I took the notepad intending to fill it out. Except that trying to describe myself only made my eyes well up, threatening the three layers of "sun-kissed," antioxidant bronzing powder he'd just applied to my face.

What had made me think that plastering my face with micro-bead this and age-defying that would make me feel wonderful about turning forty and facing the beginning of another decade with another breakup?

Because breaking up with Hector before he broke up with me is what I'd decided to do on that Friday morning, not two days after we'd been together at the St. Michel, and despite all my self-boasting about being a "successful" other woman.

I'd woken with three words on my brain: *enough—of—this*. What was I so afraid of? I had lost everything that truly mattered to me when I lost my mother. Did I die? No! I survived. And what was the worst that could happen to me really? Worst-case scenario, I'd have to buy a vibrator and learn how to use it properly. I wasn't the first, and I wouldn't be the last. And, who knew, maybe the makeup, doing something to look my best, would magically inject me with the confidence I was trying to drum up. Maybe it was just the signal I needed to alert Hector that something inside me was different. To let him (and me) know that he didn't really know me and that I was capable of changing for the better at a moment's notice. I wanted to make him wonder about all the little secrets I still held inside me. I might have been on my way out, but I still had to live mere steps from the man, and as Ellie would have said with her lame trashy-girl-imitating-ghetto-girl-to-be-cool slang, I didn't have to "go out like that."

Still, every slap, pat, and brush of makeup just felt like having the word *failure* stamped onto my face.

"What's wrong, honey?" asked the makeup boy, startled by my tears. "Oh. No. No, no, no. We can't have that. People are going to think I'm torturing you or something. Come on." He laughed. "Okay, I get it, you want me to do it for you, you tricky girl," he said, hastily taking the notepad from me as I cried. Embarrassed, I tried to smile and hoped he wouldn't think I was crying because I didn't know how to write.

"There," he said, handing it back to me after a couple of minutes. He'd filled in the blanks with:

I am .... *lush and glamorous.*

My three best features are .... *1) my black, wavy hair, 2) the way my eyes close when I smile, like a Chinese manga doll's, 3) my curvy Rockette thighs.*

What I love about myself is .... *my smile. It's a little bit gummy and fabulous and makes me look like Julia Roberts.*

I had to laugh.

"I can write good, right?"

"You know what? You really can. You also really want to sell some makeup."

"Aw, don't say that. It's nothing but the truth. And now, when you win the cruise, you can take me as your date! The word *lush* is part of the new campaign, so it shows you're a good customer."

"It shows I'm an arrogant customer."

"Nooo, it shows you're confident, like our products. There it is. You see?" He turned me toward the mirror. "Julia Roberts."

Well, I'll say this for him: I did look better in a weird, not-really-me kind of way. My eyes, shiny from the tears, were surrounded by someone else's dramatic lashes, and he'd made my lips soft, shimmery, and pin-up pouty. Still, if it were possible that I could remind anyone of Julia Roberts, it could only be of her in that teary scene in *Notting Hill* in which she tells Hugh Grant that she's "just a girl, standing in front of a boy, asking him to love her," and made me feel just as forlorn and ridiculous.

Because I *had* been just a girl, standing in front of not one, but, well, more than one boy, asking him (them) to love her, and yet here I was, about to turn forty alone, which either meant I was a girl who was pretty bad at asking to be loved or just a plain unlovable girl, and now I wasn't even that because looking at me from the other side of that mirror was someone who looked not a day less than the hard-lived middle-aged woman with no successes in her pocket, and no real skills, that she really was.

I bought the mascara and an overpriced, pinky-rose lipstick called "Kinda Sexy" from the makeup boy, and an hour later I was getting off the eight bus a few stops before I had to. Even in September, gray, rain-threatening days are so rare in Miami, I'd always found them comforting, romantic even, and perfect for a mind-clearing walk home. Plus, it would give me a chance to stop at the *frutería* to buy some fresh tomatoes and avocados for a salad.

Though their eyes never left my ass, the men loitering at the *frutería* seemed to approve of my new look, to judge by their up and down looks and their obsequious smiles. I rushed to pay, only to realize it had begun to rain, as I'd suspected. One of them opened the door for me, and I stood under the shop's whisper of an awning with him, choosing to get wet and ruin my makeup rather than go back into the *frutería* to be visually dissected. He asked my name, did I live in the area, and wasn't I cold, before realizing I wasn't about to answer any of his questions and giving up. Then he sprinted across the street and into a shop I'd never noticed before, despite probably passing it on my way home a million times.

The sign over the door read BOTÁNICA NEGRA FRANCISCA (which means "Francisca, the negress"). A *botánica* is where *santeros* and would-be *santeros* shop. And *Santería,* well, the easiest way to describe it is to say that it's as old as Christianity and blends (or tries to blend) Roman Catholic beliefs with traditional Afro-Cuban rituals and ways of seeing life and death, good and evil, love and hate. It's popular in Brazil and in Caribbean countries like the Dominican Republic, Cuba, and Puerto Rico.

You can buy folk medicine and remedies, religious candles, potions, charms, amulets, jewelry, statues of saints in every size, and other products the believing regard as the magical form of alternative medicine for whatever ails a life, from emptiness to jealousy, and from sadness to the mad, mad, mad desire for revenge.

Many *botánicas* look like a pack rat's garage and smell like incense. Most are unassuming, humble. They may have a "house doctor," usually a self-proclaimed, all-knowing, remedy-prescribing, psychic-pharmacist-psychologist who offers consultations for a set fee of anywhere from a voluntary donation to sixty dollars.

Even before my "gift" manifested with puberty, I spent quite a lot of time visiting *santeros* in *botánicas* with my mother. I wasn't even in kindergarten when I learned to *despojarme,* which is to perform a rhythmic, furious shake of your arms above your head, back to front, to send the bad spirits away.

But this *botánica* didn't look like the others. Even through the rain, it looked to me like an opera stage, with bloodred velour curtains framing the scene made by the saints in the window, arms outstretched in mercy, like actors in a play. It was the kind of place that made you imagine an old gypsy with a crystal ball on her lap and as much makeup on her face as I had on mine.

It was raining hard now. I couldn't walk in the rain and the place was calling me. Walking in, the man who'd talked to me was nowhere to be seen. I heard the same jangle of bells as before and realized they had hypnotized me into coming in. Otherwise, how was I here, suddenly surrounded by big and small gesso saints on every corner and old metal storage shelves lined with small glass bottles holding fluorescent liquids and chalky powders? A redheaded woman in her fifties wearing jeans and a purple tank top asked if she could help me and waited for God knows how long. I say this because I don't remember what I answered. And I don't remember how long before I left. All I know is that the moment my two feet were inside, I heard a loud, otherworldly crack, a single jolt of thunder stabbing some nearby inch of earth with its sword of light, and it was as if I weren't there. As if all I could do was remember who I was and feel in my very veins the sorrow I'd come from.

Chapter 10

But where *do* you come from? Who are these people you were born into? That moment, when they first hold you, and the moment in which your eyes meet theirs for the first time, are like coordinates marking the direction of your entire life. Because families are the all-important clues to the questions you will spend a lifetime answering, to your strengths and weaknesses, and sometimes, unwittingly, the cause of your sorrows.

I, for example, come from a family of non-seers who, nevertheless, had seers scattered all over their genealogical tree like freckles. This is because clairvoyance comes in strains, like a disease, and the particular variety that seemed to run in my family was partial to women, arrived with puberty, and as my mother found out much after I was born, behaved pretty much the same as blue eyes and dimples, skipping a generation like a recessive genetic trait.

Ana Cecilia Valdes, my maternal grandmother, had it. According to my mother, she was a strikingly beautiful young Cuban woman from a well-to-do Havana family that frowned on "all that nonsense and heresy."

When Ana Cecilia "got" her gift along with her first period, her maternal grandmother (my great-great-grandmother) moved into her bedroom with the pretense of keeping a better eye on her now that she was of a "dangerous" age. Using an unassuming handmade journal to write down each lesson, she began to secretly teach her all she knew about divination, intuition, white magic, and clairvoyance.

My grandmother studied it all avidly, happy to please her beloved nana, reading and rereading this bespoke clairvoyance textbook made just for her, guarding it jealously, and speaking of it to no one.

Later, in college, she began doing private readings for her friends, almost as a joke or an excuse for conversation at their living room parties, or *fiestas de marquesina,* as they were called. Until a new fellow, just arrived from some small town or other to study medicine, sat in front of her at a friend's impromptu birthday party and gave her his open palms.

"So tell me. What do you see?" he'd said, smiling.

"I don't do palms," she retorted.

"Okay. What do you do?"

"Nothing. I just . . . feel something . . . and—" She'd stopped, panicked because she could usually get a stranger's "scent" the moment he spoke to her, and here she was, incapable of thinking, feeling, or seeing anything other than the smile on this boy's half-expectant, half-curious face. "I feel something," she began again, "and just know . . . something else. And then, I tell you. And . . . it makes sense to you." She swallowed. "Or . . . it doesn't."

"So you're saying you guess?"

"No. What . . . I feel something, and then something comes . . . into my head, and feels . . . like truth."

He considered that for a moment.

"Can you 'feel' what I'm thinking right now?" he asked, roping her in with his eyes and holding her there, wherever it was he'd begun taking her with his voice from the very first word he'd said to her.

"No. Not really. I'm not getting anything right now. Maybe later. Excuse me."

But I guess she did "get" something, because she married

him against her family's wishes and moved to the town of Violeta, where she had my mother and lived a simple but happy existence, to hear my mother talk about it.

And that's the reason little Mercedes, my mother, spent her childhood hearing the wonderful things my grandmother foresaw for others while sitting at the kitchen table, and anxiously waiting for puberty (and for her own gift) to kick in. To my mother, clairvoyance was like Santa Claus: the provider of amazing gifts you got only if you were very, very good.

Then came the revolution, and my grandparents sent her to the United States as part of Operation Peter Pan. It was the early sixties, Fidel Castro was firmly in power, and there were rumors that the children of parents who opposed the Cuban revolution were going to be shipped off to Soviet work camps. The United States government (mostly the State Department and the CIA) and the Roman Catholic Archdiocese of Miami coordinated the effort, and hundreds of children were placed with friends or relatives in over thirty-five states as a preventative measure, until they could be reunited with their parents. Others, like my mother, were placed in group homes in the Midwest.

Mercedita was twelve going on thirteen when she arrived in Iowa with a valise that was bigger than she was, and her mother's inherited clairvoyance journal snug among the carefully folded clothes inside it.

You may have heard of other Pedro Pan kids. Some are famous like the writer Carlos Eire and Ana Mendieta, the famous performance artist, and I've always thought that, maybe, if my mother had had a sister to talk to about how desperately she missed her own bedroom back in Violeta, if she'd been able to understand some of what people were saying to her, or if someone at the home where she was had celebrated her first period, good-naturedly teasing her about becoming a woman like her mom and dad would have, then the fact that it didn't bring her gift with it wouldn't have hit her so hard, and she would've become a famous writer or an artist too. Instead, not knowing that it skipped a generation, she thought the cold Iowa nights had chased it away, robbing her of the only thing that could've reminded her that she was loved and missed on an island that felt farther away than it really was.

Who knows what things happened to her in the years that followed? I just know that the minute she turned eighteen, she ran away to Miami with the idea of figuring out a way to either bring her parents to the United States or go back to Cuba.

But by that time, they couldn't leave because my grandfather was a doctor, and as such, a nationalized commodity. Being a *gusana,* a worm who'd defected from her country, she was not allowed to go back, not even to visit, and not even later, for their funerals. And since having my grandparents risk their lives on a raft would have never been an option for my mother, I can see how the only path she saw was to pay someone to somehow smuggle them out.

Without a high school diploma, she began working as a waitress to sustain herself while sending money to her parents and saving even more money to get them out of Cuba.

Time passed, and I don't know when or why she gave up and decided to become a self-managed call girl. She never talked about that part of it, and she didn't leave enough random bits of runaway comments for me to piece together. But I know that it was sometime within this gray area of her life that I was born. When I was little, I'd beg to know my father's name, and she'd never tell me, until I finally realized that she really didn't remember, or didn't know, and I stopped asking.

She was clever, and fun, and kind, and five minutes after meeting her, you'd decide she really was the most beautiful woman in the entire world. You'd forget all about that separate entrance for an entire area of our house that I wasn't allowed into unless it was cleaning day or Sunday, or about the fact that our garage door would be open at predetermined times when a car would roll in, its driver staying inside it until my mother had closed the garage door and led him through a door that discreetly deposited him into the forbidden area of the house, before neighbors could catch a glimpse of him, maybe recognize him from news video of a county hearing or public zoning meeting.

Whenever people asked about her job, I was to tell them that she had a disability and couldn't work. This was designed to make people uncomfortable so they'd refrain from asking questions. I didn't like making people uncomfortable, so I just avoided making friends.

Then I hit puberty and began knowing things.

It was my mother who first caught on. After the third time of my making an out of nowhere comment about something I had no way of knowing, she took me to a *babalaó* or wise one, several spiritual pay grades above a *santera*.

"Alabaó," he said, peering down at me with his huge, round eyes, the whites of them as white against his dark cacao skin as his carefully pressed guayabera shirt. "My, my, she's got it all right, but—"

"What?" my mother asked anxiously.

He gestured to my mother to follow him to the other side of the room where I could still hear him talking in Spanish, while I sat on the little stool next to his scary altar and his life-sized gesso Yemayá.

"Mercedita, this child needs guidance. There's a lot going on there."

"Spit it out, Sergio."

"Trouble. Storms, darkness, death, and then more death! I've never seen so much turmoil in someone this young."

When my mother couldn't get him to make a more positive prognosis, we hastened out of there with her muttering all the way home, calling him too old to see his own nose in about fifty different ways that now remind me of the "your mama" jokes told by schoolkids. You know the ones: "Your mama is so old I told her to act her age and she died," or "Your mama's so old I asked for her birth certificate and she handed me a rock," etc.

Finally, she got it out of her system.

"Well, anyway, he's so old, Matusalén was his baby brother. Forget him. We'll get you read by someone else."

Which we never did. Instead, I became very, very special: the link to her long, lost family, the proof that she came from a line of "someones."

On ever-more-frequent nights without clients, we'd lie on my bed reading the tattered journal my great-great-grandmother had put together, and my own grandmother had given to her only daughter for protection in a strange country. The smell of Cuba on the pages, which my mother swore she could still smell, was long gone, but the black coffee stains remained, so faded they looked translucent, like tears someone had traced lightly around.

We were no longer lost luggage left unclaimed in the wrong airport. We were part of a family tradition. We belonged to a group of people who knew things, destined to be wise and use their gift to bring happiness and comfort to others.

Slowly, surprise at my good fortune became pride in my ability to know secrets that made people smile, believe, and hope again. A message from a loved one presumed lost was like an IV filled with life instead of fluids, and I was capable of delivering it.

I became cocky, never reading my great-great-grandmother's journal on my own, doing nothing to learn the rules and responsibilities of my gift. All I cared about was that my mother told me stories about her childhood, asked what I thought she should cook for us that afternoon, and shared her real estate plans with me, as if I knew anything about houses and money.

That was the best part: feeling like I had given something back to my mother, as if my fabulous gift was the connection that allowed her to remember she'd also had a mother who loved her once.

Just before she got sick, she looked the happiest I'd ever seen her. She seemed to have fewer but better "boyfriends," her special "niche" finally paying off in the form of generous clients "appreciating" her with properties and money that she turned into even more or bigger properties.

"You'll see, baby. Soon you'll be going off to college, and I'm going to retire so I can go with you. We'll hire someone to manage the rentals and only come back here to vacation in South Beach like the millionaires."

That's how she talked about it, by the way, as if her job and our lives were like everyone else's.

And then cancer happened.

My mother began to walk around with the shell-shocked expression of a war refugee on her face. I dropped out of school, took the high school equivalency exam, and ran from her properties to the hospital every day, doing everything she told me in order to rent the houses and apartments she owned, seven in total, before her illness took three away. Every night, I'd give her a report, as she struggled to sit up in bed and did her best to look like she was still proud of me.

But where before she'd insisted I go to college because a famous psychic had to know the world, be able to express herself when she was invited to Oprah's, now she told me it would make her feel good that I study "something."

Three times a week a hospital volunteer would pick us both up and take us to Jackson Memorial Hospital for the chemotherapy sessions. The other two days I took computer software courses in a drab room deep within the arteries of a vocational school that closely resembled a prison and was located in one of the worst parts of town close to the hospital.

It's a wonder I learned anything, spending most school days

with my head bowed, crying all over the dusty keyboards no one seemed to care much about. I was eighteen years old, and my life consisted of wrangling renters, going to computer school until I could bear it no longer, hating myself for giving my mother the false security that killed her, and watching the only person in the world who loved me wither to nothing. Of course she said it wasn't my fault. But I knew better. Less than a year later, she checked herself into the hospital one more time. And then she died.

I dealt with my regret over my failure to foresee her illness by sending clairvoyance to rest with her, forcing it out of my mind and heart. But I saved my great-great-grandmother's clairvoyance journal, unable to destroy something my mother, and her mother before her, had treasured so dearly. I no longer wanted to see beyond what was right in front of me, and I never told anyone of my "feelings," purposely thinking of something else whenever I met someone and felt "something coming."

I began automatically disregarding all of my own gut-instinct perceptions, thinking that if I "felt" it or "saw" it, it was either wrong, my own imagination, or ironically irrelevant. After a while, the dreams, the feelings, the visions, the smells, and the whispers stopped, and I could once again look people in the eye without "knowing" things about them that I had no business knowing, like I could when I was a child.

With my mother gone, I inherited the properties that were left after paying all of the hospital bills and quickly sold the house I grew up in, also in Little Havana, even hiring a contractor to turn the much smaller than I'd thought "forbidden side" into a sunlit Florida room with a bathroom and a terrace.

Besides real estate, my only other inheritance was the journal and the desperate need to be a normal person and lead a normal life the direct opposite of my mother's. No powerful men, no clairvoyance, no gifts from anyone, imagined or concrete. Just love with one man who'd go decades thinking I was the most beautiful woman in the world, the one he could not live without. One normal, kind man to love me and share my imperfect life. One love I could remember in the hours before leaving this world, and call my own.

Chapter 11

The next thing I remember was running out of the *botánica* and hurrying home in the rain, clothes sticking to me, mascara running, blisters forming with every rushed sprint and step. I hated myself for going in there, for exposing myself to the memory of stories capable of squeezing my chest for every last bit of oxygen, for falling back into my old ways of wanting to know what was beyond my eyesight, instead of taking care of things boldly, on this plane. I'd been running away from clairvoyance for over twenty years! Why had it decided to catch up with me now? Getting over the end of something as inconsequential as an affair didn't warrant a summons from otherworldly realms, did it? Had Hector gotten under my skin, or was it my own life, with all its troubles, making me think the answer was in the gift I'd had and given up?

I was soaked by the time I walked into my apartment to find my landline ringing.

"I need to see you."

Hector had remembered my birthday tomorrow! I looked at the microwave clock display. It was close to six and finally hearing his voice spelled the words "instant gratification" in my head.

"Where are you?" I asked.

"At the bookstore. Can I see you now?"

"Where? I just came in and need a bath and some food. I'm famished," I said, hinting.

"I'll see you there."

"Here?" I asked, thinking that was very odd. We never "saw" each other in the building.

"I promise I'll be careful."

"What about—"

"It's okay. You're my landlord, Mariela. We can talk."

Any other day, I'd have asked, "Are you crazy?" But.

"All right. Come through the kitchen door," I said, too surprised and curious to protest or ask more questions.

"It won't take long. I'll see you soon."

"Bye, *amor,*" I said, but he'd already hung up, while I could feel my nerves fluttering around inside my body like Miami blue butterflies. I knew the feeling, of course: It was disappointment.

Shit. I was positive the news was not going to be good, and for a minute, the imminence of the end of all the fun and excitement he'd brought into my life over the months of our affair made that time seem longer, more important. I had to make him want me back the minute he'd broken up with me. With my makeup-plastered face, maybe I could pull off the lie that I was suddenly sophisticated, blasé, understanding, and even a little excited about going on with my life, free as a firefly with a new lightbulb on her ass. Call it the Modern Mistress's Self-Preservation Protocol but, suddenly, I was all about managing my exit.

I cleaned up and got my unfinished breakup letter out of the drawer where I'd put it after I'd begun composing it the night I ran into him before his date with Olivia and tried to finish it.

But what I'd written that night was far from reflecting the sexy, playful relationship we'd had. Instead, it was a long, sarcastic, disconnected from reality, petty tirade inspired by an obscure literary figure. Definitely not the best breakup letter for my present purpose, so I crumpled it and started a fresh sheet, willing myself to recapture the feelings of the beginning in my head.

He'd seemed elegant to me in the way of people who put a premium on education over money. Hector took pride in being an intellectual, and for eight months, I'd wanted to expand like a sponge to absorb the essence of him, wanting to be cultured, well read, and ladylike, instead of being the bigmouthed *cubana* he'd at least been curious about. I thought about him, about us, until a feeling came into my head. Then I wrote:

> *September 23*
> *Amor,*
> *There is that day. A woman slows down long enough to think, wakes up, and knows the life she dreamed of is not going to happen. She will never be a famous human rights leader, rich, or loved in the way of those F. Scott Fitzgerald stories you love so much: that sweet, desperate way a man loves when obsessed and even her slightly chipped tooth makes him think of sex when she laughs.*

I smiled at that last bit, remembering how he consoled me by telling me I looked sexy after I tripped on the backyard stoop, chipping my left upper front tooth, and was unable to get it fixed for almost a month.

> *Yes, there is that day, but until today, it hadn't arrived for me. It hadn't arrived before you, and it certainly didn't show up over these past months when the occasional desire to move on and away from you was always weaker than the pull of your voice, your smell, and your mind. But things feel different now, and I just don't want to be the other woman anymore.*

I considered that line, then erased the word *the* and substituted it for the word *your* so it read:

> But today is different, and I just don't want to be
> your other woman anymore.

I wrote this because it was obvious that neither did he, but also because it was true. I was suffering. Affairs with married men that you enter into consciously (knowing they are married) aren't supposed to make you suffer, surprising you with the suddenness of their endings. I wasn't ready to say I'd fallen in love with Hector, but I was absolutely sure that I had fallen into some similar rabbit hole. And I didn't want this panic of "not having anyone," of being "left" that I'd been under for the past few days.

Perhaps I really didn't want to be the other woman anymore or maybe being his "other," as opposed to his "one," had begun to bother some part of me more than I realized.

The rain was coming down quick and thick now, and Hector would be here any minute, soaking wet if, as usual, he'd decided to walk the fifteen or so blocks from the bookstore, his precious Saab reserved only for unwalkable distances.

I kept writing.

> And so, amor, I think today is that day. For me,
> and maybe for you? I wish you well. (I began
> practicing that phrase the day I met you.) As I write
> to you knowing that it's over, and that it's what
> you're coming to say, all I want to do is thank you for
> the fun times. With love,

I considered that, then decided the letter was melodramatic enough as it was, and erased those two words, signing only:

> *M+E*

Those are my initials and the way I had been signing my notes to him lately, wanting to state my existence in his life if only through "Mission Impossible" notes destined to "self-destruct" (be thrown away) as soon as they were read.

My phone rang again. It was Iris.

"What's wrong, neighbor?" she asked when I answered as if she'd interrupted a state dinner.

"Nothing. What's up?"

"Just making sure you don't want to go to Hoy Como Ayer later. Last chance to go while you're still in your thirties."

"You know, Iris, I'm really not feeling all that well."

"Want me to go over, make you a little tea with some ginger, lemon, and honey, and some—"

"That's okay, Iris. I think I'm just going to rest up."

"You know, if I didn't know better, I'd say the Little Havana Community Committee has put a hex on Coffee Park."

The committee was her only enemy in the world. In her mind, they were a threat to the liberal way of living, almost as bad as that other type of person she had to share the earth with: conservatives.

"Nooo, I'm just tired from all that hauling of Ellie's trash we did yesterday."

"Well, I think something's definitely going on."

Shit.

"What do you mean?" I asked, making myself sound sleepy and wishing she were capable of taking a hint.

"Well, I caught Abril sniffling on the back stoop last night after she came back from her downtown meetings or errands or whatever. So I go over to Pedro's to get her extra-strength echinacea, and *he* looked worst than Abril."

"Was he sick too?" I asked.

"You could say that. Sarah left him. Went back to Madison this morning, home to her family. He's devastated."

"I'm sure," I said, remembering how he'd told her to go just a couple of days ago, but not sharing it with Iris to avoid being on the phone any longer.

"Anyway, no echinacea, not that Abril would've taken it. But it serves her right because today, of course, she came home from work sick. Been in bed with the bug since. And now you're the one who doesn't feel well, and you sound depressed. I tell you it's those damn Little Havana people putting the evil eye on us."

"Oh, Iris! You know, with the change in the weather and all the rain, I bet you that's probably what it is. We're both coming down with something. I'm sure I'll feel better tomorrow," I said, somehow knowing that Abril had not been sniffling, but crying.

"You'd better. It's not every day one turns forty, my dear."

"I know. Have fun, okay? I'll talk to you tomorrow."

"Okay then."

"Okay, bye."

"Bye then."

(You ever notice how Latinos take forever to say good-bye, as if hanging up after just one good-bye were impolite?)

I hung up and went back to the letter. I read it over, knowing I was making too much of this. It had only been eight months. Still, I couldn't help being sad. Sad and tired. I was so, so tired of endings. Even turning forty felt like another ending instead of a beginning, and I wished I could put off just a little longer this latest farewell walking toward my house at that very moment.

As if in answer to my wish, a war-of-the-worlds-like thunderbolt brought me back to the present, the sound once again affecting me like a hypnotist's second snap of the fingers.

Wait a minute, I thought. *What if I was wrong? I was always wrong!* It was the eve of my birthday. Hector was exquisite in his love of detail. Surely, he had not planned to break up with me on the eve of my birthday. Maybe there was something else he really needed to tell me. Since when was I so sure of anything?

I'd leave my options open, I decided, giving in to fear, tucking the letter I'd just written inside the journal along with the crumpled one, throwing it all inside my night table drawer, and going to put a couple of wineglasses and a bottle of locally made guava wine on the kitchen table, willing myself not to believe my own mind, as I'd gotten quite good at doing over the years. Why did I have to jump the gun? If he didn't bring up breaking up, neither would I. It was as if my mind knew it had made me suffer enough and was giving me permission to grant myself a reprieve from the messy business of send-offs. A few seconds later, I heard the low rap on my back door.

"Ey, *flaca,*" he said, slipping inside and locking my kitchen door in one move.

"You're soaking," I said, kissing him and putting my arms around his neck, not caring that I'd get wet too.

"I know. I don't have a lot of time," he said in his clipped, but perfectly sexy accent, as he untangled himself from me and grabbed some paper towels from above the sink.

I sat down at the kitchen table, stomach overcome again with that nervous flutter of loss.

"Okay then. I think it's safe to say my birthday tomorrow is not among the reasons for your urgency, so . . ."

He closed his eyes and tightened his lips in the impatient way he'd allowed me to see more of lately. Finally, he took off his scarf, as if resigned.

"Mariela, *por favor.*"

I didn't answer, wondering if that thing rising inside me was anger. What was with the attitude? If anyone had a right to an attitude, it was me.

"You know what I'm going to say, right?" he said with a "life-is-tough-what-are-you-going-to-do?" expression.

And then I was angry for sure and decided not to make it easy for him.

"No idea."

He sighed. "This is crazy."

"What is?"

"This."

"And what is 'this,' to you?"

"This is two people whose, eh, paths happened to cross . . ."

I couldn't help it. I had to laugh.

"*Somesing* funny?" he asked.

"You!" I said. "Your clichés and your arrogance, and your gall, frankly, to come to my apartment to break up with me as if this were a fast-food breakup window. I just . . . find it funny."

"You're just upset. Plus," he said, pronouncing the words *just* and *plus* as you'd pronounce the *cous* in *couscous*. "Plus, the same to do fast as to do slow, no? You'll be upset no matter what."

"Sure, I'm upset. I'm upset I put off breaking up with *you,* the way you've been acting lately. So, tell me—new lover?" I asked, barely refraining from asking who the "skanky ho" was, as my client Silvia would have, and conveniently forgetting that I'd been, until that very moment, in the very position of that skanky ho, whoever she happened to be.

How was I so sure there was someone else? Because when there isn't, a man will invariably break up with you in a soft, muddled, undefined way. He'll be nice about it. So nice you won't be sure he actually broke up with you. The reason for that is that he thinks he may still want, or need, to have sex with you and doesn't want to completely piss you off. But, when a man breaks up with you in a way that leaves no doubt that's what he's doing, trust me, he has no fear of a single lonely or boring night. He's got a strong substitute.

"I asked you a question: new lover?" I persisted.

He shook his head and smiled a little bit, not caring if I saw him for the pretentious, full-of-himself jerk he'd started to behave like the minute he decided he was done with me.

"You going to play the jealous wife? Now?"

"Jealous wife? Hector, *I* was going to break up with *you*."

"I can see you were," he said, making me angrier with every badly pronounced, well-modulated word that came out of his mouth.

"Wait here," I said, and went into my bedroom.

When I walked back into the kitchen, he was putting his scarf back on, which made me even angrier.

"Here," I said, pushing the journal with my breakup drafts, crumpled and not, sticking out of it hard onto his chest with my open palm.

He took it from me and began to read the letter I'd managed to finish just minutes earlier, then really looked at me for the first time since he'd come in.

"Well. What do you know?"

"Apparently nothing," I said.

"Look, this—I never lied to you. You'll at least admit this is, eh, a bit, pathetic?"

"Are we still speaking about you? If so, then yes, quite pathetic."

He smiled.

"I come here. To talk to you, eh, face-to-face. But you . . . you're expecting some *biiiig* pre-birthday celebration, even though I *know* I took care to write *everysing* in the wall."

"What?"

"You know, that saying, the writing. It was in the wall," he said, mimicking scribbling on a wall with his arm.

"The writing was *in* the wall?" I asked, hands on hips, too angry to correct him. "Really?"

"Sure. Yes."

"And which wall would that be?"

"It's an expre—"

"Get out."

"Mariela, come on," he said, trying to hug me.

"Get. The fuck. Out," I said, pushing him away hard.

"Jesus, lower your voice. Am I going to have to look for an apartment now too?"

"Of course not. But you will have to look for another Mariela. Good luck with that, *amor*."

He actually rolled his eyes at that.

"Show yourself out," I said, turning my back on him and unable to keep myself from finishing with, "you motherfucking asshole."

"Nice. Very elegant. I see my effort to teach you a little culture has really paid off, eh, for you. Or to you. You know what I mean."

"They're called prepositions. Learn to speak . . . *some goddamn English* and *get out!*" I screamed without even turning around again to face him, locking myself in the bathroom until I heard the back door close, the vein in my neck throbbing.

I filled the tub with warm water and got in, hearing the thunder outside and wishing some of it would land close to him and scare the smirk he'd left with right off his face. After a while, when I felt better, I tiptoed to the kitchen in my bathrobe, locked the back door, and decided to have myself that glass of guava wine to calm my nerves. The journal was on top of the table. He had drawn a happy face and written "Good Job" on the second letter, the one I'd written that night. The first one, the sarcastic, crumpled one I'd written the night I'd seen him leave with Olivia, was missing.

"Motherfucker!" I said out loud, wishing I could make him explode with the sound of my voice. Knowing him, I realized he could only have taken it to hide someplace like a trophy, a memento of the passion he was still capable of stirring. "Asshole," I said, hoping he'd be careful not to leave it lying around. The last thing I needed was a problem with Morticia.

I crumpled the one he'd left behind, opened the kitchen side door, lifted the lid off the recycling bin just outside it, and threw it inside, noticing with a sigh that the mountain of wet green trash bags filled with Ellie's things were still there, looking eerily like a black plastic wave poised to rise and swallow me.

I closed the door quickly and locked it, then filled my wineglass and dropped my bathrobe on the floor, thinking the hell with him. Another glass and I thought, the hell with her too, whoever she was. The hell with everything. Half a bottle later, I reached my bed and got into it fumblingly, turning off the light, determined to forget all about him, descending hard and fast into sleep.

Chapter 12

When I opened my eyes again, there were miles of forest around me, my vision filled with backlit trees in fast-forward, as if it were summer and I were on a horse-drawn carriage moving at high gallop. I could hear the rhythmic rustle of a thousand green leaves being left behind. The smell of wet roots was overwhelming. Still, strangely, I remember wondering what time period of human history I might be inhabiting, then thinking I should wake up, for starters, and realizing how odd it was to be aware that I was dreaming.

But then the forest gave way to Hector, drinking his watery, coffeelike mate tea and reading the business section of the newspaper, *my* newspaper, in *my* kitchen. Maybe I'd woken and gone to the kitchen for water. Otherwise, how was I standing in front of him?

He seemed to have forgotten that we'd broken up. Yet he never looked up or smiled conspiratorially. He didn't reach out with his left hand, offhandedly cupping my right breast as if to say hello. He didn't push his half-full, lukewarm cup toward me as if to ask me to pour him some more or give any sign of being aware of anything other than the paper in front of him.

He was smoking a cigar, its orange-yellow ember of a tip lighting up my entire kitchen like daylight. But when I started to ask him to be careful, to warn him that the smoke would cling to everything, to remind him that his wife, sleeping mere yards away, might recognize the smell of his smuggled Cohiba, I noticed there was no smoke and no ashes.

That's when I knew.

What I was looking at was my own memory of Hector. A live image created by me. *But why was it in my kitchen?* I would think later, upon waking. What had happened to him that he appeared unable to see or hear me? I didn't know. But if the guilt I felt enveloping me throughout the dream was any indication, what I *did* know was that, whatever it was, I was somehow responsible.

Chapter 13

When I woke up, all was as it had been when I'd gone to sleep, except for the fact that I was now officially forty, and that I couldn't get that awful dream out of my head.

It had been so real, the feeling, no, the certainty, that something not so great had happened to Hector and I was to blame. Yet, try as I did, I couldn't remember the part of the dream that had given me that impression. All I had was that image of him smoking his smokeless cigar and the lingering sensation of darkness and doom quickly coming closer, announcing itself from afar like a funeral parade whose lead float you can hear rolling toward you from twenty blocks away.

I didn't particularly like dreaming, much less dreaming trouble, but what are you going to do, right? It had obviously been just that, a dream that was over now, just like Hector.

The clock by my bed read only six thirty, but it was no use trying to fall asleep again. (God forbid that insane dream decided to pick up where it had left off.)

I shuffled over to the bathroom and stood in front of the bathroom cabinet mirror.

"Well, happy birthday, Mariela!" I said out loud, trying to put enough cheer into it to convince myself it was a heartfelt birthday wish. "It'll all be all right. Eventually," I added, realizing there wasn't enough cheer in the world to turn this day into anything other than what it was—the day after a man cared so little about me he decided to break up with me on the eve of my birthday.

Brushing my teeth, I knew that birthday or not, and breakup or not, I had more important things to do. For starters, I had to get a move on fixing up *apartamento tres* if I was going to rent it quickly and keep my finances flowing.

I trudged to the kitchen for coffee, last night's dream assaulting me as soon as I stepped onto the linoleum. *He was sitting in that same chair,* I thought, half expecting him to appear again as I opened an old but pretty pink tin can that used to hold French tea and realized I was out of coffee.

Since going without caffeine in the state I was in was not an option, I decided to walk the few blocks to the I-95 bridge and cross the trembling, groaning underpass to Tinta y Café, a little community arts café where I used to hang out in another life, while going out with Jorge, if you must know.

My plan was to get some strong Cuban coffee into me, read the paper, and kill a little time until the hardware store where Gustavo worked opened at around eight and I could get my rental apartment makeover going.

I dressed in ripped (from use), oversized, and soft (also from use) boyfriend jeans, an old chocolate-colored T-shirt reading BAD COP! NO DOUGHNUTS, and well-worn, leather flip-flops with a silver Thai bead dangling from the place where the leather met to hold the toes in place. And then, for no reason, and with no conscious premeditation, I cut myself some bangs. And when I say bangs, I mean bangs: cut straight across, stopping only when there were at least two inches between my eyebrows and the tips of the hair on my forehead. It could've been a disaster, but the effect was fresh, playful, almost flapperlike. I thought it made me look lighter, renewed.

I'd read once that when women are heartbroken, they do two things: change their hair in a drastic way and travel somewhere far away. Since I didn't have the money to travel at the moment, I decided to look at my bangs as low-cost breakup therapy and walked off in search of my coffee.

After last night's showers, the streets looked as if God himself had given them a good scrubbing, their colors bright once again. Across the street, the square looked greener than ever after its bath, except for the grays and browns of the occasional homeless person sleeping on some bench, bundled in Salvation Army anythings. Soon it would be filled with card tables and domino-playing Cubans, the overflow from those who weren't early enough to secure a seat at the Maximo Gomez Park, the official domino site for the area.

As I walked toward the I-95 underpass, sometimes on tiptoe to avoid getting my leather flip-flops wet in leftover rain puddles, Hector's face popped up as if my mind were a deck rigged to give you the same card no matter how many times you shuffled it.

I should feel relieved that it's over, I thought. Now I knew. No more wondering. No more mental limbo. And then there was the way he'd done it, so crude and heartless, so unlike him. (Or was it?) I tried to see the silver lining in that: By acting like an ass, he'd prevented me from romanticizing him, made me want to forget him faster.

Tinta y Café was empty. Only the small window and outside counter for dispensing the ready-to-eat basics—toast, *croquetas,* and coffee—was open. I asked for a *cortadito* to go (a small amount of black coffee "cut" in half by a dash of evaporated milk and sweetened with a teaspoon of brown sugar or two), and strolled toward Alvarez Locksmith, a small shop that was part locksmith, part hardware, part whatever odd and end you might need, and where Gustavo worked when he wasn't turning the scrap metal with which he occasionally littered my building's backyard into sculpture.

The shop was twelve blocks away, and I took my time walking through Little Havana, taking in its morning sounds.

I've always thought that to really "get" Little Havana in general, and Coffee Park in particular, you need to be eye level with it, be an immigrant of some sort. You have to have traveled from someplace far away and gone somewhere else altogether by something resembling choice. And then you have to arrive in this strange place, strange to you, or maybe just strange, and find something here that makes you say: "It's not my home, but it could be because I no longer fully belong to the place I've come from, couldn't return there even if I wanted to, and so this will be just fine for now, because at last, at least, I'm somewhere."

If you're Latino and live in Florida, there's a good chance you were in Little Havana when you said those words, and that that "somewhere for now" was Calle Ocho and the things I walked by that Saturday morning: the little fruit and vegetable carts where you can get six juicy tomatoes for two dollars and a humongous just-ripe Florida avocado for a buck, the Tower Theater with its marquee announcing the varied art film offerings, the Lebo mural on Eighth and Seventeenth, the record shops not admitting to, but selling, pirated Cuban music, the pawn shops bursting with hostage treasures, and the space where the old Cervantes bookstore had been on Nineteenth. And yes, where the man I'd slept with until yesterday now owned his.

At the hardware store, I found Gustavo in a sour mood, playing despondently with a handful of rusty pulleys.

"Still working on that sculpture?"

"*Qué bola,* Mariela?" he greeted me, putting the pulleys down on the old dark-stained wood counter. "Nice hair."

"Thank you, and a fair warning to you, mister: It's my birthday, so think twice before making fun of me. I'm just saying."

"*No, no. Qué va.* It looks good. *Bien loco.* I like it."

"*Bueno, oye,* thanks for helping me take care of the Ellie thing the other day."

"Man, I knew she wasn't right, but I told her *que no te hiciera una mierda,* you know, to do things right. Did she bring you your money yet?"

"Nah, and I doubt she will. I'll be happy if she just picks up her junk and moves on, you know?"

"It's not right," he said, shaking his head. "Iris said she'd never seen anything like it, and she's old as hell."

"*Chico,* let me put it to you this way: By the time you got there to change the locks, the worst was over. It was like Hurricane Andrew went through there, okay? But, you know? Onward and forward. So let's see, I need some grease remover and some superstrong glue. Also primer, a caulking gun, some spackling paste, and cleaning supplies," I finished reading from my list and followed him as he walked around the shop searching for each thing.

"Don't you worry, Mariela," he said. "I'm going to help you find another tenant, call a few friends, see who's looking."

"Thanks, Gustavo. And speaking of friends, how's Jorge? Remember him?"

That stopped him in his tracks and made him turn around and take a good long look at me before saying, "I sure do. Question is, do you?"

"What do you mean?"

"What do I mean? Let's see. I introduce you to a good friend. He falls for you like a *comemierda,* a total loser. You seem okay with that. Then, one day, you dismiss him for no reason."

"I didn't dismiss him for no reason. He did have a wife, you know."

"She was in Cuba!" he said, as if that made it all right.

"Still his wife."

"That's not the point, and you know it. You hurt him."

"I hurt *him?* What did I do?"

"You wouldn't take his calls. You refused to see him!" said Gustavo.

"That was a mutual decision and, again: He was, or is, married. How hurt could he have been?" I asked.

"You really want me to tell you?"

I didn't. It's the reason I'd never asked Gustavo about Jorge in all these months. What? And have Gustavo change my mind and drag me back into that no-win situation? Or risk him telling Jorge? Then Jorge would think I wanted him back or that I missed him, or the worst possible scenario: they'd man-talk about me. No, the worst scenario would be that they'd *Cuban man-talk* about me. You know what I mean, don't you? How once you go Cuban, you never go back, and how they're the best lovers in the world, and on and on. Don't laugh. They do talk like that. And it shouldn't surprise you. Everything Cuban is better. Bigger. Better tasting, or functioning, or whatever. It's part of our thing, and it's innocent, but I still didn't want them talking about me, because the fact of the matter is that when I decided to get Jorge out of my mind, I'd gotten him out of my mind. (True, it had taken an Argentinean to help me do it. But I'd done it.)

"Just forget I said anything," I said, feigning interest in a tube of cement-colored spackling paste.

"He was married in Cuba, which you knew when you met him. And I don't think there was a 'we' in that breakup decision. I think you decided, and he just accepted it, because what else was he going to do? Stalk you?"

"Like I said, married in Cuba is still married. And not that it's any of your business, but she was finally coming to be with him here in Miami. *She* decided to come, *then* I broke up with him. That's *why* I broke up with him. Not the other way around, okay?" I said, surprised that Jorge had shared this much about us, that I was having to defend my actions to Gustavo.

"Oh. Really? And did you tell him this? That you were breaking up with him . . . for him?"

"Yes, I told him and let's drop the subject. I was just going to ask how he was. How the marriage was going. That's all."

"Oh. Well, if that's all, he's doing fine. And the marriage is none of your business."

"Still working at Michy's?"

"Nah, thank God. Or I'd have to warn the man about the possibility of running into you there. We can't keep letting you women stomp all over us whenever you want."

"No need. And I have no intention of stalking, or stomping, anyone."

"Okay. I mean, he's a friend, you know?"

"Okay then. If I saw him, all I'd do is say hello."

"Well, don't go saying hello if you're going to leave him worse than you find him. Let him be, will you?"

"Okay. I get it. Sorry. God."

"Okay. I'm sorry too. Didn't mean to get agitated, take my things out on you."

"What things?"

But he kept trying to reach the back of a shelf, finally pulling out a black plastic bottle of degreaser, before answering my question.

"Abril broke up with me."

"Oh," I said, finally understanding his it's-just-not-right mood and wondering what unloving, sex-hating, twenty-four-hour bug had gotten hold of my neighborhood recently.

"When?"

"Yesterday morning."

He looked about to cry, and if you knew Gustavo, you'd understand how strange, how unsettling, the mere possibility seemed to me that morning. In the six years he'd lived in my building, I'd only seen him cry once, and then only because he was drunk and got to talking about his family in Cuba and about how much he missed them. Don't get me wrong—he's a sweet guy. Just not one to share his problems, complain about his life, or give out X-rays of his heart in the form of information.

Until he fell in love. The minute Abril moved into Iris's building six months ago, Gustavo threw himself at her like Batman leaping down the side of the tallest of buildings, mask forgotten in her gaze, cape carelessly draped on his arm, and his face wearing his feelings, there for all to see what love could turn a man into.

I didn't blame him. Have you ever seen a model in a fashion magazine and said to yourself, "She's not that pretty," while still having to admit that there's something about her? That's Abril. Plus, like I said before, she knew how to be mysterious.

"I'm sure you'll patch things up," I said, not telling him my feeling that somehow Henry's father, whoever he was, was behind her decision to break up with him. Maybe she'd gone back to him and would leave as mysteriously as she'd come.

"She says there's no one else," he said, reading my mind. "That it's about sacrificing for her son. What does that have to do with anything?"

He had a point.

"I'm sure you'll get to talk it out. Henry adores you."

"I know!" He shook his head, as if to say, "Exactly."

"And you know, maybe there's hope. I happen to know she was crying yesterday, *disimulando con Iris* that she didn't feel well, so at least you know she cares about you," I said, trying to console him, and thinking, *Unlike a certain Argentinean jackass.*

I didn't know what else to say, so I asked him if he was going to submit a sculpture for the East Little Havana Development Agency contest. This was its second year, and it had been a big deal the year before, with Romero Britto and Nereida Garcia Ferraz sponsoring a debut one-man show at the Miami Art Museum for the winner.

"I'm thinking about it. Kind of stuck for an idea. It would have to be something big, something that really says it all about Little Havana," he said.

"You could make it about Coffee Park instead."

"That's what Iris said, but it's Little Havana's grant, and I really don't want to stir up that kettle."

"Ah, the life of an artist, right?"

"The life of a broke artist," he said.

"Well, okay, but, you know what? Tonight, after I finish at the apartment, I'll go online and see if I find a few salvage stores willing to give you some extra material for a good cause, what do you say?"

"Que eres la mejor y la más completa," he said, which in Cuban means that I was the best.

"Okay, okay, no need to promote my greatness. I'm sure I'll be recognized when I'm dead like all the other greats."

"Well, I'm going to find a tenant for you," he said.

"An obsessive housekeeper, if possible, please. See you later," I said, stepping out and waving good-bye to him with only the last three fingers of my right hand, the rest of my arms fully occupied with my purchases.

I walked back to my building, looking at my cell phone display—eight forty a.m.—and thinking of Hector. Again. Like an annoying alarm. Good thing I was going to be very busy with the apartment. No time to think about stuff that was over. In fact, I decided, I'd make sure to be inside my apartment or Ellie's at times when he might be home so that he wouldn't be able to catch so much as a glimpse of me. I'd ask Iris, or Abril, who had a really nice voice, to record my answering machine greeting to deny him the slightest sound of me. I'd block my Facebook profile. I'd close the Twitter account I didn't yet have, I'd . . .

As I turned the corner at Eighth toward my building, a swatch of green and white fiberglass in my peripheral view brought me back from my Mariela mojo–denying plans: two Miami–Dade patrol cars. There was also a lime-yellow rescue truck, other cars I couldn't identify, and it seemed as if people from all of Coffee Park were now standing around on my block, as if waiting for something.

I thought, *Henry!* and quickened my pace. The crowd seemed thickest in the area in front of my building. I saw Abril with her ponytail all frizzed up, wearing one of Iris's designs: a hot pink T-shirt cut up to resemble a Moroccan-scrolled iron window gate and jeans. She had a dazed expression on her face as she looked toward the park, while trying to restrain Henry from running off somewhere.

Iris! Was it Iris? I walked even faster, searching for her with my eyes. There was the lady who had the huge Virgin Mary on her front lawn, wearing a house robe and curlers. There were Carmita and Betty, the couple who lived right across the park from me, with their five-foot-tall Great Dane.

Then I saw Iris above the swarm of people, probably standing on a park bench. She seemed to be trying to see something over the crowd, and I exhaled, relieved. What the hell was going on? I ran toward her now, clinging to the paper bags I was carrying.

"Iris! Iris, what happened?" I asked, cutting through the gossiping busybodies.

I'll never forget the shaken expression on her face when she turned, steadying herself to come down from the bench and hurry toward me, oblivious to the throng threatening to push her this way and that. As she reached me, she clung to my arm and turned me in the opposite direction, toward the sidewalk, only then opening her mouth to speak. But before she could say a word, somebody barked, "Excuse me! Stand back, please," and an obviously exasperated paramedic emerged from the crowd rolling a gurney right past us, taking it from sidewalk to street with a sharp thud, and toward the vehicle shaped like a small ice-cream truck.

"It's Hector Ferro, Mariela," Iris finally managed to hiss into my ear. "He's dead."

Chapter 14

The reason people go to psychics, *santeros,* psychologists, and spiritual consultants, the reason they pray with Buddhist monks, play Ouijas, pay to have their tarot decks, coffee cups, or tea leaves read, follow their horoscopes like gospel, get astral charts made, and try to decipher dreams, is to avoid regret.

Regret is worse than death. Because death, like shit, just happens, swift as a gunshot. But regret is a migraine: a pain that goes on and on and on without ever becoming urgent enough to warrant cutting off your own head, tempted as you might be.

My mother had a theory. She said that her generation, the first generation of Cubans exiled in Miami, aren't as angry as they are sad. That they act angry to forget they're sad they left the island, came here, and were never able to go back. She believed that no Miami Cuban over the age of fifty ever died of anything other than regret. Regret at having left, or at not having left in time, or at having left too soon. Regret of going to the wrong place, of not taking Pepito or Anita with them when they had a chance, not ever knowing if there was something they could've done differently. Regret that they'd never know if they'd have been strong enough to fight back, thinking the world would help them. It didn't.

They were so sure they'd be back soon, but weren't, having to settle instead into, and for, what was then an inhospitable swamp that humidity made as hazy as the dirt they pretended to have in their eyes so they could allow themselves a good cry for their beaten-black-and-blue island. Like me, they regret not having been able to see the future.

It's the chicken feed of clairvoyance, regret. Because you think if you know all the information, if you know that if you leave you'll never be able to go back (because even if you do, you'll be going back to a completely different place that just happens to be in the same location), you'll be able to escape second-guessing yourself. You think you'll be okay because in the end your mother will still be your mother. You don't know that she'll be changed. Loving you still, of course, but what you find out later is that her love now tastes different from all that time spent training to withstand distance, containing herself in order to live with impotence so strong, the phrase "so near and yet so far" was made for it. You think if you'd known all this, you'd be able to live with the results of your choices, never again wondering what would've happened if you'd never left.

Having been clairvoyant, I can understand why people think information is the antidote to regret. Maybe they think knowing will allow them to say, "I did all that I could do" or "Nothing I did was going to change that," and that this will give them peace. It's as if they could deal with it all: death, loss, illness. But the prospect of the phrase, "If only I'd known"? No—that they cannot face.

The truth is people will do what they're going to do no matter what. The best clairvoyant in the world can tell them exactly what will happen, and they'll just rationalize it and do what they will.

Still, it helps to be prepared to rationalize, which I clearly wasn't on this day that had so suddenly morphed from being "the day after my lover cared so little about me that he found it appropriate to break up with me on the eve of my birthday" to "the day I saw my dead lover's body rolled out inside a black plastic bag."

One minute he'd been telling me his neglect was just his way of writing it "in" the wall for me. The next, there was no wall, and he was rolling away on top of a gurney, his face covered from me, his eyes closed forever.

I sat there on my stoop, with my bag of cleaning supplies at my feet, looking out across the street at the crowd that seemed to cover the whole park square except for the area that had been cordoned off by police.

Someone was taking my blood pressure. Actually, there were two paramedics. I wasn't sure why two were needed when I was only one person. Had I fainted? To this day, I don't remember.

I tried to understand what was happening around me. Parked on the sidewalk, there were now two more Miami-Dade county police patrol cars. I recognized them because they were white with a green stripe. There was an ambulance, but the white vehicle resembling an ice-cream truck had left with Hector inside. From where I sat, I could see a plainclothes officer or technician taking pictures of the area at the far end of the square, where I guessed they'd found him.

There were a couple of TV station live trucks parked across the street. I remember someone asking if I wanted to go inside where it was cooler, but I don't remember who. People kept telling other people that I was the landlord, that the dead man was my tenant. That he'd been found lying under one of the benches in the square, soaking wet, wrapped in a trench coat and scarf, some blood covering his face. I heard people whispering, "Was he beaten?" "Was he mugged?" "Did he have a heart attack?" I turned my head looking for the person being asked, but invariably they'd be someone who didn't know better than to shrug their shoulders.

The dead man. How had he died? When? What had he

been doing in the park? *Maybe he'd been upset and had a heart attack,* I thought, imagining him doubling over and feeling horrified at the thought before telling myself it just wasn't like Hector. Excess emotion did not seem like the thing to kill him, and I obviously had no longer been important enough to cause such a reaction. Or had I? All my screaming to get the fuck out? Still, he'd seemed fine to me when he left last night, and definitely healthy. He'd even taken the time to draw a smiley face on my letter!

The anger and hurt I'd felt the night before now seemed so small, so petty and unimportant, as I sat on that stoop praying for this to be a nightmare, begging God to bring him back to life so that I could hate him knowing he still existed. That it all wasn't so over, so final. But it was. He was dead. I would never see him or hear his voice again. Never touch him or put my finger on the line between his brows before kissing him, magically replacing the frown with a smile.

Just when I thought my chest could not compress any farther, the tears came, and, as if my tears had called him, a man walked over to me and introduced himself as an officer belonging to the Miami-Dade crime scene investigations unit. He had a navy blue rain jacket with yellow letters and navy blue pants, and I disliked him immediately. I could see others dressed like him interviewing other people. I disliked them too.

The officer, I forgot his name as he said it, squinted to read the message on my T-shirt denying him doughnuts, then raised an eyebrow and asked me my name. He asked other questions, or rather the same question asked in different ways: Had I seen anything? Did I know of anyone who might have wanted to hurt Hector?

Then he asked me if I'd been close to the deceased, pronouncing it "disease-t," which reminded me of Hector and his terrible accent, and made me laugh, visualizing Hector as a trench-wearing, walking disease, which I'd sometimes thought he was. That was enough to get me laughing like a crazy person, kidnapped by my own nerves.

"Sorry, I'm so sorry," I said, wiping the tears that, despite my laughter, continued to march down my face, like deranged mourners compelled to dance obscenely during a funeral procession. "It's a nervous reaction. I am, I mean, I was his landlord," I said, ignoring the air-sucking way my stomach contracted again when I heard myself say "was."

"Were you close to him and his wife, Mrs. Estevez?"

"No. No. Not really."

"What can you tell me about him?"

"Nothing," I said too quickly, shrugging my shoulders like a thirteen-year-old responding "I dunno" when asked, "Whose cigarettes are these?"

"Really?" he asked with new interest.

"I didn't know him well. Didn't know them well. At all. Didn't know them—"

"Right, but, they were your tenants for years. You must know something about them."

"They have a bookstore."

"Did they get along?"

"What do you mean?"

"I mean did they get along."

"I guess."

"Did you?"

"Me?" I said, recognizing the creeping warmth of red on my face before it got there.

"Yeah, were you close to them? Did you ever drop in for dinner? That kind of thing."

He waited.

"We got along. All of us. Them. They. Me. Us."

"And they got along, you say?"

"I said I guessed."

"Yes, you did. You did say you guessed," he said, looking

into my eyes with a new squint. "Do you know if he had any enemies, someone who wished him harm?"

I knew of one person who'd wished him harm last night.

"How did he die?" I asked.

"One of your neighbors found him in the park. There was blood on his forehead, probably a concussion. Could've happened if he fell over after cardiac arrest, but we can't be sure, so we're treating it as a suspicious death for now," he said, more to himself than to me. Then he seemed to remember I was there, and added, "We don't really know yet. Could be any number of things."

All this he said as importantly and unemotionally as a headwaiter reciting a new menu of house specialties.

"Not cardiac arrest," I said, the image of him doubling over in pain doing an instant replay in my head.

"Why not?"

"He was, you know, he was healthy," I said, trying not to cry as I thought of Hector trying to breathe, caught off guard for once. Had he realized he was dying? Had he had time to open his eyes in shock, unwilling? What had he been doing in the park? Oh God, maybe he'd gone to the park to think or to reread my letter without his wife asking what he was reading. Maybe he'd tripped on something and hit his head and died from the impact.

"Well, one never knows," he said.

"And his wife?" I asked, thinking of Olivia, imagining her reaction when they told her and feeling sorrier for her than I'd ever felt during the time I'd seen fit to sleep with her husband under her very roof of sorts.

"She's catatonic, hasn't spoken."

"Catatonic?" I said, wondering what What's-His-Face's notion of "catatonic" was, because I'd always thought Olivia had been born catatonic.

"Yes. Why? Do you have reason to believe she's responsible in any way?"

"What? No! I'm just asking if she's okay."

I had asked sincerely, truly wanting to know if she was all right, thinking, and not for the first time, that there's this strange little connection "other women" have with the wives of their lovers. It's not necessarily jealousy, although there's always some of that, but more of a morbid curiosity mixed with imagined affinity, as if the wife were your sister from your father's first marriage whom you're not allowed to meet, but sometimes find yourself thinking you'd like to because you have someone in common, and probably the answer to many of each other's questions.

"Oh, well, she's as okay as can be expected. If you remember anything that can help us to rule out any foul play—"

I felt the laughter re-erupting immediately, my nerves threatening to abduct me for good.

"Again, sorry. So sorry," I finished with a barely audible squeak, wishing he'd go away so I could get ahold of myself, think, or cry, or do whatever I was suddenly desperate to be alone to do.

But he stood there looking at me for a long time.

"I'm sorry for your loss," he said. "Sometimes things like this just happen."

I looked away.

"It's hard, I know," he persisted. "This job, you know— believing in God helps."

"No," I said, anger surfacing as quickly as the laughter before it had. "Things like this don't just happen, and God has nothing to do with it," I told him, thinking that if God had done this, he would've at least made it grand, a fucking global war, a tie-dyed red sea. Instead, this had happened: a cheap, artless theater production Hector would have derided.

"You seem angry," he said.

"Of course I'm angry. My tenant . . . is dead."

"Yes. I can see how much you cared about him," said the officer now, looking at the space next to me, assessing its suitability as if planning to settle in.

Sure enough, he took some gum out of his left pant pocket, offered me some with a motion, accepted my refusal with another motion, pulled up his pant legs, and sat next to me on the stoop as if it were a throne. He smoothed back his prematurely balding jet-black hair and crossed his hands, leaning back to rest them right on his emerging beer belly, all the time chewing his gum and nodding slowly like he knew everything.

My heart sank. I wanted him to leave. I wanted to be alone to think about all I didn't understand. Like the death itself. Or the fact that it might have been a crime like a mugging.

Or that I had dreamed it, for once seeing something accurately before it actually happened, or maybe as it was happening.

"I can see you're distraught. I understand and, like I said, I'm sorry for your loss. I can also appreciate how worried you must be that some prowler may be lurking in your peaceful little neighborhood here, but I'm going to level with you about something, Mrs. Estevez. If this was murder, it doesn't look like the work of a prowler to me."

"Miss," I said because I felt stoned, drunk, and stupid, in addition to stunned. "And what do you mean?"

"Well, because of the vomit, the head trauma, and the fact that his wallet is missing, robbery is a possibility. But there's also the fact that he had no obvious reason to go to the park on a rainy night, and according to neighbors, never did, that the possible crime scene is surrounded by homes and businesses, yet nobody, including his own wife, or anyone else in your building, saw anything, despite the proximity of all your apartments to the crime scene."

"People were probably sleeping."

"Yes, that's possible. In any case, there'll be an autopsy, and we're going to need all the cooperation we can get," he finished, sliding his hand into the interior pocket of his jacket and handing me a card that smelled faintly of garlic. "If you see anyone suspicious, remember something, or think of anything that could help us, I want you to call me."

"I won't. I mean, I will. But I don't think, I don't think I'll remember anything more. I've already told you what I know," I said, knowing how I sounded but unable to soften my tone.

"Which is surprisingly little, given such a small building, such close proximity between front doors, all of your front windows facing the park," he insisted.

Well, I know an *indirecta* when I hear one, but I was silent, even as he continued to peer at me, scratching his head, letting me know with every little picky gesture that this was serious, possibly as serious as murder or manslaughter or whatever they called deaths that weren't supposed to happen.

"I see you were shopping this morning. Where did you shop?" he asked casually, trying to fool me into believing the question had just occurred to him.

"At the hardware store on Twelfth."

"Ah, yes. I've shopped there myself. They make all kinds of keys there. Were *you* making new keys?"

"No."

"Did anyone see you go there?"

"Many people."

"I only ask because maybe whoever you went with remembers seeing something when you left your apartment to go there."

"I went alone."

His cell phone started ringing, but he kept looking right at me.

"Were you in your apartment last night?"

"I was."

"But you didn't hear anything."

I shook my head no, hoping he'd strangle himself with his own tail the way he was running around in circles.

"Anyone with you who might have seen or heard something?" he said, and I realized he was just goading me now.

"Yes. At least one person," I said to goad him right back.

His phone rang again, and he stood up and turned sideways to fish his cell phone out of his left pant pocket as if he were leaving.

But then he silenced it and turned back around to face me, an unfortunate sign of intelligence revealing itself to me in his expression.

"One more question, Ms. Estevez."

"*Y dos también,*" I said, which means something along the lines of "ask away."

"When was the last time you saw or spoke to the deceased, exact time and date please, and what exactly did you talk about?"

Chapter 15

It was close to six in the afternoon by the time they finished interviewing everyone and writing down our names, addresses, and telephone numbers. A section of the park had been cordoned off with yellow crime scene tape, while upstairs, *apartamento cuatro* was silent, Olivia somewhere inside, left to mourn her husband all by herself.

I walked into my own apartment and sat in my red corduroy armchair, unable to grasp what had happened. Hector couldn't really be dead. I'd just talked to him last night. I'd even argued with him and he'd been fine. I tried to focus, to bring back the last thing he had said to me, his last glance. But all I remembered was how insanely angry I'd been and the stupid things I'd said that I'd never be able to take back. The worst of it was I'd put it all in writing, something my mother warned me a million times never to do. And hadn't it been just like him to leave my "nice" breakup letter behind for me to throw away and take the nasty, sarcastic one—for him probably the interesting one, fascinated as he was by internal conflict and human motives.

Wait a minute! The letter he took. Where was it? What had he done with it? The police would find it! Oh my God, Olivia would find it. Maybe she already had. *Everyone would find out we'd been having an affair,* I thought, beginning to hyperventilate. I had a vision of a group of people stoning me for carrying on with a tenant whose wife slept mere yards from me. My Dominican neighbors would say, *"Oh, pero que mujer más sucia"* (What a dirty woman) and my Puerto Rican neighbors would call me *la chilla* (aka skanky ho). And my friends, Iris, Gustavo, Doña Carmen, the Salvadoran lady who'd trusted me with her bank deposits for years, they'd say that I was a *descarada,* a woman without shame.

But then I remembered Hector was gone and wished I had the choice of going through a little well-deserved embarrassment if it would reverse his death, or at least bring him back long enough for me to say good-bye, make sure he hadn't suffered. But he was gone and there was nothing I could do.

I sat up.

Or was there?

After a life of running away from the possibility of contact with the dead, from the future, even from the sounds of my own mind, I'd gone from being willingly blind to wanting to reclaim my clairvoyance twice in less than one week. Except that this time was so different. Before, I'd wanted to see out of jealousy and fear. It had been a weak want, stoked by ego alone. How different it was now. The want I felt then as I sat in my apartment was fierce, fearless, radical. It made me long to talk to the darkest of the dead again, to run from one to the next asking if they'd seen him.

And what if I still could? I'd have to hurry. The longer I waited, the farther and denser his energy, I thought, imagining him walking away, his back to me, trench coat flapping against the backs of his legs, unable to hear me yelling for him to stop.

I took several deep breaths, so deep that deep whooshing sounds came out of my throat, and focused on imagining that I heard the low rap on the back door, that I felt him sitting down next to me, heard his breath very close to me. I don't remember being afraid, but only because I didn't really believe I could still cross the figurative gate of death.

If you want to know exactly what I did, I'll tell you, though I doubt it will do you much good right away. The secret to talking to the dead is not in the method, which is so simple and well-known as to be boring. The key is in the mastery you acquire by practicing, and in the quality of your inner space, energy, and your belief that you can do it. But if you ever want to try it, this is what you do:

1. Find a quiet place and sit or lie down. (I used to prefer sitting with my heels on the floor, where I could feel it vibrate as my energy changed and became lighter.)

2. Clear your mind of thoughts and worries. (The best way to do this is to make a mental note of irrefutable good things before you begin and think about them to get yourself started.)

3. Once you feel relaxed and at peace with the world (meaning okay with bad existing alongside the good because you trust in a natural order of things), construct a mental picture of the person you want to talk to.

4. Think of him or her in life until you get a sense of connection. You'll know when you have it because talking to the person will seem natural to you at that point. (Many people never lose that connection to those they were close to in life, able to talk to them every day as if they were still here.)

5. Then and only then, ask them a question. You don't have to do it out loud, unless it helps you stay focused.

(And remember, do not try to deal with the energy of a dead person before you've protected yourself with love and positivity.)

6. After you ask, you wait. Keep your vision of the person in your head. Do not put words in their mouth. Just smile and wait patiently.

I don't know how long I sat, focusing with all my might, before opening my eyes, a tenth of me expecting to feel him, the other ninety percent wishing I weren't such a mediocre medium.

But I was. I was a terrible clairvoyant who'd thrown her gift away and would now have to resign herself to never seeing, feeling, or hearing him again. The good thing is that after I forced myself to accept this, even saying it out loud, I was at least, at last, able to cry again, not knowing if I cried for the lover friend, not to be confused with a loving friend, who had taught me good and bad things in such a stylish and memorable way, or for the small, small, small man I'd become attached to despite the easy way he'd disengaged from me in the end.

Or maybe I was crying for my own screwed-up psyche, still so incapable of dealing with something as mundane and common as death, even when the deceased was someone I had told to get out of my life just hours before.

I thought of Hector, but the image that came into my head was of Abril. She looked angry, talking on the phone while putting things inside an envelope, maybe a letter. That got me to my feet and pacing, eyes wide open. What if Olivia found my letter and killed Hector because of it? And what if after, she gave it to the police to deflect attention from herself? After all, he'd died mere yards from her front door too.

Giving the police the letter would bring her revenge full circle, wouldn't it? God, what was I thinking? Sure, she was weird, but I couldn't imagine Olivia killing. Then again, neither could I imagine anyone else having done it, and he was with her when he died. He had to have been because he sure hadn't been with me.

At the thought, my heart began beating furiously. Was it a supernatural sign that Olivia was indeed involved? Or was I just imagining things? I mean, they'd been married for years and she hadn't killed him before. Why now? Then again, I had to admit cheating with a woman who lived right downstairs seemed to me like a perfectly plausible reason for killing a man. Hell, I'd wanted to kill him just for breaking up with me on the eve of my birthday. And why else would she have killed him last night of all nights? It had to be because of the letter! That was the reason for that awful dream. I was responsible for his death because she had found the letter and done something about it. Maybe, maybe, maybe.

When someone dies, taken from you forever, the pain is bearable only if you can transform it into an insatiable appetite for knowing everything. How he died, where he was, what he said, and to whom he said it. You rethink every second and its possibilities, like a sleuth in a detective novel going over odds and likelihoods, time lines and probabilities, rummaging through the wreckage of the mind for the one detail with the potential to hold the story of what happened, the key to everything, within it.

I was no murder detective, but a few things were clear to me that Saturday evening, sitting in that red armchair watching day turn into night, my own birthday forgotten:

First, Hector was really dead. I couldn't do anything to bring him back. No one could. Second, there was a very good possibility that he had not died of natural causes, given that he was in much better health than most men his age, which either meant that his wife had found out about our affair and had somehow ended his life, or that Coffee Park wasn't nearly as safe as I'd imagined. Third, even this second scenario, that someone had tried to rob him and killed him in the process, made little sense. While he was not a rich man, Hector was a pragmatic one. If someone had asked for his wallet or for the gold pinkie ring he always wore in memory of his mother, he would have handed both over with a sardonic smile. They wouldn't have needed to kill him or even hit him. And if he were in the park, that meant he'd been nowhere near his Saab, which he kept parked in front of my building unless he needed to go beyond his walking range of fifteen blocks. Carjacking wasn't even a possibility.

Then there were the things I couldn't figure out, but needed to. Like, why had he gone to the park on a rainy night? And why hadn't his body been found on our side of the square? Oh my God, of course: He was meeting someone! (A hit man for his business rival Mitch Kaplan? It was ridiculous, of course, but I smiled thinking this was just the kind of thing Hector would have said to make me laugh if he'd been sitting next to me right then. He'd have said, "If we're going to play this game, let's play it well. Where's that collection of Edgar Allan Poe stories I gave you? Best example of detecting you'll ever find is right on your shelf!")

That he'd been meeting someone was just an unsupported theory, but what I knew for sure was that if I could somehow find out why Hector had gone to the park, I'd be much closer to knowing how and why he died.

Another unresolved issue was that there was a letter, the one he'd taken, in the hands of God knew who. A mocking little letter that first one had been, clearly proving that I'd been having an affair with him and that things were not ending well between us. (This thought filled me with a terrible unease. Not only was it possible that I'd be exposed as his lover, but if that letter came to light, what was there to keep the police from thinking I'd had a reason to want him dead?) Thankfully, the other one, the nicer and blander "I wish you well" letter, was in my trash, where I'd thrown it after our fight.

I thought of the officer who interviewed me. Had it been my imagination or had he been all too willing to believe any one of us was guilty of hiding something? What would he think if he knew about the last time I'd seen or spoken to the "disease-t," and what, exactly, we'd talked about? (He'd scowled when I answered his probing with a slow shake of my head and an, "Mmmmm, you know? I really couldn't say, exactly.")

Which was a big fat lie, of course. I remembered every word of my last conversation with Hector. Wait! The trash. I couldn't leave the letter I'd thrown out there, where the police might search. I raced to the back door, wanting to keep the letter from others, but also hoping to touch one of the last things he'd touched, written on, to save it where I could use it to remember.

Except that the lid on my blue recycling bin was open, as if someone had rifled through it, the neat stack of old *Siempre Mujer* magazines I kept around for my clients scattered below and above the plastic milk jugs and water bottles. Could it have been the police? Who else would want to search through my trash? And where the hell were those damn letters—the one he'd taken and the one I'd thrown out?

As dusk began to settle in, I went from sad to frantic, visions of being whisked away to jail piercing my brain so intensely that I froze when I heard the knock coming from the other end of my apartment. Slowly, I went inside, closed the kitchen door, and walked to the living room to look through the peephole, convinced that the obnoxious policeman would be on the other side of my front door, holding the letter I had not found, ready to torture me with more questions and demanding to know why I'd concealed the true nature of my relationship with his victim.

But it was only Gustavo.

"Just heard," he said. Then, "What are you doing? Turn on some lights. You're spooking me."

I tried to muster a smile to serve as a reply, but nothing came. I switched on the lights.

"I can't believe it," he went on. "What happened? Do you know? How bad did it look? Even Abril fainted when she heard that he might have been killed. Oh, and Iris, she won't even talk about it in front of Henry, says he was pretty shook up when he heard."

"Is Abril all right?"

"She's fine. At least that's what she said when I helped her up to her apartment, just before she slammed the door in my face," he said, shaking his head, his face a frustrated scowl. "It's fine if she doesn't want to talk to me, but I'm worried about Henry."

"He'll be okay," I said.

"Notice Ellie picked up all her stuff?"

"She did?"

"Yeah. Just now on my way in I picked up some trash the crowd left in front of the building and took it around the side to throw out. Her stuff isn't there."

I'd been so distraught looking for the letter that I hadn't even noticed.

"I'm going to guess she didn't pay you?" said Gustavo.

"I didn't even see her. But that's not strange with all the people around here. You should've seen it, Gustavo. It was a circus."

Where was that damn letter?

"Well, at least she's gone, huh? But look, I just wanted to see if you were all right."

"I'm fine. It's fine," I said, feeling uncomfortable, as if I were usurping Olivia's condolences and realizing that mistresses not only have to love in secret, they have to mourn in secret too.

"You know, I'm sorry I gave you a hard time this morning. About what you said."

"What did I say?

"About Jorge?"

"Oh. Don't worry about it."

"You still want to say hello?"

This morning and what I'd wanted then already felt a few lives removed.

"Sure, of course."

Of course. Right after I found the stupid letter I'd thrown away, and figured out a way to find the one Hector had taken before anyone read it and guessed I was M.E.

"Just hello, right?" said Gustavo. "I mean, two tenants lost in one week. I figure you could use a friend."

I nodded absently, unable to concentrate on what Gustavo was saying because an idea had sprung in my head: There *was* something Jorge, and only Jorge, and his godmother, could help me with, being the only man in the world who knew my secret, and the only person I knew who could take me where I could get the answers I now wanted (No! Needed.) and trust that they'd be true.

"You know, Gustavo? You're right. I *would* like to see Jorge again."

"That's all I've been saying," he said as if I'd just confessed to the crime he knew all along I'd committed. "All right, I'll see what I can do. Right now, I'm going to make myself something to eat. Knock if you need anything, okay?"

I nodded and watched him until after he'd waved good-bye, his usually smiling mouth sad and elongated, as if his chin weighed so much it were pulling everything down. I kept watching him even after he'd turned to fish his keys out of his pocket, thinking about this old building of mine and how it would have to hold, comfort, and protect the three heartbroken souls that had somehow found their way to it and were taking refuge, alone yet together, under its roof that night.

Chapter 16

After Gustavo left, I closed the door behind me and leaned on it, once more turning off the lights, closing my eyes, and bracing myself for what lay ahead: a long night of thinking about all the death I hadn't seen coming in this lifetime.

Then . .

"Don't be afraid."

I heard it. Or maybe I just felt it. Imagined it?

Hector had said, "Don't be afraid," or rather *"eh-freid."*

I stood, frozen in place. (Had it worked after all?)

"Hector?" I whispered.

But all was silent, and suddenly, I *was* afraid. Afraid of talking, moving, or even breathing.

God! I *told* you I was a horrible clairvoyant. When was the last time you heard of a clairvoyant scared of dead people? I slithered to the floor, listening for the longest time, until I gathered enough courage to get up and turn on the lights again. Had I really heard him?

"Hector? That you?" I whispered again, looking around me, afraid of what I might see and terrified of getting an answer. I was also afraid of not getting one because I knew me and I wouldn't be able to breathe normally until I knew exactly what had happened to him and why. I had to see or hear him again, even if just once more. I had to know that he had gone peacefully to wherever it was he had gone to, to fight the notion of never, to say good-bye.

This need was so strong, it sent me crashing into the foyer closet as if propelled, opening old suitcases and boxes, almost emptying the entire space of its contents before I found what I was looking for: my great-great-grandmother's journal of clairvoyance.

"I give up!" I said to it out loud, when I held it in my hands. "I give up, okay. Here I am, but I can't do it alone." I continued in a high-pitched quivering voice, declaring my intention of "turning on" my clairvoyance again and hoping it was like riding a bike, or like sex, something you never really forgot how to do, despite my failed attempts so far.

The journal was just a tattered old book, with none of the dignified air of family heirlooms, no faint smell of long-ago mystery, no sign of the sweetness of the sea air that misted the island where it was written and where the roots of my roots still lay, sewn by nature and draped around the trunk of a jagüey tree like an old woman's shawl.

On the first page that wasn't torn, or too faded to read, "Do not be afraid" appeared like the echo of my ghost's thought in the form of my great-great-grandmother's dainty handwriting.

The dead are living and the living are dead. Without the body to tend to, we express with transparency. Sound might be guttural or whispered, touch as heavy as shame, or so light as to seem imagined. Taste and smell are gone, and sight is compromised. Only their own desire to speak can bring them forth, so you, the clairvoyant, must use this. You must understand that the image you see is the one you remember, or the one conveyed to you, consciously or not, by the person you're reading for. You are not seeing with your eyes. You are seeing with the eyes of the love that remains. The love of the living, and the desire of the dead. Use them to bring the dead angel in transition forward.

★   ★   ★

Angel in transition? Hector? I would've laughed out loud if I hadn't been so damn frightened. But I was. I was run-out-of-and-back-into-*apartamento-uno*-screaming afraid. Making-a-cross-with-my-two-index-fingers-and-walking-around-reciting-the-Holy-Father-prayer-over-and-over-again afraid.

So. Clairvoyance *was* like riding a bike.

And I'd just remembered how I'd almost broken my every limb the last time I rode it.

How all it had ever left me was death. And now it was doing it again. Not that Hector could ever be as important to me as my mother, but another person close to me had died, and I hadn't had a clue.

I opened the journal again. "Use what you have at hand. Everything is a vehicle for messages if you decide it is." But what did I have besides a dead ex-lover and the risk of being implicated in his death? I asked myself, looking around the room at my red corduroy armchair, my books, and my handmade collage of fashion photos on the wall, Coco Chanel's red lips appearing to approve of a wet Kate Moss, lifting herself up and out of a pool in a black-and-white polka dot dress, like a mermaid in black boots.

What did I have besides this old book I now held, within its pages the memories of my great-great-grandmother, writing in it so carefully, of my grandmother Ana Cecilia talking to the dead in her kitchen, of my mother always feeling like less because she couldn't see the future, and of myself, now possibly holding in my hands the answer to becoming who I was meant to be all along?

I stood up and headed for the armchair, still unsure that the book would be able to undo what years of neglect had done to my clairvoyance, but convinced that I had to try again if I was ever going to find out how Hector died and why.

Chapter 17

"He used to say my breath smelled of apples, you know," Olivia said as she poured scalding hot water into two mismatched china teacups with the most stable and precise of pulses.

She was standing next to the coffee table where she'd set the cups, so that the sound the water made while falling with precision from so many inches above its target resembled a steaming, rushing waterfall that unnerved me.

I'd spent the last two days since Hector's death holed up in my apartment, reading and rereading my great-great-grandmother's journal, gathering the strength to come see Olivia, to put compassion before shame, and worry before fear. Compassion because I knew what it was like to lose the person your life revolved around. Shame that I didn't have the dignity and the good sense to stay away from her like a good mistress, instead coming to give her my condolences on the loss of the very man I'd been nibbling from, behind her back, for months. Afraid she'd found the letter and knew everything, and too worried about the possible consequences to let pass the chance to know if she had.

"Yes?" she'd answered, wearing black ballet flats and a gray shift, the curled tendrils and ringlets I'd mocked, gone, her hair now parted in the middle and held within a tight bun at the nape of her neck. She looked younger, despite the brown-gray raccoon circles around her eyes betraying her lack of sleep.

"Sorry to disturb you. I just wanted to give you my condolences. To tell you I'm sorry . . . for your loss. Please let me know if you need anything. If I can be of help," I finished, checking with myself to see if I'd gotten through all the sentences I'd rehearsed before coming up.

"You're sorry."

She knew.

"Of course," I said, my heart beating violently.

She sighed as if relieved.

"You're the first person to come up. Won't you come in?"

She *didn't* know, I realized, following her inside the apartment.

When she excused herself to go boil some water for the tea, I started inspecting everything in the apartment. It was a little crowded and obviously furnished with things bought for a much bigger house, little tables and chairs discreetly tucked and blended into nooks and corners everywhere like the pieces of an ill-fitting wardrobe someone had refused to part with. But, even with the clutter, the original wooden floors that looked scuffed and cheap in every other apartment in the building gleamed.

"Linseed oil," she said then, as if I'd asked her about them, coming back into the living room with the teacups and napkins, then bustling back to the kitchen.

I looked around. Hector's energy, his scent even, was so strong in that room, it was like a bomb's expansive wave hitting me again and again and again.

"This is his little museum," she said, shuffling back in with spoons and a porcelain bowl filled with coarse brown sugar. "He sits on his chair, puts on his headsets, and shuts it all out," she continued, as unaware that she was talking about him in the present tense as she had to be about how seeing his things was affecting me.

When she started to head back toward the kitchen for who knows what, I thought I was home free. I needed those few seconds to blink back the tears threatening to undo me in front of her. But then she turned around as if she'd forgotten something.

"Please sit, wherever you feel most comfortable," she said, and I could almost feel the knowledge of my affair with her husband hit her when she saw my face.

Shit. I turned away, focusing my gaze on the walnut bookcase that ran the length and width of the wall, every book, DVD, and vinyl record organized by genre and author.

"Oh, don't worry," she said. "They were installed so as not to damage the wall. The bookcases, I mean. They'll be easily removed."

"Are you planning to move now . . . now that—?"

"I don't know. I don't know what I'll do. There's so much I have to decide now, finances to sort—"

"Oh, I didn't mean you had to move. It's just you said they'd be easily removed and . . ."

She just nodded and waved her hand, as if saying I needn't concern myself, that she understood what I meant.

As she served the tea, I noticed that where the living room, his "little museum," was tidy with a designated place for everything, the kitchen I could view from the sofa was a mishmash of colors and overflowing pots, pans, and cooking utensils hanging from hooks and crowding counters and windowsills. The kind of kitchen I would've had if it weren't just me, cooking for myself mostly, with the occasional treat for Henry.

"So, Mariela, tell me. What are they saying?" she asked before taking a sip of tea.

"What do you mean?" I said, also taking a sip in order to hide my discomfort with the question.

She looked at me as if to say, "Really? You've come up here

just to play that game?" and I thought that she was more like Hector than I could've ever guessed.

"This is great tea. Did you grow it yourself?" I asked to change the subject, even though it really was delicious.

"No, I order it from Colombia. It's a mix of leaves from aromatic flowers. But let's not change the subject. The police were here. Everyone knows it. People talk, right? They gossip. Hector and I, we've lived here three, almost four years. I'm wondering what they think. If they care."

"Well, of course. Hector was very friendly. He talked to, you know, to everybody about . . . about books. People were used to chatting with him, seeing him at the store. He had become part of the neighborhood in a way." I rambled, unable to stop sounding as if I were eulogizing him.

"Unlike me," she said. "I feel it, you know. You're all friends, you know each other, you visit. You talk."

The thought occurred to me that if she wanted people to talk to her, it would help if she talked to them, said hello even, once in a while.

"Everyone's different. I don't always feel like talking to people either," I said instead.

"You're being kind. But, tell me, is that why you . . . liked him?"

She knew, I thought again, putting down the cup from which I'd been about to venture taking another sip.

"Everyone liked him," I responded cautiously, remembering how my mother always said, *"del agua mansa líbreme Dios,"* which means pretty much the same as "still waters run deep."

She nodded again, then said, "Speaking of apples, did you know they can be poisonous?"

I didn't. And we weren't. Speaking of apples, that is.

"No. I didn't know," I responded, resolving not to take another sip of anything until I had a better idea of where this conversation about apples was heading.

"Yes, well, they are. Or their seeds are. But then these days you never know. It seems like everything is poisonous, isn't it?"

No. Not everything.

"You can't even . . . *eat an apple,*" she said, raising her voice so suddenly and with such feeling that I recoiled in my seat.

"I'm so sorry," she said when she saw my reaction. "I was just . . . I needed to tell you . . . there's something I need to . . . You know? It doesn't matter. I didn't mean to startle you. I'm just . . . out of sorts, nervous, a little . . . angry."

"I understand."

"I've been trying to be calm, to settle down, to collect myself, but . . ."

I wondered if I should explain that she had just done the opposite, basically screaming at me. About apples. But I decided against it because if losing the person you've shared your life with for decades doesn't shock you into acting like the very opposite of your usual self, what would?

"Sometimes I feel it makes me appear threatening, being so quiet. I want to be more talkative, but I don't always know how, and when I try, I end up scaring people. You seemed so tense, and I've made it worse. I'm sorry. I'm terrible at making friends."

After dismissing my protests that it was fine, she proceeded to go on and on about tea, about being unpopular in school, about never really feeling at home in Coffee Park despite the progressive sensibility she shared, and that's when I realized it: She needed me. She was scared of being alone with herself, and she needed me, or someone, to be there. She was trying to be my friend because she didn't have any and desperately needed one.

Suddenly, all I wanted was to make her feel better because while all I'd lost was an obnoxious lover, she'd lost the man she loved, and with him, her entire life as she knew it. I decided then that she didn't know. She couldn't and still be sitting here, chatting it up with me.

I was suddenly sure I was reading her right, and the unfamiliar feeling made me notice how ever since the day Hector began pulling away from me, I'd again begun to have episodes of sight, or what felt like sight. Still, I reminded myself, the increased sensation of assurance could just mean that the meditation sessions with my great-great-grandma's journal in hand were beginning to have an effect, and not necessarily that what I saw or felt was accurate. She could still be a killer, albeit one who was trying to make me feel comfortable and welcome, even serving me her imported tea.

"My mother always lowered her voice when she was angry," I said then, wondering where this quirky but sweet, chatty woman had been all these years.

"Right." She smiled, pleased. "Anyway, anything can be poison. Did you know a potato can kill you? A potato!"

I froze again, wishing she'd stop talking about poison so I could finish figuring her out, seal my notion of her and what she did or didn't know.

"You know, I'd scare him with it sometimes. I'd get very quiet and ask him if he wanted me to prepare him something nice, like some mashed potatoes, then tell him about their poisonous properties after he'd begun to eat," she continued, shaking her head a couple of times, as if she couldn't believe the silly things she'd done once. Then on the last shake, she left her face turned away from me, becoming so quiet, it took me a minute to realize she was crying.

"I'm going to leave now," I said after a few minutes. "But if you need anything . . . you can call me," I said, meaning it this time, relieved that she obviously didn't know and could cry over the death of her husband in peace, without having to deal with the conflict of simultaneously missing him and hating him for cheating on her. He must have thrown that stupid letter away like I had the other one, thank God.

But then her lips were trembling again.

"That night . . . he called me a *loca de mierda*. What does that mean anyway, to be shit crazy?"

I'd never wanted to know something less in my life, but I smiled comfortingly and said, "Well, who knows why men say things? And Hector wasn't one to be careful about words if it was going to get in the way of a clever phrase, was he?"

I realized my mistake, but it was too late. Olivia seemed taken aback for a second, but then peered at me, obviously recognizing the level of familiarity implied in what I'd just said, her own level of familiarity with me retreating accordingly, just when she'd been about to share something important with me, I was sure.

"They're performing the autopsy today. They think there's a possibility he was murdered. I think they think I murdered him."

I just sat there, mentally kicking myself, unable to speak.

"Anyway," she continued. "What was I saying again? Oh, yes. Potatoes. You can unwittingly kill someone with potatoes if, and only if, they've begun to turn green, and you give them enough of them."

I wondered how many would be enough, beginning to believe she really was trying to tell me something.

"I think I should go," I said again, standing now.

"Then again, so can betrayal."

I sat back down.

I'd come to find out what she knew, hadn't I?

"Marriage is so . . . fragile," she continued. "One moment you're wondering if it's all it will ever be, missing the little thrills of being a single woman, being so angry at him you think you could kill him with your own hands and, then, before you know it, he's gone. It's over."

She closed her eyes, lips trembling again, and I held my breath, waiting for it, without knowing what "it" was.

"Do you understand what I'm saying? How we betray ourselves when we marry, putting up with . . ." She remained silent for a moment and then added, "Did you know I couldn't have children?"

"I didn't know," I said. He'd never told me.

"That's how I got into naturopathy and macrobiotics. I come from a family of farmers, and we believe all solutions come from the earth, from plants, from life."

"I didn't know," I repeated.

"And did you know he never let me forget it? He made me feel it, my failure, every day for almost twenty-five years. He wouldn't adopt, but he acted like, he made me feel like he missed it, not having a child, like it was painful to him," she said, looking very angry now. "So I let him be, you know, him. I betrayed *myself* trying to make it up to him. I let him turn it all into a big lie," she said, looking straight at me. "You're so lucky, Mariela. You're free. Your life is yours."

"Olivia, I really think I should go now." I stood again.

It was the first time I'd called her by her name.

She nodded, sat there for a moment, then held up her finger as if to say "one moment" before walking off toward the bedroom saying, "The police told me not to go anywhere, not to discard anything until they finish the autopsy, but . . ."

I stood waiting, wincing at the word *autopsy*.

"How's the girl? The boy's mother? I saw when she fainted, you know," Olivia called out from what sounded like the bedroom. The one she'd shared with Hector.

"Abril? I think she's fine."

"I'm glad," she said, returning with a sheet of yellow legal paper that she placed in my hand.

My letter. The crumpled, jealous one drenched in irony that Hector took with him that night.

So she knew.

And now I knew too.

I felt a wave of repentance punching me hard on the chest when I took it from her.

"I'm sorry," I said.

"He forgot his wallet here when he came in that night. Before he left again in such a hurry, not even taking the time to change or to sit down for a proper dinner. I didn't read it. I'm not that brave. But I saw the handwriting and recognized it from the notes you post next to the mailbox to warn us of repairs or fumigation."

Of course. How hard could it have been? I thought, feeling as stupid as I must've seemed to her.

"I'm really sorry," I said again, wanting to say I had never meant to hurt her, but knowing I couldn't say it, because it wasn't the truth. I hadn't cared if I hurt her, which was different. I hadn't even considered her.

"Take it." She handed me the piece of paper. "He liked it enough to keep it. It must have meant . . . something to him."

I nodded without raising my head, then left in silence, never lifting my eyes away from her gleaming wood floors.

Chapter 18

As soon as I got inside my apartment, I leaned against the door to read the letter Hector had seen fit to save from my wrath, to fold and tuck into his wallet, to keep, even after he'd decided he didn't care to keep me.

> *Amor,*
>
> *It's been nice. But since you're not the love of my life, and I'm not the love of yours, wouldn't you agree it's time to stop it? My only problem with this letter is that I wish I could be kinder, write it so you believe I'll be suffering over you, knowing how your ego will drive you absolutely crazy over being forgotten without a fight.*
>
> *Yes, I know that it is YOU who's been planning to break up with me for days. Weeks? Since we met? I don't blame you for wanting me to accept that it was your idea. I'll give you that, even though I must confess I'd been the one waiting for you to do it first, so as not to deny your ego the pleasure.*
>
> *But you're not getting on with it, frankly, and I'm unable to sacrifice any longer. You see, I have trouble being patient with situations that have begun*

to bore me, when just days before they were, at least,
amusing me. I know you'll understand me, since you
can't stand to be bored one second, hence your chronic
infidelity of body and spirit and your occasional habit
of ruining romantic moments by complaining about
her.

   Of course I'll miss certain things about you, but
it will be so much more fun missing them than living
them. As you know, wrapped in nostalgia, even a
vulgar sardine acquires all the charm, personality, and
dignity of lobster.
   Have a nice life, amor,
   No longer yours, M + E

I remembered how I'd sat, jealous and hurt that he had
rushed his time with me in order to go out with Olivia,
searching the Internet for a literary breakup letter to base mine
on. I'd searched for Borges because Hector was always quoting
him in the most obnoxious way, but instead found inspiration in a
letter from Agnes von Kurowsky to Ernest Hemingway, in which
she begins by addressing him as "Ernie, dear boy," continuing to
pile on the digs, the sarcasm, and the condescension right until
she signs her name: Aggie, and even that, one imagines as the last
turn of the screw, a tool designed to hurt.

   I'd done it with the deliberate intention of showing him that
even though I didn't know as much as he did about literature
and language, I could still manage to sound as pompous as he
when I wanted to. I'd wanted him to know I could inhabit his
immovable feast of a world if I put my mind to it. Like Aggie, I'd
wanted to hurt him, of course, but I'd wanted to surprise and
intrigue him even more.

   I read it through again, imagining his thoughts as he read,
his chuckling at my creative pettiness, the possibility that he'd
privately conceded the originality of my approach. I compared

this to the blandness of the letter I'd given him, the "nice" one, written as he walked over, determined to break up with me.

Which was a bad idea, because once you start imagining the dead as if they were alive, you can't help but desperately wish that they were. I wanted to turn back time, not to the time before the breakup, because on some level I understood that had to happen, but definitely to the hours before his death.

Had I been in love with him? I didn't think so, but I did know I missed him. I missed his life, and the window it had opened on my own. Seeing things through his experiences had felt so exotic, global, and free, like watching a foreign movie to bask in the locations, and to dream of going wherever "there" happens to be. I missed that window that made everything strange, new, and more exciting: food, books, business, people, music, and thought were, post-Hector, forever synonymous with seduction in my mind.

And then there was Olivia. Because you didn't think I bought her story about not reading the letter, did you? And still, she'd given it back to me. And not in a mean way, though I suppose kindness could just be her dignified wife way of shaming me.

I wondered how she felt when she read it. Had she suspected all along? Had she been surprised beyond anger? Or did she feel a certain triumph about being right? About catching him "in the act" for once? Something told me Hector had been one of those men who subscribe to the strategy of "deny, deny, deny," no matter how obviously he's been caught with another woman. What am I saying? He was a man, wasn't he?

Still, an affair, even one with the landlord, didn't seem like the thing someone like her, someone who seemed to know her husband with all his bad and good traits, would kill over at this stage of her life. And what other thing could she have learned about her husband on that very day that would be anywhere near as bad?

Don't get me wrong—I know there are probably many women who would, and have, killed men over an affair with anyone, let alone one with a woman who lived in the same building. But despite her raw edges, Olivia just didn't seem like the type.

Then there was all that stuff about her inability to conceive, and his taking advantage of her feelings of inadequacy over something she couldn't help, which in itself was horrible. But she'd had plenty of time to kill him over that, and hadn't.

No, I was pretty sure it hadn't been Olivia, probably because I didn't want it to be. She'd suffered enough. The autopsy would rule out all the crazy possibilities of crime, either petty or as the result of passion, and prove Hector had died from some unknown disease, strange as that might have appeared to me at first.

And think about it: If Olivia had killed Hector over our affair, she wouldn't have given me the letter back. She would know the police would eventually find out whatever she'd done through the autopsy, and she'd have kept the letter, used it to incriminate me, to turn any suspicion that might arise away from herself.

Instead, she'd been kind to me, as if the finality of death had made her wise enough for several lives and she now knew things I still didn't grasp, like that it was useless to hate me. That whatever he'd given me obviously hadn't meant all that much to him, whereas she'd been his one and only wife for decades.

Had I had her all wrong all this time? Had I been seeing her through Hector's bored eyes, never giving the real Olivia a chance? Oh, that's right. How could I? I'd been too busy sleeping with her husband.

I realized I never asked her what she knew about how he died. Not that I'd intended to, just like I hadn't intended going inside and drinking her tea as if we were the best of friends. The grand extent of my plan had been to give her my condolences.

If she said thank you and acted reasonably pleasant, it would've meant I was in the clear. If she slammed the door in my face, I'd have had my answer. I'd been so anxious at first, and then so confused by all her talking about poisonous apples and potatoes, that I never mustered the nerve to ask. Now I didn't know what to think. On the one hand, it was possible she'd been trying to tell me something with all that talk about poison. On the other, she was a macrobiotic nutritionist. Apples, potatoes, and their curative or poisonous properties were probably all she talked about every day of her life.

Maybe I was making a big production out of stupid bad luck. Olivia had probably woken to the noise, realized Hector wasn't sleeping beside her, and found out the horrible news along with the rest of Coffee Park, the news being nothing more than that he'd had some wine, felt like smoking a cigar, and crossed the street to smoke in peace and get some fresh air. That he'd then had a mild stroke and fell, hitting his head and dying from the concussion.

Yes, and maybe, I was this much full of shit.

I was grasping for light, thinking this and that and trying to infuse each thought with the energy of true sight. But it wasn't. And I wasn't seeing a thing. Can you imagine how crazy it made me that I hadn't even been able to see what Olivia knew until she chose to reveal it to me? If after all the meditating, praying, reading, and rereading of my great-great-grandma's journal, I still couldn't see beyond my own nose, how would I ever reach Hector, find out what really happened to him, say a proper good-bye, or make my peace with death, his, and maybe my mother's?

The one good thing was that I had the letter. Well, one of them at least. The other one was probably in the bottom of the recycling bin, and I just needed to search for it a little better before the recycling truck came and destroyed it.

I went back to my red armchair where my inherited

medium's "workbook" still lay, knowing that all the reading in the world was not going to be enough, and that I'd need help if I was to get some peace by bringing Hector into my space and trying to speak to him. But it was a start, so I kept reading. The journal had sections on working with energy, clairvoyance-inducing foods, practice exercises for reaching other dimensions in a minimum of time, and a troubleshooting section titled, *"Remedios de Luz,"* or "Remedies of Light," which I read start to finish.

Did you know sex increases your psychic ability?

And that drinking coffee can kill your ability to access other dimensions, whereas clean water and very juicy or porous fruits and vegetables, such as watermelons and tomatoes, enhance it? I didn't.

And what about the fact that a mirror is one of the most powerful clairvoyance tools available?

Now, I did know that mirrors are perfect for gazing into and visualizing the person or vision you are seeking coming into the mirror, like they do in old horror movies. Not only does it help your mind more potently "get" that it's jumping between realms, but the fact that it's a light-reflecting object gives it that much more strength.

But what I didn't know was that it comes with its own way for you to test if what you're doing is working. According to my great-great-nana's *diario de clarividencia*, when your visions are about to appear, the mirror will get cloudy or dark, as if misted with vintage dew from some day long ago.

As I read through the list of tips, tricks, and other phone lines to the ghost world, it dawned on me that my mother had been wrong. Clairvoyance isn't a gift. It's a talent that has to be developed. It's a craft that needs to be worked at every day. I saw now that I'd been wrong to renounce it, believing it was an intrinsic part of me, like an arm, instead of what it was: an ability that I could practice, or not, like singing or painting.

I'd been so desperate to think that clairvoyance was as

certain as the blood shared with the grandparents I'd never met, that I fell into the trap of writers who swear the muse just "takes over" and writes everything for them. As if this muse always worked perfectly unless something were wrong with you, the way my mother thought.

For the first time, I saw that I'd just been too young when this "gift" was thrust at me. I understood that the pressure of pleasing my mother had turned something that could've been scary, but also fun and empowering, into something I was doing for the worst of all reasons: to be loved.

And then I got to the end of the book, and there, in a long-dead clairvoyant's handwriting, were the answers to all my psychic insecurities in the form of fortune cookie–like disclaimers:

★ Sight is not to be used for self-benefit alone. A higher purpose is needed, but it is possible to assist a more spiritually senior sister or brother of sight on your behalf.

★ Sight does not protect from evil. It attracts it.

★ The sight medium must have the purest of intentions when initiating contact with another realm, and be responsible for protecting herself and those she's helping from evil energy.

(See cures for protection.)

You'd think these disclaimers would have been at the beginning of the darn book, right?

And then, the next two made me gasp.

★ Sight is not perfect, clearly interpreted, or unfailing.

★ Strong emotions (love, fear, etc.) will cloud sight, especially with truth related to self, mother, father, sister, son, daughter, husband, or other that medium is bound to by love or fear, etc.

Of course I didn't see my mother's illness! I loved her too much.

So much pain, and the answer had been in this journal, a few feet from me, all this time. A surge of gratitude filled me and I dropped to my knees, thanking God and talking to my mother out loud, the words flowing from me like a torrent, my body lighter with every memory finally expressed. And even though I was not able to connect with her soul right then, I was still my mother's daughter, and she'd loved me past her death, I knew, was suddenly sure, wise once more. She'd just been confused and worried and sad, like me. She'd read this journal dozens of times and had to know I wasn't to blame. I faintly remembered her trying to tell me this, to reason with me back then, but I wasn't listening. I thought she was just saying anything to save me from my own deserved guilt. She must've died hoping I'd one day read the journal, convince myself. And now that day had come, and it was as if my mother were kissing my hair again, her arms warm around me once more.

I remembered I'd been about to do the same thing to myself again. Denying my ability and blaming myself even though I'd clearly seen Hector's death psychically. I'd just been too ignorant of my own ability to know how to interpret it and inadequately armed with the weakest of intents: soothing my squashed ego.

Well, no more. What I needed was the assistance of a real clairvoyant who could help me get my sight back, put myself back together again, and be who I'd been intended to be all along.

Dusk was approaching quickly. I slipped on my flip-flops and padded over to Gustavo's with a plan in mind, gave his door a strong pounding, and waited.

"If I want to say hello, I'll say hello. And if I want to do more than say hello, that is entirely my business and Jorge's. You have a problem with that?" I asked the moment his face appeared between door and doorframe.

"Ooooh-kay," he said, one brow raised.

"But I need you to give me his cell phone number," I said in my most dignified tone.

"I said okay. But if this is what I think it is, I want matchmaking credit for anything that develops."

"Stop being silly and give me his number."

"I could do that. Or maybe, we could let him make the first move."

"There's no move. No one's making any moves here."

"I already told him you wanted to say hello. Now, if he calls you after all the warnings I gave him, then whatever you do to him will be his own fault."

"What?"

"You heard me. I'm saying I'll feel better. It won't be my fault. Seriously, Mariela, if you'd seen his face when I told him you wanted to see him, you'd leave him alone. He's not like me, you know, with this advantage I have over the regular folk."

"Oh, yeah, and what would that be?"

"I've told you: I have a knack for knowing what people are thinking," he said, scrolling through what were apparently thousands of phone numbers on his cell phone, looking for Jorge's.

"Yes, you're a real connoisseur of human nature, Gustavo."

"It's my sculptor's hands," he said, halting his scrolling to hold his right one up. "They're like X-ray machines for seeing into other people's hearts, knowing what they want, you know what I mean? Now, when it comes to me, I'm screwed, but like you're always saying, what you gonna do, right?"

Welcome to the club, I thought, swatting a fly that had been greedily slurping away at my calf.

"Let me go get my other cell phone 'cause I can't find it in this one," he said, leaving me to hold the door open while he did a deep squat to search under the cushions of his olive-green thrift store sofa.

"Gustavo?"

"Yeah?"

"Any news about . . . Abril?" I asked, hoping it was the reason for his seemingly improved mood.

"Nope," he said from somewhere on the other side of the sofa without a second's hesitation.

"Well, then *ella se lo pierde,*" I said, believing it really was Abril's loss.

He straightened up, second cell phone in hand, and shrugged his shoulders, but his expression reminded me of a cartoon character's, face unexpectedly and resoundingly flattened by a foe's heavy frying pan.

"Times change, my friend. I've lost my touch," he said, before reading out the number for me to punch into my own cell phone. "You know, speaking of change, Mariela, Jorge sure has changed a lot. He's not the same man you knew when I used to hang out with him."

I doubted that it was as bad as Gustavo's no-joke face was making it seem. I mean, how much more pot and partying could a human being take? But I was not going to ask.

"Relax, I don't want to date him, I just want to ask him about . . . a friend of his I met once and haven't seen in a while."

Gustavo's face relaxed.

"Look at me, being nosy again."

"Very. Now go eat something. You're losing your butt from not eating."

Normally, he'd have been ready with a wisecrack. Instead, he stood there for a moment, looking at the floor.

"She won't even talk to me, Mariela."

My God, that woman! Gustavo had done nothing but love and support Abril and Henry from the day he met them. If you won't be nice to a guy for your own twisted reasons, at least you could break up with him decently because he was nice to your son.

"I'm sorry," I said to Gustavo.

"What did I ever do that she won't talk to me?"

"It's probably best that way. She may be protecting you," I said to console him.

"Protecting me? Oh, you mean, like so I don't get my hopes up?" he asked as if the concept were the most ridiculous thing he'd ever heard of.

"Exactly," I said, not believing a word of it. "You men should try it sometime."

The sound of steps on the other side of the entry door interrupted us.

"Well, this is probably a bad time, but would you believe I was in the neighborhood?"

It was Jorge.

"Speak of the devil. Was just giving Mariela your number, bro. Whassup, man?"

He looked older in a good way, with his longish, shaggy hair cut short, his loose, whitewashed jeans and leather sandals, a navy blue letterpressed T-shirt, and a thick, hammered gold wedding band.

"Mariela," he said, stepping into the foyer to take my hands in his and give me a kiss on the cheek, before turning to Gustavo and doing that slap, slap, half a hug, slight push, bring the cheeks close, finish-with-a-grin thing men do instead of kissing.

I stood there looking at their little greeting ritual and thinking about how one minute, I hadn't seen him in months and thought seeing him again couldn't be any bigger of a deal than Hector's death, and the next, I wanted to hug him.

"Mariela?" It was Gustavo bringing me to, a puzzled look on his face.

"Oh, sorry. It's been so long. How've you been, Jorge?"

"I'm good. Everything's good. Lots of changes, but all of them good."

"Still a chef?" I asked, wanting to know if he was still happily married. (As you've seen, Gustavo evaded all my digs for information, when I wouldn't come right out and ask openly for the pleasure of his male ego.)

"Always."

"And your boys?"

"Great. They're great. Eliezer got married, and we're doing a lot of things together."

Yes, I bet I had a good idea of what he and all his party-addicted chef friends were doing together, I thought, remembering just how much he'd been enjoying his life in the states when I met him, more than a decade after his arrival. The Jorge I knew equated liberty with the freedom to party until you forgot which country you were in, if not the one you'd come from.

"Jorge has become an organic chef," said Gustavo.

(What is it with us Cubans? We always sound as if we're selling something, making anything and everything so exuberantly appealing. Can we ever say something in the boring, regular, tedious way it really is? Nothing wrong with, "This is Jorge. He's just a man who cooks. Nothing special to see here, folks. Just Jorge.")

"Actually, I still let some pesticides into my cooking once in a while," he said, patting his stomach lightly. "But I *have* become very interested in cooking good, wholesome food and, my God, so sorry. Here I haven't seen you in ages, and I'm off talking about myself."

"It's all right," I said, comforted by his presence, by his obvious affection for Gustavo, and by their banter.

"It's not. How are *you?*" he asked, taking me in.

I sighed.

"I'm good, good as can be, you know? And it's good to see you."

"I've been wanting to call you, but—"

"I'm glad you're here now," I interrupted, not wanting him to make excuses when his distance was nobody's fault but mine. Still, I wouldn't have minded a heads-up and time to comb my hair and put on some decent clothes. (I was wearing the same ratty tank top and jeans I'd worn to see Olivia.)

"Gustavo said you needed to see me? What can I help with?"

I looked at Gustavo, confused. (How did he know?)

"About the tenant, Mariela. I told Jorge you wanted to say hello, but mostly to see if he knew of anyone who might be looking," he said, smiling at me conspiratorially.

Was he protecting me, keeping me from looking desperate? Or was he protecting Jorge from getting his hopes up?

"Oh, of course," said this new, more formal, more adult Jorge. "I read what happened. Must be tough."

"Oh, no," I said. "Not the same apartment. Gustavo is talking about another vacancy I had this week."

"Oh, okay, well, sure, I'll tell my guys in case they know of someone."

"No, it's okay. It needs a lot of work first anyway."

"If I can help—"

"It's nothing really. Don't worry about it. It's not that much," I said, forgetting I'd just said that it was. "But that's not what I called you about."

"I see." He nodded, looking into my eyes as if he did.

And then it was like old times and we both turned our faces toward Gustavo.

"Hey, don't look at me. It seems to me *you're* the ones blocking my doorstep," he said. "This is Gustavo in *his* house, minding his own business, *que conste*."

"Yes, Gustavo, who speaks of himself in the third person," said Jorge, smiling at me, falling into his old habit of teasing Gustavo for my benefit.

"*Oye, qué te pasa a ti,* brother?" said Gustavo, protesting our ganging up on him. "You're the lame one with your, '*Would you believe I was in the neighborhood?*' Dude, really?"

I smiled, wanting to talk to Jorge in private, but also wanting to put off having to say what I needed out loud.

"So, how's the wife?" asked Jorge, changing the subject.

"The wife?" I asked, thinking I should be the one asking him that.

"Your tenant's wife?"

"Oh. Oh my God. She's okay, I guess. I mean, we're . . . not exactly friends or anything," I said, immediately getting the strange but strong feeling that this was no longer true.

"You know, if I can help," he said again.

"It's *so* nice to see you again, Jorge," I said, surprised at how nice it really felt.

And then the vision came so quickly I didn't have time to be surprised. Jorge was kneeling on a sopping wet grass carpet, howling an extended howl that went on forever and made the tree behind him contract slightly. It was horrible . . . like "aaaah-huuuuh-aaaaggggg-hu-hu-haaaaaaaaaaaaaah-gaaaaaaaaaaaaaaaad!!!!" or something like that, impossible to describe except by actually making the sound. He'd lost someone. I wondered if it had happened recently or if Hector's death had made me hypersensitive, able to see things I never did before.

"So how did he die?" Gustavo asked, gesturing toward the stairwell to mean Hector, while I asked the same thing mentally, but about the vision I'd just received.

I was still a little shaken, but managed to muster:

"They don't know."

"Was it the wife? What do you call her?" asked Gustavo.

"I used to call her Morticia. I am sorry I did that, and her name is Olivia from now on."

"I bet she did it," he whispered to Jorge, who looked at me searchingly.

I wondered if his eyes were asking what I was thinking: Had I ever done as his godmother had directed me to? Had I overcome my fear of clairvoyance? Was I a new Mariela?

"So, Mariela, I have to get back," said Jorge. "I left a small army wreaking havoc at the restaurant and it's close to dinnertime. But I'll come by to check on you soon, and whatever you need . . ."

I hesitated for so long that Jorge looked pointedly at Gustavo, who put up his hands as if giving up and said, "I'll talk to you two later," before waving good night and closing his door.

As he looked at me, patiently but questioningly, I hesitated because as much as I needed a friend right now, he happened to be a friend I'd been in love with. A friend I might not be able to deny "benefits" to after he'd respected my wishes and stayed away, and I'd been the one who'd called him back onto my troubled road of a life.

Then again, he could be the bridge to getting my sight back, and with it, possibly the letter I hadn't recovered, the only other proof that Hector and I had been lovers.

"I have to see your godmother. I want to do what she says now."

He looked surprised, then shook his head.

"She died last year."

"Oh, no! I mean, I'm sorry. Was she sick?"

"Not at all. Died in her sleep. No pain."

"I'm glad," I said honestly, despite feeling let down.

"Exactly what kind of trouble are you in?" he asked.

"Ay, Jorge, I wish I knew. It's why I was hoping to be able to talk to your *madrina*. I don't know any other true psychics whose sight I can trust."

"Okay. Understood," he said, nodding.

"You know what? Don't worry about it. I'm really sorry about her death."

"Mariela, saying there was no love lost between you and my godmother would be putting it mildly; so I may not know what's going on with you, but when you say you were *hoping* to see her, I know it's serious."

I sighed and shook my head, words failing me.

"Tell you what," he said. "I can't take you to see *madrina*, but let me make a couple of calls. I may be able to take you to see the next best option. And you can tell me all about it on the way there. Deal?"

Chapter 19

The next day, I opened my eyes to a song made of the sounds of the neighborhood's weekday routines taking place all around my building. There was honking, and bus whistles, and people rushing by on cell phones, and kids screeching when they meant to laugh, as if someone were stealing their book bags. It was Tuesday, and these were Tuesday sounds but, somehow, they sounded different. Everything was different. Things had changed inside and around me, just like the song had predicted.

For one thing, I was finally able to really cry for Hector. It was a slow cry that took a long time, like a river trickling down a mountain from someplace within my soul's eternal earth. *He hadn't deserved to die,* I thought as I cried my strained cry. Hector was many things, and he would have been those things well into his old age, but he was also life, a mixed bag of wonders and lesser treasures each with its own purpose. Who had taken him? Who'd taken him when I wasn't looking, leaving me no choice but to cry, my tears the transport system for the toxins of impotence threatening to make me explode. Hector was like the tree in your neighbor's yard that you never notice, but whose shade you miss when the misanthrope chops it down to build a stupid terrace in its place. That's how Hector's death felt to me: stupid and unnecessary and heartbreaking, and all my tears didn't make it right, but I still cried them.

On the positive side of these changes, thank God, was a strength that had swooped in to save me from some part of me I hadn't known existed. It had warned me of Hector's death. It had pushed me to keep reading my great-great-grandmother's journal after decades of ignoring it, not resting until I'd found the words that would liberate me from the jail of sorts I'd locked myself in since my mother's illness. And it had made me want to see Jorge again, to put the fear of my own heart aside, and to seek help so I could once again see all I'd been meant to see.

And then there was Jorge himself. One day, we'd managed to stay away from each other for almost a year. He had a wife; I had a lover, and we were safe.

The next day, I'd come face-to-face with the truth of my sight and, within minutes, as if the two were connected, he'd been in front of me and it was clear that whatever used to be there, still was.

Before he left the night before, Jorge had explained that though his godmother had died just a few months earlier, there was someone else who'd never failed him, and who'd be able to help me, he was sure. He promised to pick me up tomorrow, which was today, and I hadn't stopped being nervous since.

At two on the dot, he knocked on my door, *rat-a-tat-tat,* wearing a navy blue cotton shirt, gray slacks, and the thick wedding band he'd had the day before, but never worn when we were together. He had a plain canvas tote in each hand, and several plastic bags and bundles of string and wax paper peeking out of each one.

"Okay if we eat something first?" he asked, and I said, "Of course," taking a step back and waving him in, aware of the same sensation of time stopping, with a jolt, that I'd had the night before and attributed to his showing up without notice and to my shock over Hector's death.

Thing is I recognized that jolt. It was want. And confusion over seeing him again, now more mature, clearly more comfortable with himself, looking like the man I'd wanted him to be, on unexpected loan from another life. The jolt was that craving I thought I'd suffocated, and recognizing it put me on edge, as if I were somehow cheating on Hector just by following Jorge into the kitchen.

"Trust me, you wouldn't have enjoyed seeing *madrina* again," he was saying now, switching on lights, raising the wooden blinds to let more light in through the kitchen window, while I stood at the entrance to the kitchen, watching him. "Toward the end, her predictions were off and she was grumpy, biting people's heads off, that kind of thing," he added, quickly laying out what looked like spices, some pieces of fish, and some cooked brown rice on my table before confidently opening the second upper cabinet to the right of the sink to find the cold-pressed, extra virgin olive oil in the beautiful Italian tin can that he had given me, promising it would last me for years if I always remembered to cap it tightly.

He snuck a quick glance at me to see whether it had all landed. That he remembered where everything was. That he remembered us.

"You say she was grouchy? Strange. She used to be so cheerful," I teased, waiting while he rinsed his hands to hand him a dishcloth and an apron, since it was clear that he intended to cook a meal.

"Very funny," he said, and when he tousled my bangs playfully before turning back to his ingredients, a whiff of his perfume flew from his hands and into my mind through my nose and I felt desperate to retreat to the safety of the distance I'd allowed him to breach.

I busied myself picking a knife from the ones suspended on the magnetic metal strip on the tile above my sink, intending to offer my help as an impromptu sous chef.

"You hungry?" Jorge asked.

"No. Well, not really. But it depends on what we're making

here," I said, and began peeling and slicing the piece of fresh ginger he put in front of me.

"Really? Then why are you looking at my food as if you could lick it with your eyeballs?" he said, grinning as he sliced scallions and tossed some cooked brown rice in a bowl to loosen it up.

"I'm doing no such thing."

He stopped tossing and smiling and fixed his eyes on mine until I asked, "What?"

"Need a large skillet."

"Uh, of course," I said, heading to the cabinet behind him, next to the stove. But I hadn't bent down to look for it when he grabbed my hand and spun me around to face him, wrapping his arms around my waist so forcefully and suddenly that I lost my balance.

Not that it mattered. He had me in more ways than one, and I clung to the bony outline of his shoulders, feeling the muscles of his chest through his shirt, his forearms circling me, his hands rubbing the fabric of my T-shirt up and down against the small of my back.

"What are we doing?" I asked a minute later.

But he just shook his head, not letting me go.

Finally, he leaned me against the sink.

"Why did you break up with me?" he asked, looking me in the eye.

"You know exactly why I broke up with you."

"Why did you *really* break up with me?"

"For the same reason you stayed away after I broke up with you."

"That's not fair. I called you many times. I gave up because I thought it was what you wanted. I thought you were Miss Independent, that you'd be scared if I'd told you I wanted to be with you, but needed to honor my commitment to bring

Yuleidys, to at least get her out of Cuba. That I was just bringing her over to help her."

"I know you didn't tell her that," I guffawed.

"Well, I couldn't tell her immediately. She wouldn't have accepted, I don't think. But I would have told her once she was here and settled and able to help her family. You would've had to trust me."

"It's been almost a year, Jorge. You know where I live. You could have said something."

But I knew he couldn't really. I would've bolted even further had he come wanting to be with me, to really be with me. I'd ordered him to forget about me, and then I'd gone and replaced him in my bed within a couple of months.

"You shut me out. I knew you didn't think I'd get it together and that you were scared of being with me, but—" He looked around the kitchen, as if he couldn't find a spot to rest his eyes on.

"That's not true," I said.

But I knew it was.

"Mariela, I made mistakes. I wasn't clear with you or with myself, but—"

"But nothing. You have a new life. I have . . . a life. Let's be friends."

But he kept looking at me, his eyes going from my eyes, to my cheeks, to my lips, then to the floor.

"Let's just go, okay? Let's just leave things alone and forget about the food, and just take me to whomever we were going to go see, okay? Okay?"

"Mariela, I'm freaking out here. You're next to me for five damn seconds and—"

"Jorge—"

"One kiss," he said.

"Jorge, come on."

"One kiss, Mariela."

I sighed.

"One kiss?"

"Yes. One kiss. Let's say good-bye right. And then, we'll be friends. I'll know where I stand. I'll know you're happy with whatever is going on in your life, though Gustavo says you're not—"

"Gustavo doesn't know my life."

But then he's kissing me and I'm melting and I realize how stupid I was to think I could turn a tenant into a substitute for this. His lips feel warm on mine, and my mouth recognizes them instantly, every one of my ribs, too, is welcoming the way his body is pressing against them, and I don't want him to stop, but he does.

"Okay," he says, as if that's settled. "Now, I'm going to make you my soon-to-be-famous *arroz con sushi*."

I'm confused, and I look at him knowing my face is a question, and he hugs me.

"Not like this," he says into my hair. "Not when you need me and we have to figure out what's going on with you first."

I want to understand what he's saying. I rally, try to save face, recover.

"What's this *arroz con sushi*? I'm pretty sure it's just called sushi and that rice is already a part of it."

"No, no, no, no, no. This is completely different. Here, let me teach you how to make it and let's get a move on or we'll be late."

And so, even though there was nothing I wanted to do less than to learn a recipe I was never going to make on my own, I smiled and let him teach me to make what he insisted I call Chef Jorge's *arroz con sushi*: You'll need three ounces of fish, cubed and seasoned, as if for sushi (salmon, tuna, or yellowtail work well); one cup of brown rice, precooked; two tablespoons of fresh ginger, sliced; two tablespoons of fresh garlic, minced; and two scallion stalks, chopped. Also, olive oil and sea salt to taste, and half of a large avocado.

Heat some of the olive oil in a skillet and place the strips of ginger and the minced garlic in it until they are lightly browned and crispy. Remove the ginger and garlic from the heat and set aside. Remove any excess oil from the frying pan and place the cooked rice in it, along with the scallions, until hot. Place the rice in single-serving bowls. Make some hollow spots on the mound of rice with your spoon and place your fish in. Top with the crispy ginger and garlic and garnish each side of the bowl with a sliver of the avocado. Sprinkle sea salt to taste and add a dollop of spicy mayo atop the fish, if desired.

Drink with a cup of chilled white wine.

Serves two.

Chapter 20

By four p.m., we were driving up a ramp that deposited us on the Palmetto Highway heading northbound, and all the things I still didn't know about Hector's death were back in force, troubling me.

That very morning, killing time before Jorge arrived to pick me up, I'd emptied my humongous blue recycling bin and found nothing. No sign of breakup letter number two, the one with Hector's smiley face on it that I had stupidly thrown out the morning after our blowup. I'd quaked imagining the police finding it and making God knows what out of it. And even now, as Jorge drove, stealing glances at me every few seconds and trying to keep the conversation going, I prayed the psychic we were going to see was as good as he believed, that he or she could help me see what had happened and what was in store, help me get rid of this fear of being blamed for his death.

"So tell me, what's new with you, other than that haircut and the birthday you had the other day?" he asked. (He remembered my birthday, but seemed to have forgotten the kiss we'd shared a while earlier.)

"Oh, God, don't remind me. Nothing much. Just trying to get the get-up-and-go to fix that empty apartment, but there's just so much to do, I don't know where to start."

"You know, I could help you out."

"No, I'll take care of it. I've just had a hard time focusing with all that's happened. But . . . what I *could* use is some of that great coconut soup you used to make, and maybe, for you to stop trying to make a little helpless woman out of me."

"Mariela, there's no shame in letting yourself be helped, you know?"

"I know. And I'm fine, and it's my fault for whining, so, change of subject: Tell me, how's the marriage going?" I asked, pointing to his ring with my chin and jutting out my lips, wanting to know once and for all what was happening and if that kiss had just been about giving his male ego some closure.

"You're such a woman." He laughed at my gesture.

"And don't you forget it. Now, how's the wifey?"

"There's no wifey."

Yeah, right.

"But I do have a question for you," he said.

"Shoot."

"Does the death of your tenant have something to do with your wanting to, you know, to see, after all this time?"

I said nothing, afraid I'd say too much to someone who'd always known me too well.

"All right," he said. "Let's try this: Were you and he, um, involved?"

For a moment, I wanted to tell him. But I couldn't do it yet. Besides not denying it to Olivia after it was clear that she already knew it, I'd never told a soul about Hector. It seemed pointless to start now. And besides, it was none of Jorge's business.

"No."

He seemed to exhale. "Yeah, well, you know, I'm sorry to be so curious, but you seemed so out of it on Saturday that if you were, you know, mourning, I, um, I wanted to make sure I didn't—"

"Maybe you still shouldn't."

He looked straight at me.

"Really?"

"Really," I said. It wasn't just Hector. It was me, still afraid of getting hurt. "Now, how's the wife? Where are the ten kids you were supposed to have by now?"

"Well, I'd tell you, but we're here."

It was the typical, blue-collar Hialeah house, a square, little, peach-colored house, all irregular like the city it sat on. The front windows didn't quite match, the roof looked like it was about to cave on one side from the weight of all the bright terra-cotta roof tiles, and the porch looked like an afterthought, barely held up by keystone pillars that looked like even they were ashamed to be so out of place.

A pretty woman in a housedress stuck her head out of the front door, her hands holding a bowl full of something.

"Hi, Jorge, go around back. He's waiting for you."

"Thanks, this is Mariela."

I said hello, but she just nodded and smiled at him as if my being there were a private joke between them.

We went around the back to what looked like a detached garage with doors that opened out like a barn's. There was a lot of clutter: electronic gadgets, computer parts, several chairs, textiles, and a poster of Lakshmi, the Hindu goddess of prosperity, purity, and generosity. There were also a couple of Buddha statues, one of them huge and a deep turquoise blue. And in the center of all this, with his fingers stained orange by the Doritos he was eating, was a young guy, early twenties maybe, in white jeans and a sleeveless T-shirt, also white. Black horn-rimmed glasses framed electric green eyes, and a diamond stud pierced his left earlobe.

"Dude!" he said.

"*Qué bolá, Asere?*" replied Jorge, using the international Cuban "dude" greeting. "This is Mariela. Mariela, this is Eddie."

"Nice to meet you." I held out my hand, hoping the profusion of competing religious symbols was just a sign of an inclusive mind and not a confused one.

He looked at Jorge as if I weren't there and said, *"Está bonita,"* with a smile, giving Jorge his vote of approval as far as looks were concerned, before he shook my hand. Did he think I didn't understand Spanish?

To me, he said, *"Café?"*

I nodded yes, then unable to keep from blurting out my anxiety, I asked, "So, are you a *santero?*"

"No, not really. I just mix it up in my own way, you know what I mean?"

I didn't, so I said nothing.

"Okay. Let's start," he said, bringing three little cups of coffee to the round dining table at the center of the space and placing a brand-new iPad next to them.

"I wanna take a quick look at your astral chart before we begin. Exact date, time, and place of birth?"

I looked from the laptop to Jorge, who put his hands up as if to say he had nothing to do with this.

"September 24, 1972 . . . 11:58 p.m. . . . Miami."

He typed quickly.

"Okay. Your hands?" he said, holding out his own long fingers and square, sturdy nails.

When I didn't give him mine, he motioned to a tarot deck and asked, "You want the cards instead?"

"I don't know."

"Doesn't matter. They're more for confirming what you get, and there's no need in your case." He smiled.

It was a kind smile, and I relaxed a little.

He closed his eyes, and I put my hands in his. He took them as if to warm them, then let them go as if they were infectious.

"Damn. This is not good."

It was also very fast.

Being used to this reaction by now, I waited until he composed himself enough to close his eyes, take my hands in his again, and ask, "You want me to tell you your life, or you want to know what's going to happen? Forget it. Doesn't matter. I have to tell you what's going to happen, or what's happening."

"How bad exactly?"

"Not sure. But bad."

"Then wait!" I said.

He opened his eyes, his face a question mark.

"If you're going to tell me something bad, you have to give me a minute to prepare to hear it," I explained.

"You're already prepared, but okay. Prepare."

I wanted to get out of there. I looked to Jorge, who was sharing a white vinyl armchair with several computer hard drives, smiling at me in what he thought was encouragement, but was more of a worried expression.

Eddie stared at me for a minute, then closed his eyes again and began tapping his foot, as if impatient.

"Okay. Tell me," I said.

"So you can see too."

It wasn't a question.

"I used to."

He closed his eyes again and began moving his head from side to side like Stevie Wonder singing "I Just Called to Say I Love You."

"Nah, you can still see. But you've been stupid, or afraid, same thing."

What was it with psychics calling me stupid? Was there no solidarity for a fallen sister? I thought. His words, his tone, reminded me of someone I couldn't place.

Oh, dear God. What if he was a fake? He had to be to think I could still see beyond my own nose.

"Okay. I'll tell you as much as I can. Slowly. But you have to hear this, so listen."

I waited, really wanting to know for once. Tired of running and needing to get it over with.

"This man you're seeing . . . he's over."

Wow, I thought. But then he said, "Or he'll be over like, now, or very soon. It'll be ugly, like, really, really, really . . . you know, ugly. But as a result of this . . . bad stuff . . . he'll finally get on his knees before you."

I exhaled, deflated. I'd felt so hopeful when he started talking. And then he'd ruined it. He *was* a fake. He'd guessed my visit was man-related and assumed commitment issues, a pretty safe assumption when a middle-aged woman wearing no wedding band gives you her hands to read in the middle of a weekday afternoon. He thought I was some chick-lit heroine trying to find out if my boyfriend would ever marry me. He'd gotten my attention by scaring me, and then tried to slip in the happy ending that would ensure a generous "donation" for the reading.

I looked at Jorge, furious, weighing whether to tell Eddie the psychic that even if Hector weren't dead and could get on his knees, he couldn't possibly propose because he was already married, just so I could watch the look on his face at being caught faking it. But I decided against it. Why give him, and Jorge, more information?

"And when he does, you're finally going to get the only thing you ever really wanted from him."

"Right," I said, swallowing the last sip of coffee in the cup and thinking that if there was one thing I'd never wanted from Hector, it was a marriage proposal. "Well, thank you."

"You don't believe me," he said.

"No."

"It's okay. I knew you wouldn't," he said, as I got up and went to the glass bowl filled with money that sat next to the makeshift coffee-making station to drop in a twenty-dollar bill. I figured he needed the money more than I if he needed to make his living ripping people off.

"No, please don't put any money in there. When you believe me, you come back and put in whatever you like."

Once again, he wasn't asking, so I just nodded and said, "Sorry."

"Don't be sorry. Jorge here is family. You should both come back sometime. My mom makes killer black beans, right, Jorge?"

We said uncomfortable good-byes, got back into the car, and within seconds were driving over streets lit up from above by the sun's spurting of the afternoon's last orange-pink gasps.

"You're mad at me."

"Why would I be mad at you?"

"Bad judgment when it comes to psychics?"

He did have a point.

"You were just trying to help," I said.

"You wanted to see *madrina,* and Eddie is *madrina*'s only grandson."

Of course. No wonder his electric green eyes had seemed familiar. And another gifted child? Well, that certainly explained things. After a while, Jorge said, "I'll tell you this: Whatever you're looking for, I think you should keep looking."

"Oh, really, and why is that?"

"So you can come back to your life."

"I'm here."

"Nah. You're only half here. You used to be three-quarters here, but now . . ."

You'll recognize the feeling: Something inside me said "yes!" to what he was saying the minute he said it. Yes, I'd been missing from my own life. It's what happens when you refuse to see: You also refuse to live. To be here.

I smiled, thinking he was pretty instinctive himself. I wondered if this new demeanor of his had to do with his listening to his instincts when it came to his life. I wondered if he was happy.

"You know what you've always had?" I asked.

"Irresistible sex appeal?"

"Ah, yes, yes, that, and the modesty, of course."

"Above all things, the modesty," he said, laughing easily, his eyes crinkling.

"But what I was going to say is that you always had this knack for really, really seeing me," I told him.

"Well, you always were easy to look at," he said, smiling the smile I remembered.

But then, just as quickly it was gone, the feeling of being comfortable around him. Suddenly it all felt wrong again, and Hector was back in my thoughts.

"Mariela, you know, I have some leftover building materials from this project I've been working on. You're welcome to have it. I'll even drop it off, if you want. Might come in handy to fix your rental."

"No, no, but tell me about this project. Did you and your wife buy a house?" I asked, insisting on my fishing out of pure compulsion.

"No, Mariela. We didn't buy a house. I was just working at fixing up this locale, and I have leftover material: wood, plaster, some shelving, some cabinets, a counter," he said with a questioning look, no doubt noticing the shift in me and thinking it had to do with his marital situation instead of with my own extramarital one.

When we neared Le Jeune Road, not too far from the St. Michel, and my old Coral Gables neighborhood, I asked him to drop me off at Books and Books.

"Sure you don't want to grab a bite?"

"I'm sure. Need to clear my head a little, you know?"

I also wanted him to kiss me again and hated myself for it.

"Sure," he said, and was silent the rest of the way.

When we got there, I scooted over to his side and gave him a kiss on the cheek.

"Take care of yourself," he said then, and I thought, *Good*. He'd used the phrase people use to break up with each other these days. No wonder when a man tells me to take care of myself, what I hear in my head is "Fuck you." So, good. He'd gotten the message. Asking him for help today had complicated nothing, unlike I'd feared.

I waved him good-bye and turned to go in, ignoring the magazines next to the entry gate and the people eating organic fare in the courtyard. I'd hoped to hop straight over to the new age section, but the back of a man in multipocketed khaki shorts prevented me from it. A professional-looking camera rested on his right shoulder, and a dark-haired woman in heavy makeup and a light orange shift stood beside him, effectively blocking me.

Then I saw who they were getting ready to interview. It was Mitchell Kaplan, the owner of the bookstore. The man Hector had hated with such passion. I'd often told him that he needed to get over Mitch. I'd muse that he sounded like the Joker in Batman, bemoaning the cool gadgets the other guy had, while dying of envy and the desire to get ahold of them for himself. Hector would always snort, snarl, and harrumph before telling me the comparison didn't deserve an answer. I knew better: He had a hard time with comebacks when truly flustered.

The reporter was saying, "Mitchell Kaplan is the founder of Miami's foremost literary haven, Books and Books, and of the Miami Book Fair International. He's agreed to chat with us today from his Coral Gables location about the state of publishing. How are you, Mitch?"

"Nice to see you again."

"Tell us, how is Books and Books dealing with the ascent of the e-book and the fall of the brick-and-mortar bookstore?"

"Brick-and-mortar is out? We hadn't noticed," he said, smiling.

I smiled too.

"In my world, it's in!" he continued. "I love the physical book, and I'm attached to the physical book, but I am also about those third places where people congregate to talk about the books, digital or not. Like right here. You think this is out?"

"Well, obviously you can't see it here," said the reporter, waving around and noticing the place was packed, she the one "obviously" out of her depth in the rattling-the-interviewee department. "Care to share your secrets with us?"

"Well, we've always been a home for book lovers. Lately, we are working even harder to bring authors and readers together. We hold events almost every night in each of our four stores . . . and, just continuing to do what we do. I don't know that I'd call it a secret, but there it is."

Oh, he was good. No wonder Hector had hated his guts so much. He'd turned the reporter's premise into one that allowed him to get his piece in and managed to sound humble doing it. Despicable.

"Good enough? You got everything you need?" he asked the reporter a few minutes later, handing the cameraman his lavalier and already focused on the people who'd assembled around me, curious.

"Yes, excellent, thank you," said the reporter, frowning.

"And how are you?" he said to me. "I hope we weren't keeping you from the books."

"Oh, no. Not at all. It was . . . interesting," I said inanely, entranced by his easy smile, good hair, and huge blue eyes. I remember thinking, what would it be like to own your world? To walk around with the effortless knowledge that you are doing what you are supposed to be doing where you are supposed to be doing it? And just like that, I envied him, just like Hector had.

The excitement over, I headed for the occult section, and why not? Books had been my best friends in life, and they'd been Hector's. Maybe I could turn to them like he often had and they'd come through, I hoped, as I searched for the one that would speak to me. My great-great-nana's manual had been a start, but it had been three days of reading and rereading it, and I had yet to feel anything remotely resembling Hector's presence. No sense of peace or love upon connection, as I'd get when I first got my gift more than twenty-five years ago.

One thing was certain: In those twenty-five years, clairvoyance had gone mainstream. I'd thought my great-great-grandmother's diary was unique, but there in front of me were dozens of books showing how to concoct spells, how to "open to channel," describing witches' commandments, Wiccan techniques, Celtic chants for talking to angels, and even voodoo strategies for the modern practitioner. There were also books about silence, gratitude, self-induced happiness, and self-love as psychic tools. I felt hopeful. Maybe I could reteach myself clairvoyance after all, get myself to that incredible feeling of loving the world again. And if I learned it right this time, maybe I could still help people, and help myself by ridding my days of all the garbage that regret, mourning, guilt, and self-loathing had stored in the garage of my life.

Last night, after seeing Jorge, and knowing we'd be meeting with a psychic today, I'd tried all the things prescribed by my great-great-grandmother in her journal. I'd lit candles, played music, prayed, visualized, and held the books Hector had given me during our time together because he'd imbued each one with intention, and they'd each inspired an emotion in me. Seeing them, I'd realized these bound clairvoyants had correctly predicted each curve and turn of our relationship. There was the beginning, desperate and sexy in *Love in the Time of Cholera*. *White Teeth* by Zadie Smith was funny and charming, delighting me in the most carefree way, like our middle. And there among them was *Chiquita,* which had predicted our ending, with help from Hector himself. But no Hector that I could feel, despite hours of running my hands over them, praying and wishing to communicate with him one last time.

Yet now, here, surrounded by books and the people who

loved them enough to keep trying to sell them, I suddenly believed I'd reach Hector if I just kept at it. That I'd talk to him and find out what happened, and that once I did, I'd be protected from the police finding out I'd been the last person he'd seen and blaming me for his death. Then I'd be able to separate myself from this paranoid dread and mourn his death and the way things ended, maybe even find peace with the death of people I loved, with myself.

That afternoon among words, I understood that I couldn't leave things to someone else. That no psychic was going to magically appear and see what I couldn't see for myself. But the realization didn't weaken me, as it would have before. Instead, it made me hopeful that I could put myself back together, the woman and the clairvoyant, both made whole, united in some way.

I kept searching for more books pointing in that direction: going within, gratitude rituals, creating a psychic space, playing with images as a way to turn intuition on, and many other things that sounded to me like things everyone should do regularly, like a pedicure or a haircut. Natural things. Things that pointed to your being part of a whole, as opposed to some isolated freak by virtue of being able to see, feel, and hear what others appeared unable to.

A few minutes later, I'd chosen *Opening to Channel* by Sanaya Roman and Duane Packer, *How to Rule the World from Your Couch* by Laura Day, the classic *Life After Life* by Raymond A. Moody Jr., and, almost as an afterthought, *101 Ways to Jump-Start Your Intuition* by John Holland. They'd do for a start.

I took a taxi home, and when the cab neared the intersection of Twentieth Avenue and Calle Ocho, the corner where Hector had dropped me off just days ago, I paid and stood there, reliving that last afternoon we'd spent together, as the foreword in one of the books I'd just bought recommended. Then I walked the block or so to Del Tingo al Tango, feeling focused on my goal: connecting with Hector, understanding how he'd died and why, and making peace with his death, and with my not having seen it in time to prevent it.

His bookstore looked so beautiful, like a woman, lovely in her mourning, the *Cerrado Hasta Nuevo Aviso* (Closed Until Further Notice) sign like a Victorian locket around her shiny glass neck. Then I ran my hand over Del Tingo al Tango's doorknob, and the shift was immediate. Intense goose bumps shot from the inside of my right wrist to the inside of my right elbow until I withdrew my hand, my breath quick, listening, until I caught, if barely, the sound of a faraway radio blaring some Tito "El Bambino" song about forgiveness. Was it a message? If so, it was saying that my first order of business was forgiving Hector? Myself? My mom? Whoa, where had that come from?

I stayed a little longer waiting for another sign, then gave up and walked the rest of the way home, knowing that, my urgency be damned, my reeducation as a clairvoyant would take place at its own pace. And I could either walk away from my sight with nothing to show for all my suffering or stand fast, be right here when, and if, it returned.

Chapter 21

Do you know what it's like to sleep with a dead man? To feel his presence underneath your sheets, but not his morning rise, the space between his legs not really there, except for the anger of impossibility pulsing through onto this realm from some level of him. But don't get me wrong. You will feel something when you're sleeping with a dead man, the urgency of his urge manifesting in unexpected ways. You might, for example, feel his essence, cool and pointing, poking, or trying to poke, the space between the fleshy part of your buttocks like a laser beam, or a narrow field of energy.

The reason for that is that you don't have to be alive to be delusional. I never gave Hector my ass when he was alive. What was making him think I'd do it now? Crazy man to death and beyond it, which goes to prove all you've heard at wakes and funerals is bullshit. Death does not make you a better, more aware, or more profound soul.

"Flaca?" I heard the casual Argentinean term of endearment, which literally means "skinny one," but kept my eyes and mouth closed.

"Flaca? I know you here."

Shit.

Shit, shit, and shit.

"I know . . . I know you . . . meeee."

I made myself still as a bar of soap, wanting to make sure I was really hearing what I thought I was hearing.

"I know you . . . hear me," he said now, followed by something unintelligible.

"What?" I actually whispered back this time, realizing that even if he could guess I was listening, he couldn't know I was utterly unable to understand him. Can you imagine? My possibly murdered lover back from the dead, and I couldn't comprehend a word.

And then he was on me, like water when it feels solid because of the sheer amount of it, and the speed at which you're hitting it, or it's hitting you.

"You're choking me."

"Flaca?"

"Don't *'flaca'* me. Get off!"

It was like having a heart attack, this enormous pressuring weight crushing my chest. Did Hector want to kill me? Maybe he thought I'd killed him and was trying to pay me back by taking me with him. So I struggled, thrashing about like an evil green-faced teenager in dire need of an exorcism.

"Please, please, Mariela," he said, though it sounded more like *Merry Ella.* "I need you . . . listen, please. I can't go."

"Get off. Now!"

And off he went. I felt him go, or rather felt the big space in the place where there'd been an urgent energy.

"Wait!" I said after I'd caught my breath.

Nothing.

"Hector?"

"This better?" he muttered from somewhere in the vicinity of the far end of the hallway.

"Better," I said after a few seconds.

"I did *somesing* bad."

"You did, but it's better now, when you're not so close."

"No . . . I did *somesing* bad."

"What?"

"Don't know!"

Well, he didn't have to get snappy.

"Did you . . . do this? Did you . . . kill yourself?" I asked his soul or whatever other part of him was in the room, invisible to me.

He didn't answer in words I could hear, but I felt his answer, like a "harrumph," as in, "Are you kidding me?"

"*Flaca* . . . I did *somesing* bad. So . . . so . . . soooorry . . ."

"Hector, I can hear you. I never thought I could, and I'm, and I'm sorry too. Listen, I'm sorry I wished you dead, I'm sorry for how I acted, and I'm so, so sorry you're gone," I said, rushing my words for fear I'd lose him again, and overcome with emotion, amazement, and gratitude at being able to hear his voice.

"They're *caaahl-ming.*"

"Who's calming? Hector?"

"Going now."

"No, wait, don't go. Tell me what happened. Who did this to you?" I asked, trying to hold on to him, wondering if I had lost my mind to think I could hear him when I couldn't possibly, not after so many years of strictly enforcing a "no ghosts allowed" policy on my life.

"For you," he said.

"For me?" (He died for me? Because of me?)

"They're *caaahl . . . ming.*"

I was suddenly very afraid. So afraid, a little gasp escaped my throat when I heard two decisive thumps on my door.

I got out of bed, threw on my pink kimono, and rushed out of the bedroom to find that, unlike my bedroom, the living room was bright with blinding sunlight.

"Yes?" I asked the two police officers I'd never seen before. They weren't uniformed, but they showed me their badges and offered me business cards.

"Mariela Estevez?"

"Yes."

"We'd like to ask you to accompany us down to the station."

"Why?"

"There've been some new developments in the case of your tenant's death, and it would be convenient if you could come with us to help shed light on some of the new information."

They were talking, but I wasn't listening. I was so nervous, I kept waiting for one of them to reach out, grab my wrist, handcuff me, and say I was under arrest for the murder of Hector Ferro.

"Can't we talk here? I'm not even dressed. Was just waking up."

"We'd prefer it if you'd come down. You don't have to come now. You have our cards. Come down at your convenience, but it would help if you—"

"No, no, you know what? I don't have a car, and I don't leave the neighborhood much. I, I have no idea where this is," I said, looking at the card. "If you'll just wait a few minutes so I can get dressed?"

I needed to know what had happened to Hector, didn't I? Well, apparently, here was my chance.

"What's going on? What's wrong? Mariela?"

It was Gustavo, leaving for work and finding the detectives blocking his view of me.

"I'm fine, Gustavo. But will you let Iris know that I'm going to the police station to answer some questions for these officers?"

"Why?"

"Not sure."

"Then why are you going? Wait, are you arresting her?"

The detectives turned fully toward him now. One said, "Why would we be arresting her?" even as the other one said, "We're not arresting her, sir."

"What's going on, Mariela?" he asked me, ignoring them and making it clear he didn't trust or believe them.

"Nothing, Gustavo. It's nothing. Don't worry. Just make sure Iris knows where I am, okay?" I said, giving him the card the detectives had given me.

I went inside to dress, trembling like a crumbling bridge. I felt like taking a shower, but was so nervous, my space so invaded, first by Hector and then by the police, that I couldn't think. Was this it? Did they really think I'd had something to do with this? How was I going to prove I'd been sleeping all night the night Hector died?

I threw on some jeans and a hoodie rescued from my heap of a hamper, all the time looking over my shoulders, expecting Hector to come back and tell me what he'd been trying to say. I thought it couldn't be a coincidence that I'd been able to hear him just before the police came for me.

When I stepped out, hobo bag slung over my shoulder, I knew this was the moment I'd been fearing since the night before his death. Gustavo was still standing in the foyer, arms crossed, watching the detectives like a gargoyle, while they stood their ground and glared right back at him.

"It's fine, Gustavo. Don't worry. Just call Iris," I said, before following them into the unmarked car I imagined speeding off toward some corner of hell destined for people stupid enough to refuse seeing to such a level of blindness, that they manage to get themselves wrongly accused of the one thing they could never do.

Chapter 22

So what happened was everyone found out about Hector and me. It seems Gustavo ran over to Iris's and blurted out that I'd been taken away by the police and that it was about Hector's death, before noticing she was on the phone with Carmita's partner Betty, who was so psychologically incapable of keeping a secret, she should've been a journalist.

That, and the fact that, unbeknownst to me, Ellie had been making the rounds of Coffee Park cafés, the laundromat, and even the naturopathy pharmacy, telling anyone who'd listen that I'd been having an affair with Hector, that she'd heard us break up the night before he was found, and that the reason she knew all this was I was a crazy bitch who'd kicked her out for no good reason, causing her to come upon the scene when she was picking up the very lot of personal items that I'd thrown out and on a rainy night, no less.

I could just imagine her, coming back for her things and hiding in the bushes when she overheard us fighting. She was probably still there when, minutes after he left, I threw out the letter. She'd probably picked it out of the bin, figuring it could be useful, easy payback for putting her out, a gift from the god of potty-mouthed Valley Girl wannabes.

Which meant that the story had been making the rounds for over a week now, even as both Olivia and I were crying over

Hector's death and waiting for the results of his autopsy. Betty's confirmation, heard straight from Gustavo's mouth, was just the stamp of proof my neighbors needed to let loose.

Ellie's vendetta was also the reason I'd been summoned.

After planting enough poison to kill an entire village, or at least my relationship with the people in it, she'd gone and turned the damn letter in to a police officer who frequented the McDonald's where she worked. The letter that specifically confirmed, in my own handwriting, that I was not only expecting to see Hector on the evening of his death, but also that I anticipated that he would break up with me that very night. The added fact that Ellie found the letter in my trash can, with Hector's "good job" written on it with his pen and in his handwriting, well, that was just the dome on the cathedral, from where the police stood.

"Why get rid of the evidence if you had nothing to hide?" one of the detectives, Martinez, I think his name was, asked me that morning.

"I didn't know it was evidence of anything when I threw it out!"

"Then why throw it out?"

"Why not?"

"Wouldn't you want to keep something so private?"

"No. And you know what? I think the fact that I threw it away should tell you I had nothing to do with this."

Then again, it hadn't helped that I'd almost fainted when after a few minutes of questioning, they'd shown me the letter I'd so desperately wanted to get my hands on before they did.

"We never said you did," said the other one, a detective whose name I can't remember, but who looked more like a male model than a policeman, all big eyes, long nose, and juicy lips on smooth black skin, as he typed out the statement I'd been asked to write on a simple sheet of plain white paper, the contents of which they were "just reviewing" with me now.

"But out of curiosity, why would it prove you weren't involved?" asked Detective Martinez.

"Because if I'd known I was going to kill him, I wouldn't have thrown the letter out in my own recycling bin, where anyone could find it and know it was mine."

I had him there, I thought, sitting back for the first time while he considered this.

"Maybe you didn't know you were going to kill him, and just forgot the letter in the heat of things."

"You know what? Are we done here? Because I'm a little tired, and whatever I had to say, I already wrote."

"I understand, but let's just follow your own hypothetical logic here. If you have nothing to hide, why would you conceal the extent of your relationship with Mr. Ferro after something as serious as his death under suspicious circumstances happens right across the street from you?"

Now he had *me,* because even I had to admit that my silence made me look more than a bit guilty, even if only over the affair.

I kept answering their questions, each one more invasive than the last, making me worry and wonder whether this was the point where I needed to ask for a lawyer, but afraid to ask for one.

It was all clearer now. Unaware of Ellie's gossiping and distraught by Hector's death, I hadn't put two and two together, but now I realized that the reason people had been crossing the street on their way to pick up their kids from school rather than walk in front of my stoop wasn't because they were uncomfortable with death. It was because there was always the chance I'd be sitting at my laptop, by the window, and they'd have to say hello or decide to turn their heads, awkward as that would be. I could almost see their faces upon reading the headlines if I were arrested for Hector's death: The *Miami Herald* would read "Landlord Kills Married Tenant/Lover." The *Miami New Times* would call me the Murdering Mistress of Coffee Park. Even WTVJ's channel 6 would lead their five o'clock newscast live from my empty stoop to recount how I'd been dragged from home by police and arrested in connection with the murder of my alleged lover, a prominent Little Havana businessman and patron of the literary world, whose wife happened to be my tenant and lived right upstairs just a few steps away from where the beautiful, young, hip reporter would be standing. Trust me: I'd be the wrong kind of famous by all of Coffee Park standards.

Unfortunately, after answering all of the detective's questions and being released for the time being, I got home only to have to hear the stories from Iris. Apparently, she came close to clocking the lady who owned The Little Vintage Shop Down the Street for saying she worried that my "involvement" in Hector's murder would keep customers afraid of crime away from her Coffee Park shop.

"That bitch," Iris said to me that Saturday night. "It's all because of the time you told her she should shorten that long-ass shop name of hers. Let me tell you, if something scares people away from her shop, it'll be that thirty-pound hissing queen of a black cat she allows to roam around and sit on the merchandise like he owns the place."

Still, said Iris, trying to make me feel better, there were plenty of people who said nothing at all, refusing to get on the gossip bus. But even she had to admit it wasn't because they believed I was innocent. It was because they didn't want to give Little Havana people another reason to deride Coffee Park and its reputation as a liberal lifestyle oasis. Bottom line? I was now persona non too grata in my own neighborhood, which goes to prove it's not true what people say: Liberals do draw the line at actual murder.

Or do they? Because according to Iris, the issue wasn't the murdering. It was the "mistressing." Well, in fairness, not so much the "mistressing" as the convenient location in which I'd chosen to do it. Had Olivia lived even a couple of blocks away, there would've been money pools organized on my behalf and painted "We Support Mariela Estevez" signs denouncing police overreach. But not when I'd had the *descaro* of carrying on with Hector so close to his wife's very flowerpots. There were thousands, if not millions, of unfaithful men in Miami. I couldn't have picked another one? Apparently not, and *that* they could not forgive, not that I blamed them.

Since the conversation with Olivia, I'd reconsidered the affair too and decided I was sorry about Hector. Sorry I'd ever been stupid enough to convince myself married men were fair game. Sorry about all of it.

When I'd been the one being cheated on, I'd felt ugly, inside and out. Worthless. An unfeminine joke. A fool. So I'd somehow decided it was justified to create rules that would protect me from ever having to occupy that place again. Let some other idiot be the trusting wife for once. Let someone else be the one divested of any self-love she might have possessed, the thing not good enough being returned to the store to be exchanged for something better.

I didn't entirely realize it at the time, but that day with Olivia, I'd seen something amazing. Instead of an example of the ugly, unworthy woman I thought I'd been when I'd been the one cheated on, I'd seen a self-possessed person, elegant, flowing and true to who she was, and to the good and bad decisions she'd made in her life. Even in her mourning craziness, and possibly even in her guilt, she'd been whole, open, a presence no one, not even Hector, had been able to minimize. I'd truly seen Olivia for the first time that afternoon, and understood that shame need never attach to the victim. The wife is still also a woman, the marriage is whatever both husband and wife make of it, and the decision of either partner to be with someone else doesn't make the other any less of a whole person.

As for me, I hadn't even had love for an excuse. I'd only had loneliness and insecurity, but was that as good an excuse as love? That day I thought not and, apparently, so did my neighbors. (I've since changed my mind about that too. I don't think I'll be having affairs with married men again anytime soon, but, understanding firsthand what a deeply insistent lacerating bitch loneliness can be, I won't be rushing to judge someone who does either.)

"Screw the whole lot of 'em," Iris said to us the following Saturday evening from the tight backseat/storage area of Gustavo's Chinese-red Tacoma pickup as we drove to do our grocery shopping on Twenty-Seventh Avenue, considered the outskirts of Little Havana, to avoid the busybodies, the staring, and the whispering. "They'll get over it, darling, and if they don't, so fucking what? Like they all don't have some crazy shit poking out of their recycling bins. They're lucky I don't talk, 'cause if I did—"

"I still want to hear what they're saying behind my back. Come on, you can tell me," I insisted, sounding like Olivia.

"Nothing to me. They all know better than to mess with me when I'm stressed. But this one." She jutted out her chin toward Gustavo, who pretended to concentrate on driving. "It's like he has a promise to the heavens: Be Mr. Nice Guy to all these sons of b—"

"Iris! Now come on, *vieja*. Is that the way a fashion designer speaks?" said Gustavo.

"Don't *vieja* me. I know what that means, and calling me old is not going to make me stop, so there."

"It's a respectful endearment, and I only say it because I love you," he said to her before whispering to me, "Ñooooo . . . She's been cursing darts all day."

"It's the nerves, Mariela. When Gustavo ran in with his face translucent as a spring roll wrapper, I thought I'd die imagining all the things they could do to you. I hate to tell you, my friend, but I don't think you'd survive in jail. I just wish I had some fuck-you money to give you so you could move to wherever you wanted, not have to put up with these mother—"

"Who says I'm going to jail?" I interrupted her. "And what in the world is fuck-you money?"

"It's when you have enough money to say fuck you to any job, husband, or neighborhood trying to mess with you. Have you thought about how much this is going to affect your business? Who's going to give you their taxes to do? Who's going to rent that apartment, right across from where a man you supposedly killed lived?"

I had, but had put it out of my mind because I had bigger problems at the moment, like a couple of questioning policemen who hadn't sounded like they were done with me when I'd left their precinct.

Later, when we were on our way back from the market, Iris asked, "So what are you going to do about Morticia?"

"Olivia," I corrected her.

"Yes, that's who I meant, the frigid bitch," muttered Iris.

"Now, Iris, why is she the bitch? It's not like she owes me any favors," I said.

"Still," said Iris stubbornly. "And she does owe you if she killed him, Mariela. She has turned you into a pariah in your own hood, and you don't think she owes you for that?"

"But notice how she only challenged the bitch part, Iris?" said Gustavo in a weak attempt to distract us from bickering, because when Iris wanted to dislike someone, there was no stopping her. "I think she knows something we don't."

What *I* knew was that, as grateful as I was to Gustavo and Iris, I suddenly felt alone. Like being there but not, exiled despite having gone nowhere, existing in a space where no one could really meet me.

"We're sorry, Mariela, but what I don't understand is why Hector?" asked Gustavo.

See what I mean? Not even my friends were immune. Maybe I had taken them, their love for me, and even their socially liberal views about living and letting live for granted. Maybe they were secretly as disappointed with me as everyone else seemed to be.

"I don't know, Gustavo. Let's just say I'm a big whore and be done, okay?"

"No, what he means is," said Iris, faux-smacking him over the head, "did you love him?"

"Oh," I said, realizing they were just trying to understand and, as my friends, deserved an answer to their question. "I never really found out. What I know is that he was there at a time when I needed someone, anyone, to be there, and if that's love, then I loved him," I said, surprised at how easily I could characterize my relationship with Hector to them, but fail when explaining it to myself.

Gustavo nodded and said, "Okay, so, good deal then, let's worry about what needs worrying, and that's finding a good lawyer, you know, just in case."

"In case what?"

"Haven't you been listening? In case the police decide to keep harassing you when you have no fuck-you money."

We'd gotten to the fourplex by then, and I was about to get out of the car when Iris's hand shot out like a retractable blade and grabbed me.

"Uhn-uhn. Remember: The windows are watching. Chin up, back straight, shoulders down, boobs up, and *always* looking forward."

Gustavo parked in his space facing the building, but Iris didn't let go of me until I'd smiled, straightened up, and stepped out of that truck with my bag of groceries determined to look like I'd nothing to be ashamed of.

I kissed and thanked them and was about to go inside when I saw Abril and Henry walking toward us. Abril was wearing a black dress with a slightly flared skirt, and Henry had gray pants, a white shirt, and a black tie. I thought he looked adorable, and then I realized the direction they were coming from: the church.

Of course. With a funeral delayed because of the autopsy, there must have been a mass for Hector at the Coffee Park Unitarian Church and nobody had told me, probably because the people who could've told me weren't speaking to me, and the ones who were, well, let's just say now I understood Iris's and Gustavo's insistence on doing groceries as far away as possible from Coffee Park on that very night.

"Abril, Abril." Iris waved to her, thinking she hadn't seen us. But Abril didn't hurry or acknowledge her. When she got to us, she stopped right in front of me and glowered as if she were about to slap me. Then she said, "I'm sorry, Iris. I can't be a hypocrite and talk to her as if nothing were going on," and kept on walking without a word to Gustavo. I looked at Henry being dragged away by his mother, turning back to steal a glance at me, his smile more timid than I'd ever seen it. The pain in my chest was so acute, I swear to you I think I heard the sound a lightbulb makes when it goes out: a swift pop followed by the sad tinkling of minute glass shards inside me.

"So there was a memorial?" I asked, still watching Henry, wanting to have been at the church and, despite myself, having the nerve to be upset that Olivia hadn't invited me to Hector's mass.

"Yes, there was a service, but it was organized by the nature center where the wife volunteered. They didn't really invite anyone formally. Just posted it in a few places around the park. We thought it would be better for you not to go, so we didn't tell you," admitted Iris, picking up her grocery bags, one in each arm. "I'm sorry, Mariela. Listen, I'm going to go talk to Abril. She's just still in a little bit of a shock. You know she's not judgmental. The service must've freaked her out."

I had no idea what Abril was or wasn't, but I said to Iris, "No, no. Don't talk to her. Let her be. It's okay."

And it really was, because in the split second I'd lived inside Abril's angry stare, I'd seen something. Something that felt important: Abril and Hector, standing very close, facing each other. In my vision, there was tension, as if they were adversaries squaring off, not exactly what you'd get from new lovers. And yet, it was an electric tension that suggested something more between them. Could they have been having an affair too? I wasn't sure if that clarified his death or confused it, but it would make her attitude and his sudden interest in ending our relationship just before he died that much clearer. Then again, could I trust this sudden vision? Was my sight coming back? I mean, I'd been able to hear Hector just that morning, hadn't I? Could my efforts finally be paying off? Could Abril be the missing clue to Hector's murder?

But then I remembered how, in the weeks before his death, she'd been going out of her way to be friends with them both, Hector and Olivia. That wasn't something a woman having an affair would do. And she'd gone to the memorial service. Maybe I was wrong after all.

Iris hurried off after Abril and Henry, and I turned to wave at Gustavo before heading inside, but the sight of him stopped me. It's amazing how instantly a lost love can change the arrangement of the pores on a person's face. The corners of his mouth looked as if they held weights that were forcing them downward and misaligning everything else. His pupils were fidgety, like they belonged in blind man eyes.

"It'll be all right," I told us both, then I ran inside with my bags, dropping them on the floor, taking off my clothes as I walked, and heading straight for the bathroom, already hearing inside my head the rush of warm water filling the tub, so desperate was I to sink my body into it, to forget this whole day, this whole week, this whole month.

"Well, is about time."

"*Aaaaaaaaaaaaaaaaaaaaaaaaarghhhh!*"

It was Hector!

"Oh my God, you scared *the hell out of me!*"

"You need to use the bathroom?"

So I really *had* heard the water filling the tub, and Hector really had spoken to me that morning, because how else could he be in my bathroom, fully dressed with his tan cotton scarf, khakis, and trench, but barefoot, only his head and toes sticking out of the clear water on each end of the claw foot iron tub I'd painted and glazed just last summer?

"I can see you! Wait. What're you doing here?"

"Waiting for you," he answered. "What else?"

"They had a service for you tonight."

"Humph," he said, looking away.

"My God. It's really you. I can really see you," I said, staring at him, unable to believe I'd done it.

"Yes. It took me a while to get, how you say? The hanging of it, but am working on it. Nice hair," he added, nodding in the general direction of my bangs.

"I'm so glad to see you, and . . . I'm so, so sorry, Hector."

"For *war?*" he said, still struggling to pronounce, or maybe it was me, struggling to understand.

"For being so angry at you, for the things I said."

"I'm dead, Merry Ella. Who cares about that?"

He had that right.

"You're right. I'm sorry. It doesn't matter now, and I'm glad you waited for me because I don't know if I'm still in trouble, and I need you to tell me . . . how it happened."

"This is why I'm here," he said, then going into what sounded like a lengthy explanation I couldn't understand at all.

"Okay, I hate to be demanding here, but I can hardly understand you. Maybe you can do something to—"

"You want me to 'learn English'?" he managed.

"Okay, okay. I'm sorry about that. And anyway, what I actually said was 'learn to speak some goddamn English.' "

"Very funny," he said, though the word *funny* sounded like he'd said *hunny*, the volume of his voice was a few levels lower this time, and his reflection faded and trembled like the water he appeared to be soaking in.

"Wait. Where're you going?"

"I'm still here," he said from somewhere in, on, or below the bathtub, though I could barely see him, or the water, now.

I'd have to focus to keep as much of his energy here if I wanted to get the truth about what had happened to him, but at least now I knew I could really do this.

"Hold on," I said, though I had no idea where exactly he might be able to go if he tried.

I went to the bedroom, searched for the books I'd bought the day before, and picked up Raymond Moody's *Life After Life*, scanning the table of contents for what had made me buy the book.

"I no have a lot of time, Merry Ellaaaaaa," he wailed, his voice even lower this time, as I came back into the bathroom with the book, and sat cross-legged on the toilet.

"I'm trying to bring you forth again. Help me! Concentrate on wanting to be here."

"I *am* here. Please . . . just . . . help me."

"Of course," I said, closing the book. "I'm so sorry."

"Why you *furry?*" he said.

I had to laugh a little.

"I'm sorry . . . that you're going through this," I said. "Tell me why you're here. Tell me what happened? I'll be quiet. I'll listen."

He didn't answer. But I felt the coolness of his long, drawn-out sigh swirl around me like a gust of winter wind. It was the sound of a spirit beaten, perplexed, bewildered, like a dog after the blow he didn't expect, all his life confident he was the apple of his master's eye.

"I do not . . . I do not . . . know how. I do not know why," he said finally.

"You don't know how or why you died?" I asked, beginning to get him a little better by uniting the sounds he made in my head and translating them into words with the help of my intuition, which just meant what I felt he might be trying to tell me.

"I," he said, and then nothing. I waited a few seconds, listening intently, but nothing more came out of him.

"Okay, listen, let me try to bring you closer. I can't really hear anything you're saying right now. But this is progress, so just hang on, okay?"

No answer, but I thought I could still feel him.

I went to the section in the book titled "Meditation and Mediumship." It advised against coffee, alcohol, and heavy meals. I hadn't had a heavy meal in days, so that was good, I guessed. It also advised lots of meditation. No wonder I could see him now! Ellie's "outing" me as a mistress had resulted in less social, more silent days, even if I hadn't realized it just then. Talking less must've made me light, spiritually and energetically. That and barely eating, plus the fact that in an effort to keep myself from going insane, I had meditated (actually prayed) more during the past six days than I had over the entire twelve months preceding Hector's death. The book also said comfortable clothes were vital, so I took off my jeans and sat on the toilet again in my T-shirt and panties.

"Trying to tempt me?"

"Shut up," I said.

"I no have all day!" he said before doing more of his unintelligible mumbling.

"Hang on. I can barely understand you."

I breathed in and out as the book instructed until I felt myself become heavy, as in stable and centered, like a tree securely planted right onto the toilet, my roots snug somewhere beneath the bowl, alongside the drainage.

I concentrated on thoughts of love and imagined the bathroom bursting with beautiful pink and gold light, and as the light in my head and heart became brighter, my fear of death seemed to dissolve. Nothing else mattered beyond the moment.

Then I felt a question inside, a question I was sure was not coming from my own mind: What was my intention? And the answer, swift, if clunky: Be love.

Be love? How did you become love, exactly? And how could I do it before Hector disappeared again? How could I love Hector now that would be different from how I loved him before? And again, the answer came quickly from somewhere I couldn't quite pinpoint, simple and true: By wanting to help him more than I wanted to help myself. By being unequivocal in my intention of love.

The tears came then, marching to the rhythm of my breathing, warm and flowing down my cheeks like beads on a bracelet strung by the thinnest of silk strings. I remembered the sessions of my youth then. Some friend of my mother's would sit in front of me and give me her hands, and I'd feel the pain that shook and slung her every which way, and I'd want to help, and immediately I'd feel, hear, or know something I wanted to say to her. It's how it had always been. I'd just forgotten.

I thought about Hector. I tried to remember something good. Books! He'd wanted me to learn things. He'd shared the thing he valued most with me. I had loved that. I could be grateful for that. I could . . . open my eyes . . . and . . . there he was, looking at me as if I were deader than he.

"You're back!" I said.

"Where to go?" he said, shrugging his shoulders.

"Right. Listen. Tell me what I can do? What do you need?"

"I need . . . you . . . to help . . . meeee to know," he said as if I were learning disabled and he was losing patience with me.

How can I tell you what was in my heart in that moment? It was all so ridiculous, and yet, there he was, asking for help, my memory of his face now bent and twisted in worry and pain, and I didn't have to make an effort anymore. I just wanted to make it better, to help him rest. Wanting to help by seeing what someone else could not was the reason I was there, in that moment, and maybe the reason Hector and I had "crossed paths."

"I will help you, Hector. I just don't know how. You can see how hard it is for me to see and hear you. I don't know what more I can do."

"You have . . . have to tell me why . . . and how," he tried.

"Okay, I understand. Well, I think . . . the police think . . . you were . . . murdered."

"Moistened?"

"No, murdered."

"*Ass* what I said!"

"Anyway, that's what they're saying. But you have to tell me what you remember. Who did this to you?"

"I . . . I . . . I saw . . . she haaaaated me."

"She hated you? Olivia hated you? Was it because of us?"

Silence. I could still see him, but he wasn't speaking, so, afraid I wouldn't be able to bring him forth if I lost connection, I decided to ask my questions quickly.

"Hector? Not sure if you can still hear me, but tell me all you remember last. Who was there? What did you see?"

More silence. Then:

"You look *goot*."

"Yes, well . . ."

"Last night, you looked . . . good too. And hot. You were hot."

Did he mean . . . ? Wait a damn minute.

"Could you hear me calling you? Tossing and turning all night?"

He sighed and said, "Of course," though it sounded like *"off curse."*

"So why didn't you come to me until now?"

"You had tears. Not my *sing.*"

"Really? Women crying not your thing?"

"You look *goot,*" he said, fading again.

"All right, Hector, forget that and please listen to me. We don't have much time. What happened?"

"I don't *know.*"

"You don't remember?"

"I . . . I know . . . she did this. I saw her . . . hate me."

"Who's she? Olivia?"

"But I don't know how!"

"Hang on!" I said to his fading outline, feeling the air lighter and lighter around me with every passing second. "Are you saying Olivia murdered you?"

And then from somewhere in the empty, dry bathtub, came his very distraught lament.

"Just help me. Please."

"I'll help you, Hector. I promise. No matter what, I will help you. Now, why did you go to the park?"

Nothing.

"Hector?"

I was alone again and felt with certainty that he was no longer where I could reach him, at least that night. It was just me now, alone with my shock. Olivia had murdered him after all? But how had she done it? And why after all these years?

There was just no other explanation. She'd known I'd go seeking for the letter and had given it to me to throw me off. She'd murdered him when she first found it. But how?

I could understand why Hector couldn't rest until he knew.

But how come he didn't know? He had to have been there. Had she somehow made him unconscious before she hit him with some heavy object? Had she injected him with something? I got up and headed toward the kitchen, knowing I'd be much better able to think after I'd eaten something and put my groceries away. Despite everything, it felt so good to have heard his voice, to have seen him, almost as if he were alive again.

I'd just finished putting everything I'd bought away when someone knocked on my door. The police again? I was still in my panties, so I went over and looked through the peephole. A short guy wearing jeans, a T-shirt, and a red baseball cap covering half his face stood on the other side.

"Can I help you?" I yelled through the door.

"Delivery."

"I didn't order anything," I said.

"Mariela Estevez?"

"That's me."

"Well, this is for you. And it's kinda steaming, so—"

"But I told you. I didn't order anything."

"Just the delivery boy here."

One could never be too cautious, so I slipped him a five-dollar bill through the slot tenants used to leave me notes or their rent, had him leave it next to the door, and leave, then opened up just enough to snatch the big brown paper bag into my apartment before locking the door again and tiptoeing back to the kitchen with it.

There were many small cellophane and aluminum containers, the contents of each one written in cursive with a thin-tipped Sharpie. There was a milk shake cup holding what looked like a mango yogurt drink, a piece of pungent goat cheese, and a simple green salad that had been drizzled with some kind of fig-flavored vinegar. There was also a small baguette and a slender white fish filet that had been lightly grilled and smelled faintly of cilantro, garlic, and lime. At the very bottom of the bag, there was a flourless chocolate soufflé that filled my kitchen with the smell of fresh butter and a bowl of coconut soup with avocado, bacon, and a dollop of sour cream as garnish. Tied to it with raffia string was a note from Jorge:

> *Querida Mariela, here are organic versions of things I hadn't cooked in a long time. Things you used to love, that remind me of you. I know you don't like favors, or accepting help from others, but this is my way of telling you that I'm here for you, no strings attached. (Not too many, anyway.)*

It was a good thing that, being a chef, Jorge slept when people gossiped and worked when people slept, because it was clear he hadn't heard about the little visit police had paid me.

> *I just thought you'd be in no mood to cook, because let's face it, when were you ever? Now, if someone who cared about me sent me soup, I'd accept it and think it was the best thing I'd ever tasted. So, at least taste the soup. It might not be the best you've ever had, but it was sent by someone who will always care.*

Chapter 23

Attorney Consuelo de Pokkos advertised as a "spiritual lawyer."
Iris warned me that she was a bit unorthodox, but said she
couldn't have gotten back on her feet after her husband's death
without her and I should come see her because she would
advise me well, allay my fears, and only charge what she thought
I could pay, which, right now, was very close to nothing.

That Friday, the bus left me a few steps from the weird little
building where Attorney Consuelo kept an office. I looked again
at the name, address, and phone number Iris had written down
for me. Attorney Consuelo? What kind of lawyer without a
daytime TV show calls herself by her first name?

I waited for the bus fumes to dissolve and crossed the street
toward the narrow, two-story building. A bistro called Fresco
California occupied the entire ground floor, sporting a chronic
inability to make up its mind in the form of a green awning that
read: PASTA PIZZA SALADS TACOS BURRITOS.

Upstairs, the door to the only other business led directly
into a waiting area with no receptionist and no waiting chairs,
just a daybed with a night table holding a small lamp that had an
open-winged Murano glass bird hanging from the brass-colored
pull and copies of *Tricycle, Good,* and *Shambhala Sun* magazines
next to it. Was I going to be waiting that long? I looked at the
bed with the knitted blanket laid carelessly on it. It seemed to be

telling me, "What're you, slow? When have you seen a bed in a waiting room? You're going to be waiting so long, you're going to want to take a nap. And the magazines? Just here in case you're one of those people who can't sleep if they don't read first."

I wasn't. But Hector had been.

"Every night?" I'd asked incredulously, watching him smoke after sex.

"Every night."

"What if you want to have sex with your wife? Do you read before or after?"

"Mariela—"

"All right, all right, I'm sorry," I'd said, not knowing that just a few weeks later he'd finish the sentence by telling me not to do "that," whatever else I might do, or that he would soon thereafter be unable to tell me much of anything at all.

I could now hear the faint sound of voices coming from the office on the other side of the door. What kind of lawyer had such thin walls? I looked at the daybed, the magazines, and the blanket that I had to admit seemed to beckon me to take refuge under it, feeling as if I'd entered a parallel universe.

After a few minutes, I considered leaving, but Iris had taken the trouble to make this appointment for me and I didn't want her to think I didn't appreciate it. Worst-case scenario was I'd listen to what the lawyer had to say, get some information in case I was questioned again, and leave it at that. I hadn't been accused of anything, at least not yet.

Instead, I tiptoed over to the closed door and put my ear to it. (Yes, I know it's wrong to snoop, but you can see how having been clairvoyant as a teen helped erase my scruples about listening to other people's business, especially when their lawyers weren't smart enough to install soundproofing.)

A woman was crying. Then another woman's voice said, "You're human, you love, the person you love humiliates you, replaces you, forgets about you. You say you want to 'understand,' but if you really wanted to, you would have. What you really want is for him to have to continue to explain himself so that he can feel guilty, realize he's made a mistake, and come back to you."

The other woman stopped sniffling abruptly.

"Is it so bad to want things to be the way they were?" she said after a few seconds.

"Of course not. That's just how stupid we all are. But even if you get back with him, you'll need your little revenge, and you know why? Because you don't want to feel you allowed the infidelity. You want to feel you did something about it, stood up for yourself, refused to be an accomplice."

"But I did."

"But you didn't. Your worst-case scenario has already happened and, at some level, you allowed it to."

Oh my God! It was as if someone had opened a window and given me a light to shine into Olivia's mind. Olivia had gotten tired of allowing Hector's infidelities. One happening so close to her home, a space she obviously valued and took good care of, had been more than she could stand. It wasn't complicated. It was simple. She had finally become angry and hurt enough to kill.

Though the idea still didn't feel right inside me, I now knew that being so close to the questions I was asking, my intuition was on shaky territory. As much as I was trying to trust myself again, I had to remember that, in this case, the fact that something didn't "feel" right to me didn't mean it wasn't true.

Just that morning, and as part of my resolve to relearn to see and recapture my gift, I'd begun reading Laura Day's *How to Rule the World from Your Couch*. She'd written, "Intuition may not show you the whole picture, but if it is working right, it will draw your attention to what you need to know for your question or goal."

And then a few hours later I stumble on this gem of a

conversation? What else could this be if not my intuitive guidance trying to tell me something?

The woman inside was saying, "But what does that mean? That he has the right to go on with his life without care or pain? Without mourning us for so much as a single minute? It's just not fair. I want this ending to hurt. We should both be hurting."

I stood there with my ear to that door and my heart pounding hard, listening as if someone's death, or at least the quality of his post-death life, depended on it, because maybe it did. Laura Day said we rely on symbols, and that metaphors were tools that our subconscious sometimes uses to show us the truth of a situation, but dressed as something else, so that we can see it more clearly. I knew that's what this was: a story that was there to tell me another story. This woman's words, her hurt, were Olivia's hurt. Maybe this was a gift, a message to help me jump-start my own compromised intuition.

The attorney was saying, "I thought you just wanted to understand, to validate, thought you didn't want money—"

"I don't. Not really. But there has to be something I can do here because I can't live with this anger in my chest."

Hearing her, it was as if Olivia were inside me. I could see what I'd done to her and what Hector had done to her. I'd made infidelity impossible to ignore. He'd made her hate him. Together, we'd forced her to decide to live without him, and I couldn't be sorrier. Somehow, I now knew that Hector's ghost was right: She'd hated him, and then she'd killed him. But why? Or why now?

On the other side of the door: "Never fails: Show me a woman who doesn't want revenge, and I'll show you a woman who secretly hopes to reconcile with her husband. The minute they see the light . . . Erika, fighting for more money than is due you or delaying the divorce is not going to help your self-esteem or your pride, and it certainly won't make you happy. It will just make you old. And fat, causing you more than one blister and a couple of bunions, but you can do it, if it's what you really want. Your decision."

Olivia had finally decided she didn't want him, and that she'd take her revenge instead?

"It's not about revenge," the Erika woman said. "I thought you were a real lawyer."

"I am. I thought you were a coward, and you are. Why aren't you embarrassed to admit you want to take your husband back, yet you won't admit you want your revenge first? Do you want it for free? Ah, you want Attorney Consuelo to do everything! You want me to ruin my 'karmic' record, get the wrinkles, gain the extra pounds and the bunions! Well, I won't if you won't do your part."

This lawyer was nuts! I thought of leaving again, doubting Iris knew Attorney Consuelo had lost her mind since the last time she'd consulted her. But I was hooked. I needed to know everything about the client on the other side of the door. Somehow, she'd become Olivia in my mind. She'd become the woman I'd never felt I'd really been and always been curious about: the wife.

The voices were lower now, calmer. I held my breath and got ready to scramble to the other side of the room if the Erika woman's voice came closer to the door, but it didn't.

"Now then, do you want to take revenge against your husband, yes or no?" Attorney Consuelo was asking.

"Well, yes," said Erika this time.

I would've felt the same way she sounded: defeated, drained, unable to think.

"Good," said the lawyer, who was crazy with a capital *L* for crazy-ass lunatic.

I looked around the office and found what I was looking for: a candy dish filled with business cards next to the small lamp, each one with a picture of Attorney Consuelo to help me put a face to the voice. In the picture, she looked to be in her early to mid fifties with the roundest face I'd ever seen, brown curly hair, big brown eyes, and a huge mouth she seemed to think she needed to enhance with bright red lipstick.

My cell phone rang then. It was Gustavo, but I let his call go to voice mail along with the other missed calls from clients who hadn't yet heard of my sordid present. Seemed like everyone and their mother had decided to call me today, except Jorge. I thought that for a guy who'd put so much effort into doing something that would put a smile on my face, he had tremendous restraint when it came to seeing the actual smile. I also realized I wanted him to call and wondered what had made him kiss me, then stick to his "one kiss" promise as if it had told him all he needed to know.

The cell phone had alerted Attorney Consuelo and her client of my presence and now the door to the lawyer's office opened and a young, tall, elegant woman with glasses and long curly hair hurried out. Her face was red from crying, and I busied myself with the magazines so she wouldn't be embarrassed. Soon the other woman, Miss Red Lips from the picture on the business cards, was waving me inside.

"So."

"So," I answered.

"Mariela Mia Estevez Valdes," she said, reading from her appointment book.

"That's right," I said.

"I like it."

"Thank you."

"You're welcome. You're also afraid of being accused of murder?"

"Yes."

"So did you do it?"

"Of course not!"

"Of course not! Just checking," she said, smiling as she stared at me.

I was staring at her too, because the moment I'd come in, I'd begun to hear the low but insistent sound of invisible glass wind chimes being swayed by a breeze.

"Are you ever going to sit down?" she asked.

I wanted to, but I couldn't. The office was a vortex of energy, and thoughts, and sounds, and the chair, well, the chair had just too much to say.

Finally, I decided to tell her the truth.

"I'm getting something from that chair."

"How could you be getting something from the chair if you haven't sat on it yet? And, whatever it is, you really can't get it while fully dressed, that much I know."

"No, I mean . . . I'm psychic," I said, believing it for the first time in decades.

"Yes, I know."

"You know? How do you know?"

Instead of answering, she extended her long arm and index finger as long as she could and pointed to a hand-painted sign above her window.

"What does it say there?" she asked.

"Attorney Consuelo de Pokkos, spiritual attorney at law," I read.

"Exactly. Spiritual Attorney Consuelo. That's me."

"Right."

"And I'll give you the psychic thing, but you'll have to sit in the chair and tell me what you get."

Of course she didn't believe me. She was either testing me or making fun of me, which was fine with me since I had a hard time believing she could've passed the Florida Bar, or any legal exam, so we were even in that respect.

"Okay then," I said, sitting on the chair and closing my eyes. The message was sudden and clear, as if it had been inside me all along, as if I were the message, or rather the situation the woman had been crying about.

"It's about the woman who just . . ."

"Erika. Her name is Erika. What can you tell me?"

"He's going to come back to her."

"Oh, no! Really? Are you sure? It's a shame. She deserves better. We all do."

I wanted to shush her, but didn't want to lose the feeling of definitive knowledge I hadn't felt in so long.

"But it'll be a lie. He's . . . not a good person . . . his soul is in constant pain. He doesn't know *how* to be a good person."

"So I've heard."

"But she'll be okay."

"Tell me something I don't know."

"Sorry, that's all I get. Not even sure it's right," I lied.

"Oh, it's right, all right," she said, chewing on the pink side tip of a pencil. "So, getting back to you. I made a few calls. Police say death happened inside a very narrow time window because of the poison used, uh, let's see, belladonna is its name. I did some checking, and the plant doesn't grow naturally anywhere in Miami and, apparently, if ingested, a poisonous reaction can happen anywhere within ten minutes to an hour," she finished, sounding fascinated with her own ability to Google stuff.

"What's belladonna?"

She showed me an Internet picture of a five-tipped green leaf from which hung a single black fruit resembling a berry. The caption read "Atropa belladonna."

"Other names for it are deadly nightshade, devil's herb, love apple, sorcerer's cherry, murderer's berry, witch's berry, devil's cherry, and naughty man's cherries," she read, in case I wasn't getting the idea.

"So it's poison . . . for unfaithful men?"

"Seems that way."

"I feel sick."

"You should. But. Who has the most to gain from punishing a wayward man?"

"His wife?"

"His wife, who thankfully lives right upstairs, so even though they may be right about time of death, they'd have to be exact to the minute, since Mr. Ferro could've gone from your apartment to the one shared with his wife within a literal few of those."

"That's . . . great? But how can I be sure?" I asked.

"All they have is a breakup letter that proves you were having an affair, and ending it, if only because you expected him to end it first if you didn't. It seems to me you have nothing to worry about."

Then why did I still feel this weight, this sense of doom surrounding me?

"Look, they just got the tox report results yesterday. My guess is they're going to go after the wife."

You'd think I'd be relieved, but I wasn't.

"So what now, Attorney de Pokkos?"

"Consuelo," she said, waving the air with her hand, as if she were clearing the air of formality.

"Consuelo," I repeated.

"No, no, Attorney Consuelo," she corrected me again with a freakishly virtuous grin that would have been useful to show a person less desperate than me that she was absolutely and irreparably insane, alerting them they should find themselves another lawyer.

But since I *was* desperate and had little money . . .

"Okay. So, what now, Attorney, um, Consuelo?"

"*Um* is not part of my name, but okay, the answer is nothing. You do nothing. You're not a suspect. And if they want you to answer any more questions, you call me and wait for me before you say anything."

"What should I do in the meantime? And what do I owe you?" I asked, holding out my hand as I stood.

"For now, just one dollar. As a retainer, so that our conversation can be considered confidential. Not that I think you'll need me. But just in case, lay low, stay out of trouble. No, wait. Wait," she said, standing, putting the tips of all her fingers on the desk, and closing her eyes for a moment before saying, "As your attorney, Mariela Mia Estevez Valdes, I'm going to tell you what I tell all my clients: In the meantime, you go do whatever you want, whatever fills your heart. You go live, while you have a life."

Chapter 24

I never told Attorney Consuelo that there was a third person who also lived just a minute or two away, and at whose apartment Hector could have chosen to stop before heading to his own on the night of his death: Abril.

In my vision, the one I had when we'd crossed paths on the sidewalk as she was returning from Hector's memorial service, I'd seen Abril and Hector facing each other like the opposite ends of a rubber band about to snap. Had they been lovers? Or had there been something else going on? How could I be sure the tension I saw was sexual, and not adversarial, as I'd thought at first?

Oh, please, I scolded myself. What else could it be? She was a beautiful young woman, and he was a philanderer who wasn't above having affairs close to home. There was also the fact that she inexplicably broke up with Gustavo on the same day Hector broke up with me. Maybe Hector had mistaken her overt friendliness for flirting. On the other hand, she might really have been flirting with him. Maybe she was tired of struggling, figured Hector for an easy sugar daddy, and traded Gustavo in for the older model, convincing herself she was doing it for her son. Maybe that's why she was so angry: She thought I'd killed the man who could've made her life a little easier.

No, none of it felt right, but I knew there was definitely

something there, even if I couldn't figure out what the something was. I could feel it in the way my heart accelerated its beating every time the image of them together assaulted me, which it did, repeatedly and compulsively, every minute of the bus ride back to Calle Ocho.

Just that morning, when my newly exercised instincts wouldn't leave me alone, I'd followed her. I knew what time she usually left her apartment and I'd waited to hear the sound of her straw wedges coming down Iris's stoop. I'd followed from a not-too-safe distance, knowing Abril was not the kind to turn around when she heard sounds, her mind always somewhere else, and had taken my steps in time with hers, the raspy scratch of her wedges and my own flip-flops against the sidewalk sounding like two old women who've smoked all their lives, their gravelly voices in deep whisper, rasp, rasp, rasping away about others.

I'd made the decision to follow her in the lull of sleepiness from which I'd now been jolted by the cool morning air and the adrenaline of my hunt, though what I was hunting for exactly, I couldn't have said then.

Meanwhile, Abril turned the corner and stopped to cross Calle Ocho toward the bus stop, trailing a pink scarf tattooed with yellow peonies, posture perfect, suntanned face fixed forward in determination. I stood still, waiting for her to turn around when she got to the bus stop, wondering if she'd notice me looking at her from a distance. But she didn't stop at the bus stop. She kept right on walking west, weaving purposely through morning street vendors and ladies sweeping the sidewalk. I followed with a racing heart until I saw her stop at the entrance of Hector's bookstore. What was she doing there?

Then a stocky, blond man wearing dark sunglasses caught up to her, and they shook hands, turned around, and began walking in my direction. They were probably just walking to the café that was a few doors down from Hector's bookstore, but I couldn't risk their seeing me. So, heart like a marching band tuba, I turned around, struggling to walk calmly and not call attention to myself. Damn it, I'd really wanted to get a better glimpse of the man. What if he was the motherfucking lawyer Iris and I had been speculating about? Or a hit man for Henry's father?! (After that last thought, I made a mental note to spend just a little less time with Iris.)

By the time I unlocked my front door a few minutes later, I'd made a decision to channel Hector again if it took me all day and all night. Especially now that I'd heard from Attorney Consuelo what the police thought they knew, that he'd been poisoned, I couldn't wait to ask him to give remembering another try. Whose face had been the last he saw before blacking out? He said he'd seen Olivia "hate him," but that didn't mean she'd poisoned him. Then again, she was the only person I could think of who knew enough about plants to have a clue to what belladonna was, how to get it, and what amount might be needed to kill a grown man weighing some one hundred and eighty pounds.

As I ran through the possibilities in my mind, I didn't want it to be Olivia. I also didn't want it to be Abril, because what would happen to Henry if she were accused?

The one positive thing in all of this was that I could feel my sight slowly coming back to me. It wasn't just being able to hear and see Hector, albeit with a lot of effort. It was also feeling open, a little less afraid of life with every passing day. And just in time too, because in my apartment was the soul of a dead man who'd be spending his "days" moaning and sighing while "soaking" in my bathtub, unless I could help him remember who'd killed him exactly and why.

And it was this quest that now felt more important than anything else. What had before weighed heavily on the problems' scale: the breakup, the ruined apartment, the drug-addicted tenant, and even the lost letter, felt small and insignificant now. The old troubles seemed to have solved themselves somehow, while the new one—solving the mystery of Hector's death—called not only for all my faith and focus, but also for the recapturing of my skills. For a change of life and for a change in me.

So far, Hector had not been much help. Piecing together his moans and half words took a lot of energy out of me, and I still didn't have the faintest image of those minutes before he died. For example, I felt that Abril and the vision I'd gotten of her the other day were a clue or at least a symbol of what had happened to Hector. But if I asked him, would he understand what I was asking? Would he tell the truth, if he did? Would he be able to focus long enough to tell me what we both needed to know? No, I decided. I had to figure out another way to find out if Abril had been involved with him, and if not, what my vision of her meant.

Walking home from Attorney Consuelo's, I considered coaxing some information out of Iris, but discarded the idea immediately. (You know those people with no filter between brain and mouth? That's Iris.) Then a dangerous idea sprang into my head: I lived right next door. Iris had the keys to Abril's apartment, knew all her comings and goings, and would probably share it innocently with very little prodding. Maybe what I couldn't get via clairvoyance, I could get the good old physical way. I knew where Iris kept her tenants' keys and could "borrow" Abril's duplicate without her noticing. Once I had the key, I could just coax info about her schedule from Iris by feigning wanting to talk to Abril about what she'd said to me on the sidewalk, and then later sneak in when she was certain to be away for a few hours. It would take me a bit of time, but I knew I could do it. I no longer cared if Abril had been Hector's lover, but if she had killed him, that I had to know, even if it made me ache for Henry's sake.

In the throes of planning the newest escapade by which I'd be sure to get myself into more trouble than I might already be in, I almost walked right past Jorge's house.

Oh, that's right. You want to know when I'd decided to go to the house of a man I'd, until recently, avoided. It was during the bus ride home. While half my brain had been plotting the discovery of a possible secret connection between Abril and Hector, the other had been looking at my cell phone. Hadn't he sent me a gift of food? Hadn't he said he cared? Hadn't he kissed me? Why didn't he call?

Finally, I convinced myself that, having enjoyed his cooking, it was only proper that I thank him. It was just good manners. I didn't have to wait for Jorge to call me in order to thank him. I'd pass by his house. As a friend. And this way, I would meet his wife once and for all. Get whatever unfaithful plan was covertly hatching in his head and mine out in the open. Maybe even dispose of the evil thing. At least that's what I told myself as I walked over from the bus stop.

His house was located on the street directly behind Little Havana's historic Tower Theater, which was separated from Domino Park by a small skateboard area outlined in mosaic cement tile. (The "park" itself is made up of cement instead of grass, benches instead of trees, and flanked by murals made famous by the locals who actually play dominoes there.) Because of the corner position of his house and the open space made necessary by the skateboard walk-through, you could see Jorge's house from Calle Ocho, even though it actually faced the theater's "backstage" entrance.

But though the house itself was right where I remembered it, most of its facade was not. The enclosed porch I remembered had been demolished and a modern, open-space portico had been built in its place and painted a rich, creamy white. The cement around the new, huge, black, loftlike windows was still fresh and unpainted, but somehow the final effect was sophisticated-rustic instead of unfinished. There was new landscaping, and the architectural lines of the two palm trees, one on each side of the walkway to the front entrance, gave the house an air of romantic simplicity. I liked it. It reminded me of Jorge's cooking. Unpretentious. Simple. With just a touch of elegance and just a touch of sexy. Like a vase with a single pink rose and plain white cotton sheets on a four-poster bed.

The wrought iron gate was open, so I walked right up to the door, a glass and black steel affair. I'd been at the house only once or twice before because it had felt weird to be in a house that was always undergoing some preparation for a woman who was being held back in Cuba, but whose arrival was always impending. Maybe because of that, it had never seemed special to me, but now, well, now it looked absolutely stunning.

"Can I help you?"

A brunette in her early thirties answered the door. Behind her I could see boxes, tools, even an electric sander that had very probably sanded and polished the newly laid wooden planks in this house.

"Hi, I'm looking for Jorge."

"He's not here," she answered with a very slight accent.

"Oh, that's a shame. I'm Mariela," I said, extending my hand with a smile despite the once-over, so unapologetic and intrusive she could've been in charge of pat downs at the airport.

"Mariela?" she asked, tight-lipped and frowning, as if she'd never heard the name before and wanted to spit out the taste it left in her mouth. "Are you a vendor?"

"No, actually, I'm a friend of Jorge's," I said, noticing she wasn't wearing hcr ring when she finally consented to shaking my outstretched hand.

"Well, he's not here right now."

I could've said I'd wait for him just to annoy her, but I'd done enough annoying of wives to last me a lifetime.

"You're remodeling," I said instead.

"Yes."

"Looks fabulous."

"It's not finished."

"Well, you can tell it's going to be fabulous. Would you please tell Jorge I came by?"

"Can I tell him what this is in regards to?"

It wasn't her words. It was her tone and the way she kept looking me up and down, one hand on her hip.

"Of course," I said, knowing exactly what I was doing. "Tell him Mariela came to thank him for the other night. Food was delicious," I said, looking her in the eye and smiling wickedly.

She looked thrown for a minute, then basically slammed the door in my face, but since it was mostly glass, I stood there watching her pick up a box and walk away down the hall, her impossibly rounded butt constrained by light blue jeans, her hair swinging dismissively until she disappeared into a room.

I guessed she wasn't about to give him my message now. Just as well. I could always call his cell, tell him I'd seen the house, and that I thought it was beautiful.

Turning to look back at it as I walked away was like looking at myself in a mirror and seeing how incredibly judgmental I'd been whenever he'd mentioned his life, his restaurant, or his "guys," probably his kitchen help team. I'd chosen to hang on to the image of who he'd been when he'd been with me: a party animal with a good-enough-heart, but few responsibilities or long-term plans.

But now, with that last look at the gorgeous house that had his good taste sanded right into its cement walls, I knew what I wanted to do: Next time I saw him, I'd show some gratitude and encouragement for someone who'd done nothing but be supportive when almost everyone else had decided to desert me. I'd even tell him he had a beautiful wife and close the door on all of this. This is why he hadn't called. He'd needed closure. He had it. It was really over now.

And now, I had a job to do before I lost my nerve. I'd get home, change into something sexy for a supposed date, then drop by Iris's knowing that she'd pepper me with questions and be more focused on my romantic prospects than on the spare keys she kept underneath the phone. I hoped she still labeled them, knowing I had to move quickly and then keep Abril's key only long enough to make a spare key so I'd be ready the next time Abril left the house for any length of time.

But the second I stepped inside my apartment . . .

"Don't scream," he said, perched on the living room windowsill in his immortal khaki garb. "No screaming right now."

My mouth had already opened to do just that, but I closed it again, surprised at being able to understand him without strain for the first time since he died.

"Your words are clearer."

"I must be speaking goddamn English."

I wondered if it would make him happy to point out that at least his sarcasm seemed to have escaped death intact.

"Again: I'm sorry I was so hard on you about that when we were together."

"Soh-kay." He shrugged.

"You were always making me feel like I didn't know anything and . . ."

"Was trying to teach you."

"I know, and I appreciated it, but sometimes it made me feel dumb, made me want to point out the things *you* didn't know," I said, realizing as I spoke how much I'd resented him for this and wondering how married people manage to stay together for decades, pulverizing all those little resentments that creep up between folks who share a bed, in order not to let death do them part before it was time.

"Very annoying," he said.

I wanted to say no more annoying than his bringing it up now, but, again, I let it go. My great-great-grandmother's journal had warned me against the foul moods of new spirits, especially of those who are stuck and can't leave, so I took a deep breath and determined to "walk in his shoes" for a few minutes as the books advised.

"I been creamed today," he said.

Creamed? Cremated! Of course my impatience with him evaporated. I even took a step toward him, wanting to touch him, but when I saw he faded perceptibly as I approached, I stepped back.

"The good thing is you're here now and we're talking," I said instead.

"Yes, there you go. Is great," he said, looking out the window with a blank expression and a wistful air that confirmed my thoughts.

"Okay, well, good. This is good, right? Progress. And just in time because I have to ask you something important."

"So ask."

"The police say . . . you were poisoned."

He grunted and began to fade again, and I figured being here during the cremation was taking its toll on him. Maybe this was why he couldn't remember his death. It was too painful for him to watch, to remember. Which was bad news for me. If each time I asked him to remember that day, his energy would fade and make it impossible for him to recall anything, then he was not going to be any help in solving the mystery that would give him his rest, and me my peace, and my apartment, back.

"Okay. Well, they say the poison used is a plant," I pressed, pausing to let this sink in, knowing that it pointed to Olivia. "And that it's called belladonna. Is the name familiar to you?"

"Belladonna . . . *bella donna* . . . beautiful woman . . . how ironic," he spat.

"I'm sorry, Hector."

"Is done, no?" he said, a few degrees more transparent.

"Well, yes, but, as you know," I said, realizing he was unconcerned about the fact that I could be a suspect for what was "done," "they questioned me in the matter of your . . . possible murder."

"Is not you," he said as if he couldn't believe the level of idiocy of anyone who could believe I killed him.

"Well, of course, *I* know that and *you* know that, but it's not as if you can testify on my behalf, if it ever came to that, can you?"

"I'm dead, Merry Ella. Dead!" he thundered suddenly.

"Okay, point taken. Actually, that was *exactly* my point—"

"*Dead,* okay?"

Wait a minute. I was so intent on keeping the connection I'd only just realized that he was "screaming" at me.

"You know, Hector. I want to help you, I do . . . but this is hard on me too. So, this is it. You tell me: Why are you here? If you think Olivia murdered you, then why aren't you upstairs giving her the hard time?"

"Because."

"Because what?"

"Because. Don't want to scare her."

"Well, it's good to see you care about someone's well-being."

"How come . . . you never . . . toll . . . told me you spoke to . . . to others . . . like me."

"You mean to arrogant ghosts like yourself?" I said, because it was time to stop pussyfooting around him as if all this were my fault. "Or to dead people who think they're the only ones with problems?"

"Why you never told me you did this?"

"Because I didn't. You're the first one in a long time."

"Where I heard that before?" he said.

"Hector, you know, this isn't a joke. It's serious for a lot of people. Now, tell me. Why are you really here?"

"Told you. I have to be sure is her, Merry Ella. And I . . . have . . . to know why."

"What about Abril?"

"Who?" he asked, fading again.

"Henry's mother? Little Henry? From next door? And stop doing that fading thing. You're like a damn neon sign."

"Who?"

"Abril. Don't you remember who she is?"

"I know who."

"If you know, why do you ask who? Never mind, just tell me about her."

"I know whoooo . . . Henrieeee . . ."

"You're talking funny again."

"Wuuuuuu," he began, followed by his first mumbling of the day.

"What're you trying to say, Hector?"

But he just kept moaning and fading with every moan, his expression so comical I considered that he might be faking disconnection to avoid my questions. But why? I hadn't forced him to seek my help.

"Hector? How well, exactly, did you know Abril?"

"He's *cahl-ming.*"

"Who's coming?" I asked, alarmed, because the last time he'd warned me of someone's coming, it had not precisely turned out to be the Messiah, and, instead, I'd ended up cooped up for hours somewhere inside a police station, answering questions.

"*A rey muerto, rey puesto,*" he said, which means something like "to a dead king, a king crowned," and is often used to reproach the quick replacement of significant others.

"What're you talking about? Don't you leave without giving me an answer about Abril! Hector? Hector?"

"Don't worry about meeee . . . is *cahl-ming.*"

Sure enough, someone knocked on the door, but this time, Hector told me exactly who it was before I opened it. I could no longer see him, but his voice dripped a mix of hopelessness and irony so thick it could've condensed into a cloud right there in my living room.

"Open the door, Merry Ella. Is your boyfriend."

Chapter 25

Sure enough, there was Jorge when I opened the door, wearing dark green khakis and a loose-fitting screen-printed T-shirt that read: I DISAGREE WITH YOU, BUT I'M PRETTY SURE YOU'RE NOT HITLER.

"You went by the house!" he said in place of "hello."

"Yep, and good thing I remembered the address because, otherwise, I wouldn't have recognized it," I said, waving him inside, my heart beating faster than when I realized Hector was still camping in my apartment.

"And? What'd you think?"

"What did I think? What did I think . . . mmm, let's see—" I played, pretending I didn't see that his face was all lit up in anticipation of what I'd finally say.

"Stop torturing me, woman, and tell me you loved it!" he said, taking me by the shoulders and mock shaking me.

"Torturing you? *Ché,* you have no idea what torturing is," said Hector from wherever he'd faded to.

"Of course I did, you silly man. It's beautiful," I said to the guy with the pulse standing in the middle of my living room.

"It's coming along, eh? I bought it right after—"

"You bought it? Wait? Is there a rich uncle I don't know about?"

"The owners were going to lose it in the mortgage crisis, so

I offered to buy it in a short sale. It was a good deal because it needed so much work."

"That I remember," I said.

"Whoooo is this guy?" said Hector.

"Wow, so you're a homeowner now," I said.

"Actually, I'm a restaurant owner. Can you believe the house has dual commercial and residential zoning? It's because it's so close to the Tower Theater."

"Oh my God, that's fantastic. I'm so happy for you," I said, motioning for him to sit on the sofa, then sitting at my desk, so I'd be occupying the space between him and the windowsill behind me, which is where I'd last seen Hector sitting (floating?).

"I want to keep it feeling like a house, like you're going to a friend's home for dinner. So, every room will be a separate dining room with a different atmosphere, and . . ."

"Blah, blah-blah, blah-blah, blah-blah," groused Hector.

"The porch will be one ambiance, the dining room another, the bedroom will look out onto the backyard and be more intimate, more romantic," Jorge was saying.

"But where will you live?" I asked.

"That's the beauty of it: I'm turning the detached garage into a great little tree-house apartment with a side entrance and a view of Calle Ocho."

"Oooh, I could *die,* it's so fan-taaaas-tic! *Pero qué* incredible, *ché,*" said Hector, loudly slurring his words, and even using Spanglish in protest, as if he were drunk instead of just dead to the world.

"Hoping to open by Halloween. You'll have to come."

"Of course! Oh, and thank you so much for the delicious food you sent last night. It was really amazing."

"Yes, soooo dee-licious," Hector said so close to my ear that I shot out of my seat as if my butt had been spanked into springing out like a jack-in-the-box's.

"Thought you could use it. Gustavo told me, you know, about the police coming," Jorge said, getting up and coming toward me as if to give me the bear hug that would finally do away with this new stiff civility, this nervous formality between us.

But when he touched me, I was so tense he had to step back, unaware that it was the sarcastic dead guy's presence making me edgy and not the possibility of his touch.

"I'm really glad you came over," I said, trying to erase the hurt look on his face.

"Really?" he asked. "I know I was a bit of a jerk the other day."

"No, you weren't. I understood. You needed closure."

Jorge protested, but I couldn't hear him because someone else was talking:

"Oh, for God's sake, get a broom already," griped Hector.

"You want some wine? Coffee?" I said, motioning him into the kitchen where I hoped Hector would have a bit of a hard time following us, and pouring him a glass of rioja.

Once in the kitchen, I got right to it, doing something I'd (stupidly) never done before in my relationships with men: speaking clearly upfront.

"Jorge, I am going to share what's going on with me because I really need a friend."

"I'm here."

"Yes, but I need to know why."

"Why what? Why I'm here?"

"Exactly. I need to know your motives, so no one gets hurt. So I don't get hurt."

He thought for a minute then started to laugh, shaking his head as if I were unbelievable.

"You really don't know?"

I shook my head no, even as I heard Hector snorting and harrumphing from the living room that even he knew.

"You know, I'd been here over a decade by the time I met

you, but I never felt I was here, never felt like I belonged, never wanted to do more than work just enough to send money to Cuba every month, have fun, live life. Even marrying Yuleidys was about proving to myself that I could settle down, live like normal people."

"And you did."

"And I did, but you'd changed me."

"Don't say that. We had an affair. It was not—"

"How do you know what it was not? I don't," he interrupted me. "Anyway, later, months later, I noticed the little changes. I noticed I wanted to do better, be better. I noticed I wanted to do all those things so I could come find you, show you."

"You wanted to show me what I was missing, huh?" I said, making a joke, but feeling flattered in spite of myself.

"We have something, woman. You and me," he said, smiling. "I don't know what it is, but there's something."

"What you have is a wife."

"Had."

"He's ly-iiiing!" wailed Hector from the living room.

"Have," I said, afraid Jorge would prove Hector right and lie to me, ruining the good feeling I was starting to feel about him. "I just spoke to her today," I said, pointing to the hammered gold wedding band he always wore now.

"This is my father's wedding ring. He gave it to me before he died last Christmas."

So he was the man I'd seen him cry over in my vision when Jorge had first come over last week.

"I'm sorry. I didn't know."

"And the woman you saw today isn't Yuleidys. Yuleidys went back three months after coming here."

"Are you kidding me?"

"No, she didn't like it here. Hated everything about it. The whole learning to drive thing, the learning English thing, the following rules she wasn't used to thing, plus, she really missed her family, and, to top it off, it probably didn't help to realize that she wasn't really in love with me, and that I wasn't really in love with her."

"How horrible for you both," I said, remembering how he'd tried to hide his excitement about her coming back then. "And what about all the money you saved to bring her?"

"To tell you the truth, I was so relieved when she decided to go, that I didn't even care about the money. I knew almost right away that getting married and pulling her away from all she knew had been a big mistake. You know, Mariela, *La Yuma* isn't for everybody."

La Yuma. It had been so long since I'd heard the term. *La Yuma* is a mirage wearing an American dream costume. The only way to look at it is in reverse, as if through a mirror, it's what *los de alla* (the ones over there) think coming over here is. Everyone wears designer jeans in *La Yuma*. They have huge houses, and cars, and even boats. They go on vacations and say whatever they want without consequences in *La Yuma*.

"No wonder you've grown up. More?" I asked, pouring him another glass of rioja when he nodded. "And so she left?"

"Yes, but by then I knew what made me happy: feeding people, having them over, watching them relax and enjoy themselves at my own place," he said, swirling his wine before taking a swig.

"I do remember how much you liked to have people over. Still doing those crazy cook-ins at two in the morning? I could never understand how you guys could spend all night cooking at a restaurant, then get to the house of any one of you and cook for each other, with all that loud music, and pot, and wine, almost every night. I confess, that drove me crazy about you."

"It *was* crazy, I'll admit it. Maybe it was a phase. My new-immigrant-welcome-to-America phase. But then you broke up with me, and all I heard was your voice telling me how talented

I was, and what a good cook I was, and how I could do anything I wanted to do, so, I decided to do something about it."

"I'm impressed, but wait, so who was Miss Smarty-Pants at the house today?"

He looked at his feet as if he hadn't heard me.

"You don't have to say."

"That's Omayra. My . . . friend."

"Your friend?"

"My friend. Ex. Girlfriend. Ex live-in ex-girlfriend, and now my finally moving-out girlfriend."

"Ohhh."

"She was almost done moving out when you came to the house. I left to give her space. How was I to know you'd go by? I thought you'd forgotten where it was, the way you stayed away all this time."

"Well, you know, I imagined you were happily married. Didn't want to intrude," I said, realizing how much I'd cared about him, but also how much I'd wanted to believe happy marriages could exist.

Jorge placed his forearms on his knees, leaning toward me with wineglass still in hand, and smiled a wistful smile before saying, "I missed you, you know?"

"What you probably miss is your little girlfriend who just moved out. That's what you miss," I said, downing my wine and looking around for Hector, unable to keep from feeling how I was feeling, once again so close to Jorge. To a now unmarried Jorge sitting across from a woman who felt, for the first time in years, like she could really try to love an available man, this available man, for a change.

But Hector had apparently decided to be quiet now and stay in the living room, the denseness of his energy probably hard to move around.

"Nah, it was a long time coming. She's a nice girl. Just not for me," said Jorge.

"Right," I said. "Still, glad to know you haven't been lonely."

"You were saying you needed a friend," he said.

"I do," I said, letting him change the subject.

"Okay?"

"I need to commit a small crime."

"What?"

"I need to break into a neighbor's apartment."

"Why? What are you stealing?"

"Nothing. You remember Gustavo's girlfriend, Abril?"

"Sure. Just saw her."

"Where?"

"She was walking down the street with her son, just now. Why do you need to break into her apartment?"

"I think she might know something about Hector's death."

"Mariela, everything's going to be okay. The police are going to come to the conclusion that you had nothing to do with it because it's the truth."

"And you're that sure?"

"Of course. It's not so easy to accuse someone of murder," he said.

"No, I mean, you're that sure that I didn't do it."

He looked straight into my eyes and said, "Never in a billion years."

I could feel them now, the butterflies of possibility bringing Jorge closer to me and making me afraid in a good way.

"But," he continued. "If you insist on breaking into her apartment, we're going to have to hurry because it didn't look like she was going to be out too long."

Chapter 26

"Can I tell you just how much I wanted a remote-controlled car like this one when I was kid?" Jorge said, running his hand slowly over the top of one of Henry's RCs, a dreamy look in his big brown eyes.

"No remote cars in Havana?"

"Woman, and here I thought you were Cuban! No, of course no remote-controlled toys in Havana, at least not for kids without family in exile with money to send one to them."

"Okay, well, I promise to buy you one of those if you stand close to the door and be a good lookout like you promised."

"I got you in, didn't I?"

"That you did, and I thank you because I really didn't want to take that key from Iris."

We were inside Abril's apartment, and as Jorge dutifully stood beside the front door with Henry's car still in hand, I proceeded to look around for a diary, a letter, or a copy of any Gabriel García Márquez book with a sticker identifying it as having come from Del Tingo al Tango. I was also keeping an eye out for a belladonna plant or for leftover leaves, even though I knew Abril would never leave something with the ability to be even remotely dangerous lying around where Henry could find it.

I wanted to know if they'd been lovers. But more important,

I felt, was finding proof of the depth of the relationship, if it existed. You see, if it had been a quick fling, then the only one with enough of a reason to kill him was Olivia. On the other hand, if the relationship had been long and intense, then maybe Abril had real motive. That said, I wondered exactly how intense a relationship can really be with a man who already has a wife he lives with and a mistress he sees regularly? And if it had been going on for a long time, how had I not known? Then again, maybe I hadn't noticed in exactly the same way Olivia had failed to catch on about Hector and me. Maybe he'd just been that good of a liar. Or maybe, and a lot more likely, we'd all been that good at not seeing.

I did a mental inventory of things in my apartment that would be symbols of my relationship with Hector to someone who'd known him and scanned the living room for possible matches: a forgotten linen scarf, a classic novel, a blues jazz fusion CD.

Nothing. At first glance, Abril's home was as unrevealing as Abril herself. The living room was sparsely decorated with a sofa, a couple of wooden rocking chairs that looked like inherited heirlooms belonging on a tropical balcony, a tube TV set, and three big plastic bins with Henry's toys carefully sorted: one for cars and robots, another for games and puzzles, and what I guessed was the "everything else" bin with coloring books, crayons, and some old plush Beanie Babies that had obviously been smothered, kissed, cried into, hysterically thrown during tantrums over the years, and then rescued just in time to be preserved like honored members of the family, reminders for his grown-up self of who he really was, as reflected in who he'd really been.

Between the living room and the kitchen was a very small dining room with a square-shaped Formica table, three chairs, and a filing cabinet. I pulled at its top drawer, but it was locked, so I picked it with the errant bobby pin that manages to always be left behind in my hair. The drawer contained a few manila envelopes and a small pinkish-peach Capezio ballet flats shoe box full of papers: plane tickets, hospital records, and a copy of Henry's birth certificate, as well as receipts for his baby formula, his clothes through the years, his orthopedic doctor bills, food, books, toys, glasses, immunizations, and a few school trip permission forms.

Among these, one receipt caught my attention. It was from a detective agency and identified the service rendered in a single word with capital letters: HENRY, as if he were a government agency and not a sweet boy with a smile so honest it could make you happy to be alive all by itself. Underneath his name, it read, CONTACT INFO RETRIEVAL.

I spread the contents of the box on the Formica tabletop and could almost see the invoices, corresponding receipts, and canceled checks drawing a southbound dotted line from New York City, where Henry was born, to his present life in Miami.

I opened one of the manila envelopes, and dozens of pictures of Henry fell out onto the table, almost covering the receipts. Together, pictures and receipts looked like the elements of a baby book someone had forgotten to make and made it clear to me that Abril had come back to Miami with the intention of bringing Henry's father to justice, or at least to court, and had slowly and painstakingly prepared for the task, documenting her child's life and the cost of the sacrifices she'd had to make along the way.

I wondered what Abril was really hoping to get from this man. Was it the child support owed her? Did she want a relationship with her son's father? Or was she just trying to force him to hold Henry in his arms, teach him to throw a baseball, and call him "son"?

I began to put everything back as carefully as I could. *How hard could it be to find a man?* I thought looking at it all. That's when it occurred to me that he was probably dead. It was the only way that all this paperwork wouldn't have already led Abril to Henry's father. Maybe he'd been rich and Abril was trying to build a posthumous case for Henry's rightful inheritance or suing his estate for child support, which would explain all the receipts. Or maybe he was dead, but she didn't know it yet. Maybe she'd have to wait until the next detective agency revealed it to her. The news would, of course, be delivered in the form of a receipt: *Subject of search no longer at last known address. New address beyond this detective's scope.*

"You know, I think we should hurry," said Jorge, opening the door a crack to peek out down the hall.

"I thought you said you saw her carrying a clothes hamper."

"I did, but it was one hamper, not three. How long can it take to wash and dry one load?"

"I'm almost done," I said now, heading down the short hallway in Abril's apartment, past a light blue bathroom, to the only bedroom, right above Iris's.

Abril and Henry's bedroom was in keeping with the rest of their home: sparse and neat, a light yellow chenille bedspread on the only bed in the house, queen-sized, providing the frill factor in the room.

I went straight to the single night table. There were just some barrettes, a tube of Neosporin, and a faxed confirmation of an order for a school dictionary. I closed the drawer and quickly opened the top two drawers of the white laminate bureau facing the bed. I felt along the underside of the mattress's edge, finding nothing.

I was giving the room one last glance to make sure everything was as I'd found it when it dawned on me. The force of the realization was so strong, it closed my eyes and almost made me sit on the bed, catching myself just before my butt disturbed the perfect alignment of the chenille popcorn detail on the bedspread.

I opened the drawer on the night table again and picked up the fax confirmation sheet knowing exactly what I was going to find, for why would Abril, who didn't even own a computer of her own, fax a confirmation to buy a dictionary for Henry or anyone else?

Sure enough, the fax confirmation had been sent to Del Tingo al Tango by a teacher for twenty copies of *El Pequeño Larousse Ilustrado 2010* (*The Little Larousse Illustrated 2010— Spanish Edition*). I turned it around and read the handwritten scribble: "Coffee Park 11 p.m., if okay with your boyfriend."

I wasn't sure about the handwriting, but the sarcastic tone was unmistakably Hector's, the "your boyfriend" like an echo of his ghost's announcement of Jorge at my door less than an hour ago. And now the vision came again like a hammer on my head. There was Hector facing Abril, but the feeling was definitely tense, adversarial, and painful. What had I been thinking? This woman didn't care about affairs! This woman only cared about her son's father, about finding him and making him pay, or something.

I couldn't believe it. *How could I not have seen this?* I thought, walking back into the living room.

"Mariela, we should really get out of here," said Jorge, eyes trained on the hallway through the narrow slit of the slightly open door.

Abril hadn't been trying to make Hector stand in for Henry's missing father. Hector *was* Henry's father.

"Are you okay, Mariela? What's wrong?" Jorge said, closing the door and coming toward me as if intending to carry me out of there by force if he had to.

But I ignored him, shocked out of my skull, all the events of the past year sprouting new meanings in my head, and went back to the file cabinet and to the detective's invoice I'd put back into the shoe box. The attached receipts were all from just before Abril moved into this apartment and corresponded to coffee shops and cafeterias that were next to, or right across from, Hector's bookstore. The man meeting her that morning had been a detective.

"Come on, *Tatica*. Let's go!" Jorge said, in his desperation, using his old nickname for me, which I'd always loosely translated as "my sweet girl," but had any number of meanings along the same lines. "I don't want to have to leave this apartment by jumping off a ledge."

"Jorge, I think I know," I breathed.

"You know who killed him?" asked Jorge, eyes wide.

"No, but I know something just as important."

And that's when we both heard it, coming from the street below and through the window: Henry's voice.

"How is it fair that it's always after? Why can't I have ice cream *while* I do my homework? It's still going into my stomach."

"I don't want you to be distracted," Abril was saying, her voice now directly underneath the window, meaning she and Henry were standing on the stoop, probably looking for her keys while balancing her folded clothes.

"Who gets distracted by ice cream? It's just ice cream!" whined Henry.

"Stop it, Henry. No ice cream until you're finished with all your homework. Now, come on, help me with the key," said Abril, a minute before the entry door swooshed open, then closed with a clean click.

"Damn it, Mariela. We have to get out *now!*" whispered Jorge, putting his arm around my waist and basically towing me toward the door, the voice of the little boy I now knew was at the center of this entire mess still echoing in my head.

Chapter 27

I'd been so scared when I realized Abril and Henry were back from the Laundromat that I'd allowed Jorge to carry me out before he locked the door to her apartment and took my hand to steady me.

"Relax," he'd said, slowing me down to a stroll. "We're not going to make it. They're going to see us, so let's not look like someone who just broke into another someone's apartment."

And then they were upon us.

"Mariela!" said Henry, grinning at me.

"Hi, Henry," I said, touching his chin with the tips of my fingers. "I've missed you."

"What are you doing up here?" asked Abril, pulling Henry back.

"I came to see if Mr.—" I gestured toward the door of the apartment facing hers.

"Mrs."

"Right, if Mrs . . . the lady who lives there . . . was home."

"That lady's crazy, right, *Mami?*" said Henry.

"Henry!" said Abril. "She's not crazy. She's sick."

"Oh, well, maybe that's why she didn't hear me knocking, and by the way, this is Jorge. Jorge, Abril. Abril, Jorge."

"We've met," she said, giving us a wary look before turning to open her door without so much as a good night.

"Yes, of course. You're Gustavo's ex," said Jorge.

"I'm Gustavo's friend," she said with her back to us.

I couldn't help snorting at that.

"Okay, well, now that that's all cleared up, um, good night," said Jorge.

"Good night!" said Henry. "Don't let the bedbugs bite."

I smiled, looking into his beautiful, innocent dark eyes, searching for (and finding!) Hector in his face, before waving good-bye to him and following Jorge down the stairs and onto the sidewalk. I walked slowly, my hand still in his, my eyes shut tight with fear and dread of all that lay ahead. It was true: Abril and Hector. Maybe not now, but at some time.

When we got to my stoop, I turned to go up the stairs, while Jorge turned toward the sidewalk, pulling me.

"Where we going?" I asked, eyes wide open now.

"Across the street," he said, gesturing toward the park.

"I can't."

"Yes, you can. Now come on."

"I can't, Jorge."

"Would you rather go by yourself?"

"No."

"Are you going to avoid the park you live across from forever?"

I couldn't do that either. The park, that apparently inconsequential square patch of green and brown, was the heart of Coffee Park, of this place that had sheltered me after every one of life's blows.

So I went.

As we neared the bench where Hector's body was found, my body began to quake. My knees, like poorly secured stilts under an old, creaky beach house, started to sway left, then right, until I had to sit down on the bench right across from it.

Coffee Park was silent, all shadows and rustling leaves.

"How do you feel?" Jorge asked.

"I don't know."

"You were lovers," he said.

"Yes," I admitted this time.

"Okay. How do you feel?"

"Sad."

"Were you in love with him?"

"I think I might have been. His smarts, his brain, how he made things interesting. I think I wanted to be the feminine version of him, and yet I didn't want to marry him, or even live with him. Does that make sense?"

"I'll make it make sense," he said.

It was something he'd say to me when we were together, and back then it had been enough to make me feel safe when he was close.

I kissed him, and he kissed me back, his tongue tasting faintly of coffee and cinnamon.

"Okay. Not what I brought you here for," he said after a few seconds, putting his hands on my arms and gently pushing me to rest my back on the bench.

"Well, this is no fun," I joked.

"You're avoiding it."

"Avoiding what?"

"Mariela, you just broke into a person's apartment to find out what happened to him. There are obviously things you need to deal with. Now we're here. Where he died. Talk about him, think about what happened, remember him, cry, whatever, but face it."

When I didn't answer, he said, "Here, I'll help you. Tell me about him."

"No."

"Come on. Please."

"Uhn-uhn," I said.

"Talk to me, woman," he said in mock exasperation.

"Since when are you such a grown-up?"

"Start talking."

So I told him everything up to Hector's death. And then I cried, and he hugged me, and the hugs turned into kisses that felt good, but also good for me. And then *he* told me everything. About Yuleidys, and how mind-blowing it had been to realize he missed me while being with her. About how he'd kept on missing me, but hadn't known how to approach me or what to say. About the day that had turned him around: He'd gone to work high on pot and screamed at a customer who'd sent back his signature dish—baked white fish on a bed of mango, avocado, cucumber, and crabmeat. The customer's wife had looked at his enraged face and begun to cry.

"I will never forget her face. She was afraid of me! She thought I would hurt them. That's when I decided I needed to do something with my life. Get over Cuba already, carry it with me without letting it drag me down, and put down some roots here, you know? Get high on life, as they say."

He told me how he'd thought of me as he worked on turning his house into a proper restaurant, fantasizing he'd invite me to his place, to see everything he'd done, and how he'd changed, and that I'd be proud of him.

I listened to him in that place that had recently witnessed death, but also, no doubt, life, and children's squeals, and the banter of friends. I wanted to tell him how much he was making me want to believe in the existence of happy possibilities. That sitting next to him, I could almost see myself having a good life, a loving life free from fear of my own sight, strong enough to see what I was meant to see, and wise enough to use what I saw to help myself and others.

"I'm afraid," I said instead.

He let out a huge laugh and put one hand on each of my cheeks as if he couldn't believe the clock had somehow turned itself back to this place, the "place" where time and space and circumstance had intersected to let us meet again.

"Mariela, I get it. You're working through some stuff now, and I don't want to rush anything, but—"

"Jorge, I don't even know what will happen or what I'm feeling. A part of me is still grieving for something without knowing exactly what that something is, and there's all this unfinished business surrounding Hector's death."

Not the least of which was his ghost, living in my house.

"I know. I know. When you're ready. And if it's a no-go, fine. I think I've proven to you I can take a hint. But. If it's even close to being a maybe. Then we'll figure out how to take it one day at a time. How's that? Deal?"

"Deal," I said, happy to be offered a short-term layaway while I mourned Hector and thought about the little boy to whom he'd never teach the joys of a good book.

Chapter 28

In case you've wondered, people don't change just because they've died. And if my early experiences connecting people with dead loved ones are any indication, this is especially true of men.

Two whole days had passed since I'd discovered the secret of Henry's paternity. Or at least, the pieces of evidence that pointed to the fact, since what I'd found fell rather short of being the equivalent of a smoking DNA gun.

Still, Hector refused to show his face, or whatever it was he'd been showing during our post-death conversations, which, to me, was proof enough.

"Hector, this isn't the way it works. You can't just show up when you feel like it, and then refuse to come when I call you. Hector? Hector!"

Nothing, and I'd tried it all. I'd held objects of his, mostly books like the copy of *Chiquita* that he'd given me that last time at the St. Michel. I'd filled the bathtub and sat on the toilet clinking my Tibetan bells, thinking of specific moments of our time together and trying to connect with him through shared memories. I'd chanted repetitively for him to make his presence known to me, substituting legitimate chants with funny words like *knock-knock, mango,* and *guavaberry* (my cell phone's alias) and singing them in the most ceremonious tone I could manage, trying to make it impossible for him to refrain from a snarky comment. Exasperated, I'd read positive newspaper stories about the Miami Book Fair, cofounded by his mortal enemy, Mitchell Kaplan, thinking his jealous ego wouldn't be able to resist, and had finished by further provoking him: "Now there's someone who knows how to sell a book, I tell you." But not even a snort.

Finally, I'd tried talking to him, promising not to judge or say a word about what I was sure I knew, to understand anything, no matter how horrible. But no Hector. Trust a man to disappear when you need him most.

The police had been by a few times. But the plainclothes officers had gone right past my door and up to Olivia's apartment. If she'd ever had to accompany them as I had, I didn't see it.

Still, no Hector.

Knowing him, I'd considered the possibility he might be jealous of how quickly my "boyfriend" and I seemed to have fallen back into a hybrid courtship/rekindled friendship since that evening in Abril's apartment.

And then, weeks later, after I'd almost convinced myself I'd lost my abilities again, he came back.

It was 5:55 a.m. on a Miami winter's Monday, according to my microwave's digital readout, and narrow, pinkish mango slivers of light had begun to sneak in through the slats of the wooden blind covering the little window that took up the upper half of my kitchen door.

"You want me on my knees?" Hector had asked after a while.

Before I could explain to him how little that would solve in his present state, he'd slid toward the floor, a mass mostly made up of a crumpled khaki trench coat and slacks, barely held together by my memory of his tanned skin and dignified manner. This stance, so proud and self-assured even now, was Hector's version of kneeling.

When he "hit" the floor, we'd already been at this for almost an hour: him begging me to protect Olivia from danger he had not been able to articulate in any way I could understand. Me, seated at the kitchen table, leaning forward with knees pressed together and arms crossed in front of my chest, as much because I was feeling the evening's misty cold giving way to the peaceful quiet of morning in Coffee Park as because I wanted to create a bit of a barrier against the intensity of his dead energy.

I'd walked into the dark kitchen for a glass of water and found him sitting at the kitchen table, moaning softly and sitting in the same chair of the dream that warned me of his death weeks before, only, this time, there was no cigar and no newspaper.

"Please, Merry Ella. I'm begging you!" he demanded again now, his eyes, usually mischievous in life, now frantic, piercing, and haunted.

"Okay, again: How do you even know Olivia's in danger? Or is it that you think the police are coming after her?" I asked, thinking of how he'd known when they were coming to fetch me for interrogation.

"I don't know! I *sink* she wants to hurt herself. You have to tell her. Tell her is not her fault. Tell her I'm sorry, please, tell her I'm sorry," he said.

"Hector, I told you: Olivia knows about you and me. She doesn't want my help."

"I know she's in trouble, I knooooow . . . I know . . . whooooooo . . . whooooooo . . . who-whoooo-whoooo . . ."

He'd finally broken down, defeated, crying his futile tears like the ghost he was having a hard time understanding he was. It was like watching a junkie agonize. But don't think of a strange junkie, a junkie you don't know. Think about a junkie who's your brother, or the son or daughter born out of your womb, a junkie you care about. It was like watching that junkie thrash and tremble, sweat and sob, and it was unbearable.

"Please don't cry, Hector. I promise I'll figure something out."

I'd told him I knew all about Henry the minute I'd seen him sitting there in my kitchen after so many silent days. I'd asked him how he could have done something so terrible to his own son. But he'd just grown even more frenetic, refusing to talk about Abril or Henry and insisting I go to Olivia that minute.

"Sorry, Hector. Not until you tell me the truth about them. I mean, don't you care about Henry? How can you be so coldhearted?"

That's what had brought on all the kneeling and begging and sobbing: All my chanting and calling him forth since finding out about Henry had forced him to remember. He'd remembered that somehow Olivia knew about Henry and Abril. He was sure that's why her last look had been one of hate, effectively handcuffing him to this world. That was the reason for all of this, he said, wailing his pain with "wooohooohooos" again and again, until I could no longer stand it.

"Enough! If you can't tell me what happened, then I don't want to keep talking to you."

"It's, it's . . . I can't, I . . . I can't," he managed, stressing the sounds, wanting me to understand every word.

And then I saw. It was regret! Regret had paralyzed him. He couldn't move in any significant way because the pain was blinding him so, making him heavy, unable to see, just like me.

I began to say words, synonyms of *light* and *love* to try to calm him down, as I'd read from the family journal I'd almost memorized in a matter of weeks.

"Love, mercy, light, good, beauty, friendship, soul, whole, good," I repeated again and again until I no longer felt him wailing.

"Hector, I can't help you if I don't know what happened to you, and I can't put it all together without what you know about what happened that night."

"I just said! *Somesing* bad."

"You mean like evil?"

"Eh," he said sadly, shaking his head wistfully like an old Jewish grandma, as if I were close, but not quite, and trying to explain it to me were of no use.

"Okay. Something bad. Maybe like shame? Or blame?" I said, feeling strongly that I was on the right track.

"Woo-hoo-hooooo!" wailed Hector again, sections of him appearing and disappearing before my eyes.

"It hurts? Painful? Remorse? Guilt? Is it guilt?" I kept tossing out options at him like a game show contestant racing against a thirty-second clock.

I knew when I'd gotten it right because the second I said guilt, his wailing got louder and he covered his ears, out of habit I guess, as they were no more really there than his trench coat.

"Okay, okay. Stop it. I get it. It hurts. But it's too late now. There's nothing either one of us can do. You'll have to take the guilt with you. It will go away in time, I promise."

"How can you of all people say that to meeee, Merry Ella? Don't you know I can't go . . . like this?" he wanted to know.

He was right. How could I? I knew all about guilt. I'd been carrying it with me like a favorite purse all my life. I'd made a decision born of guilt and suffering over my mother's death when I was eighteen, and then been too stubborn and too blind to the fact that I didn't have all the facts, and refused to change it, denying myself the memory of my mother's love until just a few weeks ago, when Hector's death had cracked me open. The result was an entire life shaped by that one decision, by that one absence of self-love. So many opportunities to create my own happiness wasted.

So I got it now. That's why Hector was still here. Guilt and regret, two sides of the same coin. Guilt of the kind so painful and powerful it springs at you from around every corner, keeping you from sleeping, from resting, even from dying. I understood now. But understanding it didn't mean I had the remedy for it.

"You have to help Olivia," he said again.

"Tell me about Henry."

"I need you to help Olivia," he said, standing his ground. "I don't want her to pay for this. I owe her."

"Tell me about Henry and Abril, or I'm going back to sleep," I said, ignoring the fact that he'd basically conceded Olivia was behind his death, the pain involved in accepting this one fact probably the reason he'd stayed away after I'd mentioned that belladonna had killed him. Of course he'd known then. He must've known immediately.

But even though I could feel bad for what he was going through, the truth is I was really angry with him just then. Here he was, back from the dead, going on and on about Olivia and the supposed danger she was in, while apparently not caring one bit about a child who hadn't asked to be brought into this world.

"Start talking, or I'm walking right back to bed and getting under those covers, and don't even think of getting in there with me because I swear I'll start chanting the rosary if I have to."

"I'm not perfect, Merry Ella."

"Don't you give me that, Hector Ferro. Who the hell asked you to be perfect?"

"Please don't say hell," he said quietly.

"What kind of man doesn't care about a child? His child!" I insisted.

He was very quiet for a few seconds, as if weighing his options, then got up, or that's what it looked like to me, and "sat" on the chair across from me again.

"She wanted me to be a father. I told her to break up with her boyfriend," he said, relenting at last.

"You mean, Abril? Oh, Hector! How could you do such a thing?"

"I'm baaaad," he said, shaking his head again.

"Forget you. How could you do this to Henry?"

Then he told me how he'd been giving Abril cash for Henry after a detective contacted him threatening with proofs of paternity. How he'd thought he was doing the right thing by protecting Olivia, while giving Abril what he could honestly give. He really hadn't seen how telling Henry that he was his father could do anybody any good. He'd told Abril that he'd continue to help her secretly, but she insisted that her son had a right to be loved by his father.

"He does," I said.

"He's a good boy, Merry Ella. I could take responsibility, but she say that was not enough. She wanted me to love him, spend time with him. But I never wanted to be a father!"

"You should've thought of that before sleeping with her. And you told Olivia you did!"

"I did no such *sing!*"

"You didn't say you wanted a child?"

"I did not say it to make her feel *anysing.*"

"Yes, you did, you horrible, horrible man. You shamed her all these years, lied to her, made her feel worthless," I insisted, not caring that I was making him writhe with every word. And when he didn't answer, I kept right on going, as if I knew anything about his marriage.

"Say something, damn it!" I said finally, pounding the table with my fist.

"So I deserve this, then?" he asked, unruly brows vibrating like pond water, his words feeling as if the table had punched me back.

"Okay. So what happened? What really happened?" I asked, yielding.

"She wanted me to tell Olivia *everysing*. That it was the reason I sold the house, put the money in Olivia's name."

"Was it? In case she came back demanding child support?"

"I told her she had to break up with her boyfriend if she wanted meeee to destroy my marriage," he said, ignoring my question.

"Oh, Hector."

"How to know she was going to do it?"

"Right, you just wanted to sleep with her. And when she showed you she was willing to do anything to get you to do the right thing, you decided to go for it, have your little fling again. That's why you were in such a rush to break up with me, wasn't it?" I said, seeing it all as if I were reading it right out of my grandmother's journal.

He was silent again.

"Come on, admit it. You couldn't wait to toss me like last month's paper, just so you could, what? Prove to yourself how irresistible you were?"

"I said: I was baaad."

"And for what?" I continued, on a roll. "Olivia would have forgiven you. I would've gotten over it. Instead you hurt me, you hurt Gustavo too, you hurt Abril and Henry, just to sleep with her? To prove you could steal her from a younger man? What was it?"

"I don't know! Maybe. I don't know. Leave meee alone," he said, breaking up again.

"You're kidding, right? Because unless you were going to leave Olivia, this makes no sense."

"What? No! No, no, no. No, no. But, I felt, eh, you know, eh, macho. She always said 'your son, your son.' It was very, you know, macho. For me."

"Padre no es el que engendra," I said in my most disgusted tone, half of a saying that means "father isn't he who engenders, but he who raises."

He just shook his head, as if to himself.

"Stupid, I know. I know I did baaad."

He didn't remember why he'd been in the park or how Olivia could have known about Henry. All he remembered was the hate in her eyes, and then, nothing. And I saw this now; it was all he cared about. Which made me realize the futility of wanting him to be a better person in death than he'd been in life. It just doesn't work that way. Like all egotistical philanderers, Hector had felt entitled to everything: the one loving wife that he loved back "in his own way" and the myriad dalliances, which were just that, the entertaining drama and variety he felt deserving of in the same way he felt deserving of good books, art, and music. You know, the other joys of life.

"Will you help me, Merry Ella? Will you . . . be . . . a friend? Help Olivia?" he pled again, as if to remind me that nothing mattered now that he was dead, that there was no use berating him for what was done.

"What can I possibly do?"

"Tell her. Tell her I'm ssssorry."

Now there was something I was absolutely *not* going to do.

"How can I tell her that, Hector? You're dead!"

"Tell her. Merry Ella, I told you: I sink she wants . . . to hurt herself."

I sighed, hoping he'd understand I'd try my best, but also that he'd be unable to see inside my mind and know there was no way in hell I was going to tell Olivia I'd been speaking with her dead ex-husband.

"Merry Ella?"

"Yes, Hector."

"I want you . . . to forgive meee. For how . . . I was. I didn't *sink* about you. I'm ssorrry I hurt you so much," he said, back "on" the floor, looking up at me with those eyes that seemed as alive as ever, the intensity of their gaze unchanged as he knelt in front of me, just like Eddie the psychic had said he would.

"It's okay, Hector. It's okay. You didn't hurt me that much. You didn't. And you gave me good things too."

"Like what?" he asked, unbelieving but expecting an answer.

"Like love of life. You know, of . . . art, books, music. Good stuff, and—"

"You are beautiful, Merry Ella. You are . . . good. I can see that now," he said, stressing every syllable, making a huge energetic effort to speak clearly. I could tell because with each word, his image became more and more like a Venetian fresco seeping into the plaster of the wall behind it, to be hidden from history for centuries. "Forgive meee?"

"I forgive you, Hector," I said, wanting him to believe, to know, that he'd never be alone. "I know Olivia forgave you too. You know that, right?"

He started to sob again, doing that who-whoing thing he did. "Hector?"

"Tell her. She was always. My Olivia. No, tell her she was my olive tree. Tell her that, please. And that I loved her."

I believed him. He'd faded almost to nothing in order to muster the strength to say those words as clearly as he could, to make absolution and his love for Olivia his last intention.

So I let him go, letting go also of the diversion this whole mystery had provided, and that I was only now able to admit to myself I'd held on to, like a crutch, to help me deal with the loss of him in my life.

It had been much too long for him, this roaming of days,

unable to go, unable to be here. It was time for him to rest, and for the two women he'd hurt the most to live.

When he'd gone, I was no longer cold and could hear the sounds of Coffee Park, fully awake and ready to face the day. I was ready too, and now that I knew what I had to do, there was no time to waste.

Chapter 29

"For months, I knew something was wrong, but when I'd asked him, he'd just grumbled some nonsense about the cost of the booths for the Miami Book Fair. I knew he was lying, but . . ."

Olivia was on her bed now, where I'd convinced her to lie after she'd finally answered my insistent knocking and opened the door, trembling and unstable from lack of food and sleep and peace.

She'd waved me away when I tried to cover her with the shabby floral comforter by her bed, but didn't object to my going into the kitchen in search of something for her to eat. Wasn't she afraid I'd find her belladonna? Or was she beyond caring?

Opening cabinet doors (and loudly banging them closed) in my quest for eatable food, I was tempted to search for it, as confirmation, but stopped myself. I already knew what I knew. Plus, I'd promised Hector I'd help Olivia, not come up here to do the police's job for them.

In the cabinets, I found cans: chickpeas, sweet corn, and white sardines in lemon. In the fridge, I discovered the last quarter of a red onion and some leftover shiitake mushrooms, which I chopped and threw, along with the contents of all three cans, into a ceramic bowl, followed by the last handful of feta cheese crumbles miraculously preserved inside the sturdy plastic supermarket container they'd been sold in.

There were no greens or fresh vegetables for a proper salad, so I doused what I had with some expensive extra virgin, cold-pressed, organic olive oil I found under the counter and sprinkled it all with Celtic sea salt that was thick and rough and almost as expensive as the olive oil.

I swirled my mix in the bowl until the oil coated everything, making it shiny and colorful. Then, not finding a proper (or a clean) tray, I put the salad of sorts atop a turquoise dinner plate and brought it into the bedroom for Olivia.

The room, like the rest of the house, was a complete mess. She'd obviously given up doing anything but the most basic things: going to the bathroom, drinking water, and bathing, maybe.

I placed the food on the night table next to her and started to pick up a little, noticing a small suitcase and a change of clothes on the chair by the window, but continuing to tidy up until I saw her eye the bowl a couple of times out of the corner of my eye.

"Here, let me help you," I said, sitting on the edge of the bed, taking the plate in one hand and holding the spoon up to her mouth with the other, very matter-of-factly, as if I did this every day.

After just a couple of mouthfuls, she shook her head, lips closed.

"You have to eat," I said, wondering if I should ask Gustavo to help me take her to a hospital.

"I knew something was wrong. His mood, his absence even when he was here, but I thought whatever it was, whoever she was, would go away, like it always did. I decided to find a project. That always helped," she said, looking intently at her hangnails, picking at them.

"A project?"

"A remedy, a recipe. I thought I'd help the boy. Henry. With his eyes."

"The belladonna," I said.

She looked at me then, surprised that I knew.

"I spent a lot of time reading about myopia. Some say that it isn't hereditary, but I found that with the very extreme cases, as in degenerative myopia, it is."

"But Abril told you she doesn't have myopia."

She looked away abruptly, fixating her gaze on the wall, and I knew that Hector had been right. She knew about Henry. But how?

After minutes of silence, I insisted: "The belladonna, didn't you know it was deadly?"

She breathed deeply, as if bracing herself, then motioned for me to give her the bowl again and took an enthusiastic spoonful or two of my concoction before speaking again, already looking better. God only knew when she'd eaten last.

"I wasn't going to have him ingest it. I was going to use it to dilate his pupils so that the secret ingredient in my remedy would work better," she said, adding, "It's shiitake mushrooms," after it was clear I wasn't very curious about naturopathy and wasn't going to ask her what it was.

She was all business now, energy coming to her from the act of speaking about something she knew.

"I was so meticulous. I worked for days to carefully extract liquid from the belladonna leaves I'd ordered, drying them until the remaining liquid turned an almost perfect consistency, like a resin. And this with leaves from a plant that's not even native. Well, I could have managed to grow it, but I didn't want to risk one of those sudden Miami weather changes rendering it unusable."

"You said you ordered it? Where?" I asked, not knowing what she would say before she said it, but knowing that she was telling me the truth, getting that feeling of confirmation each time she dropped another detail on my lap.

"At Pedro's Pharmacy. They ordered it for me weeks ago," she said as if I'd asked a stupid question, and I thought again how much like Hector she could be when it came to the little things.

"Who ordered for you—Pedro?" I asked.

When she shook her head no, I knew why they hadn't arrested her yet.

But before I tell you how I knew, let me shoot you a Polaroid picture of the hybrid nature of Coffee Park shops. Like the locksmith whose wife also bakes empanadas and makes *lulo* juice for lunch, as if his shop were a cafeteria, or the yoga studio where they also give massages and teach beading classes, and the pharmacy, of course, which functioned like a remedy store, stocking everything from ointments, to herbs, to imported tonics and leaves from every part of the world. In other words, our shops, they're, let's say, informal.

Then there were Pedro and Sarah.

Sarah had been the only other person who ever tended the register or processed special orders. I remembered how distracted she'd been toward the end of their relationship. And how I'd thought it was all the fighting with Pedro that made her forget to write down what you were buying, forget to make the order sheet with the duplicate that would have served as your receipt, forgetting also to put the cash inside the register, "distractedly" saving, I saw now, for her getaway.

Since it was a cash-only establishment, there was no credit card to track and, thanks to Sarah, no record of the order. But even though Sarah would have remembered a belladonna purchase, she wouldn't have told the police a thing. That is, if she'd been around to tell, which she hadn't been, having gone back home the very week of Hector's death, if I remembered Iris's account of it correctly.

I was sure the police had searched all the nearby pharmacies for orders of belladonna plants, leaves, or seeds, starting with

Coffee Park's. But if Sarah had not written it down, I doubted Pedro would have thought to say anything other than "We would have had to order it, and I see no record of that on our special-order pad." I wondered if, when double-checking for the police, even looking at Sarah's handwriting on that pad had made him miss her, and if in his sadness, he could have been less than concerned about helping the policeman or woman, who'd be, in any case, just another outsider to him, if not the outright law-enforcing enemy.

"So did you dilate Henry's eyes with the belladonna?" I prodded.

But Olivia just looked into her food for a while, then:

"Have you ever been in love, Mariela?"

"What do you mean? I mean . . . I guess, maybe," I said, unsure of where she was going.

"You meet a man. A wonderful god of a man. He makes you laugh, he makes you think, he makes everything fascinating, exuberant, and wonderful. You're in love and you're loved and nothing else matters. And then, something terrible happens. You can't give him the one thing he says he wants the most: a child. And you watch this man be sad, so sad, that you offer to let him go, to go about his life without you, to find happiness somewhere else even though you know that the minute he's gone, your life will become as small and dark and airless as a crowded coat closet."

She'd started trembling like she did the day she'd given me tea and returned my breakup letter, so I took the bowl she still held in her hands away from her and set it on the night table. Then I sat on the edge of the bed, took her hands in mine, and closing my eyes, I listened.

"But he wouldn't leave me. Can you imagine the sacrifice? He said I was his wife and we'd stay together. And then he kept his word: When there was trouble at the university with the economic crisis and my parents wouldn't help us, he didn't hesitate. He decided to come here, and he worked hard, and we bought the house, and later the bookstore. Then, just a bit before the whole mortgage mess a few years ago, he took charge again. He said, 'Olivia, you're my home, and I am your home. We don't need these walls, this roof.' So we sold it and paid off the mortgage on the bookstore, which he placed in my name. He'd joke I could leave him penniless if I ever wanted to. But he knew I wouldn't. Never. No matter what."

Her hands moved violently within mine, like those flashing vibrating gizmos they give you at franchise restaurants to alert you when your table is ready, but I held on.

"That was Hector on a good day," she said, a lone tear rolling down her sunken left cheek and landing on my hand.

"And on bad ones?"

"On bad ones he'd be hurtful. Couldn't help making me feel inadequate, ugly, a silly hen. He'd tell me all my suspicions of infidelity were my own inferiority complex making me crazy. He'd say I needed professional help. Sometimes, I'd be reading or gardening in the balcony or cooking in the kitchen, and in he'd come and ask me how much we had saved up, and when I'd tell him, he'd say the amount wouldn't even begin to cover my psychiatric hospital costs the way I was going."

I listened, knowing both Hectors were true Hectors.

"About a year ago, I told him about you."

"About me?"

"I told him I knew all about you. I told him I didn't know if he was sleeping with you, but that if he hadn't, he would, and I promised him I'd leave him when he did. The next day he brought me a Spanish-language copy of Sylvia Plath's *The Bell Jar*. Told me to read it and decide if that was the life I wanted, because I sounded just like the crazy, suicidal woman in those pages. That I saw women everywhere, that I was delusional. He said that he didn't mind carrying one burden, but that my torturing him was just too much. Sometimes, he'd even convince me, make me apologize."

I hugged her then, letting her cry on my shoulder, knowing, absolutely knowing, that she wasn't telling me everything, that things had been worse than she was sharing.

Someone else, someone not a woman, might ask why she hadn't just left him. But I knew the truth of us: If we could, we'd leave them all—the chronic bad boys, the frauds, the violent abusers, the unreliable, the lazy, the egotistical, the bad in bed, even the ones who pose as "good men" but have the relentless ability to turn every single happy moment into a day trip to the nearest latrine. We hang on, looking and feeling, and taking notes right on our hearts, until we manage to be able to breathe, to stand, to tell ourselves we're not crazy. That what we are is strong. And then, we leave.

Or we kill them. Was that the way it had happened? I still couldn't see Olivia poisoning Hector.

She was pushing me away now, dabbing at her eyes as she got up and walked to the bathroom, raising her shift to her waist with the door open, not caring that I could see her drop her panties and sit down to pee, still crying.

I busied myself propping up her sweaty pillows, until she came back and sat on the chair, right on top of the change of clothes someone—she, I assumed—had laid out.

"So I put together the remedy. When the belladonna tincture was ready, I called the boy's mother. She'd given me her number about a dozen times, always when she saw me with Hector. I'd always thought she was just friendly, if a bit irritating. Now I know it was her way of threatening him with telling me about the boy. But that day, I just told her what I was doing and asked her if Henry was allergic to anything."

"Oh, God," I gasped, seeing everything as she spoke, like watching a movie trailer after the movie has premiered, my clairvoyance no better than an old DVD when it came to Hector's mess.

"She said, 'Do you know your husband is a son of a bitch?' I told her I knew no such thing. That calling her had been a bad idea. Because I knew. I knew what she was about to tell me, and I didn't want to hear about another betrayal. I even remember thinking I didn't want her to tell me because I'd have to move. And I didn't want to move again. Now, isn't that silly?" she said, smiling a forlorn half smile.

"And that's when she told you?"

"How Hector had seduced her and then refused to do anything but give her money for an abortion. How she'd been too scared and alone to know what to do. How she had planned to be proud, to call him when her son was president of the United States, only to hear him weep with remorse."

That certainly felt like Abril.

"What changed her mind?" I asked.

"Her family, I think. They were asking questions, telling her she was being a bad mother. That a child needed to know who his father was. So she came back prepared to do God knows what. But we'd moved, sold the house."

"You moved here."

"Yes, and so did she when she found him, which didn't take long. There was, of course, the bookstore, which I'd all but stopped tending or even visiting as I got more involved with my work at the nature center. She told me the plan had been to let him see how wonderful Henry was, how smart, how much like him. She thought he'd change his mind without having to take him to court. But he didn't. Instead, she says, he pressured her to sleep with him. She told me he'd taunt her, telling her I would never leave him. That he had nothing, which is true because by then all we had was in my name, and that all she'd get would be a handout dictated by a court."

"Well, he was wrong," I told her. "The only way that would have been true is if you had been divorced. Otherwise, your assets were still half his assets."

"That was Hector. Always thinking he was smarter than everybody else. That no one was smart enough to get him. Anyway, she told me she'd tried giving up, going about her life, dating the man downstairs . . . Gonzalo?"

"Gustavo."

"Yes, Gustavo. She said Hector was very jealous. She said he told her he could see her future, bearing many sons of different fathers, all different colors like test-tube aberrations."

"My God," was all I could say. Could Hector really have said such horrible things?

"She said, 'You want to know how much of a son of a bitch your husband is, lady?' I just held on to the phone, not saying a word. But she kept on screaming at me, said he promised her that if she broke up with Gustavo and slept with him one last time, he'd tell me about Henry."

I thought, knowing Hector, that "one last time" had not been the extent of his plan, until he tired of her being more likely.

"She said she'd sue us both, assured me she'd already been to see a lawyer. She told me he'd pay for what he was doing to her son, that he wouldn't get away with it."

"But she didn't see a lawyer," I said. The threats had been about getting Hector to spend time with Henry, sure as any mother would be, that once he did, he'd love their son as much as she. It had been a good plan. But she'd completely miscalculated Hector's narcissism or his apparent lack of fatherly genes.

"Then she said something about how he was going to have to wait the entire night at the park because she was through playing his game," said Olivia.

"The park!" I gasped, wondering if I'd been mistaken, if

we'd all been mistaken: Hector, me, even the police in thinking it was the belladonna that had killed him instead of the furious mother of a child scorned too long.

"Yes. She told me that she'd agreed to see him in the park at eleven that night, but only because all she wanted was for her son to know himself loved by his father," said Olivia, confirming my suspicions about Abril's motives. "But that now—hearing me 'condescendingly' ask about her son's allergies as if I were asking about his diseases, as she put it, which I'm sure I did not do— she'd changed her mind. She said she was glad I knew it all now because if I stayed with him, I'd know who I was staying with and we could both rot in hell. How was her sleeping with my husband my fault, Mariela, tell me that?"

It wasn't. Abril had just exploded after years of impotence. Plus, I was sure Olivia underestimated how condescending she could sound. She didn't realize how her own shyness made her out to be the superior witch we'd all imagined.

"What did you do?"

"Nothing," she said. "I sat here like a stupid woman, remembering all the times he'd told me he would've given anything for a child of his own, and I knew: He never did. He never did, Mariela. All he really wanted to do was torture me. Bring me down. Manipulate me into turning a blind eye to his, to his women!" she said, looking at me, no doubt wanting to call Hector's women by another name, but remembering I'd been one of them and catching herself.

"It was all a game to him," she continued. "By the time he came in that night from being with you, or with her, or whoever, I was consumed with rage. I couldn't think, or breathe, or even look at him."

She looked consumed with rage now: Her eyes were stretched wide, as if struggling to free themselves of their sockets, her temples pulsing.

"He made fun of me, asked me what I was doing sitting in

the dark with my mess all over the kitchen. He started picking at food, talking and talking, not noticing anything. Not noticing me. And I felt the hate of decades. *Do you know what that is? Do you know what that feels like?* My life, Mariela. He'd made it miserable for nothing. He didn't want a child. He didn't love me. He loved and wanted nothing but himself."

"Olivia, please calm down. You don't look well." I walked over to her, a little afraid I admit, and tried to get her to leave the chair where she'd sat, to come over to the bed.

"And then he saunters over to the counter and just rambles on, looks at the cutting table, at the leaves and lemons and the honey I had there to add in case a thicker consistency were needed, and says, 'I'm going out again,' and then as if I were completely stupid, 'Meeting with some bookstore people. Don't wait up.' And I looked at him and I saw it: the boy. I hadn't been able to put my finger on it, but there had been something about his face that had always seemed familiar to me. And that was it. For the first time, I wanted him gone. Away from me, from her, from all women. Away where he couldn't hurt anyone, and I . . ."

She looked at me for a few seconds, then turned away.

"You what," I pressed.

Still, she was silent for a few long minutes.

"Sometime after the first decade of marriage, when you know him like you know your own face, you feel it, the bulk of the debris that has been accumulating, making a lump there, against your side. It's just as possible for you to love him as it is to hate him, the line between the two varying first from year to year, then from season to season, month to month, week to week, and finally, it happens frequently, quickly, scaring you."

"What did you do, Olivia?" I whispered.

"I let it happen," she choked out.

I didn't understand, but I waited.

"He kept tasting everything, making an even bigger mess, and I knew he'd stick his fingers into the belladonna resin I'd prepped in such a way as to maintain its effectiveness, bringing out the power of the alkaloids, its curative compounds, but also its most poisonous properties if ingested. I knew he would and I did nothing. Knowing he smoked, knowing he had respiratory issues."

"What did that matter?"

"It's belladonna's insurance policy. It may or may not kill a person who swallows it. Many people are only able to get high on it. But it will almost certainly kill a smoker, or an asthmatic, if ingested. The alkaloids—"

"Oh my God. What did you do?"

"Nothing. I stood there, looking at him, hating him, watching him put his fingers into everything, watching him lie to me, again. After a few minutes, he turned a little pale, and I almost said something, but I couldn't speak. Even after he walked out, I wanted to run after him, but I couldn't move. I killed him. I killed him for me. I killed him for the little boy. I killed him. I killed him. I killed him . . ."

She kept repeating it as if she'd had all those "I killed him's" inside of her and needed to vomit them. Then she cried for a long time. I sat there with her until she dropped back onto the pillows from pure exhaustion and fell into a shaky, tortured sleep.

Then I got to work. I found her cleaning supplies. And I cleaned her apartment, wiping everything, trying to get rid of all her pain. It had been a second of hate, born of years of love. She hadn't planned it. And she was paying for it, wasn't she? Doing something about it was not my business, and it wouldn't bring Hector back, not that he wanted me to do something about it, quite the contrary, I reminded myself, my decision strengthening inside me.

I cleaned and thought and cleaned and thought, realizing he had loved her in his own way, and she'd loved him, and yet, this is how it ended.

I wondered how many marriages were that one hateful second away from a precipice they wouldn't be able to back away from. And here I'd thought my marriages had been dangerous. Well, I'd had no idea how bad they could've been, I thought.

A couple of hours later, I heard a noise and went in to check on her, finding her fully dressed with the clothes that had been on the chair.

"Where're you going? You're not strong enough."

"Turning myself in."

"Please don't."

"I have to. I can't live like this, knowing—"

Had he known she was going to do this? He'd thought she was going to hurt herself, commit suicide. This was different. Should I let her turn herself in? But before I knew it, my heart spoke for me.

"You can't do it because Hector doesn't want you to."

"What?"

"I . . . had a dream."

"You had a dream?"

"Yes." I swallowed.

"Please, don't patronize me."

"I'm not, I swear. I actually came up to help you . . . to tell you something . . . you know, when I came up."

She sat down on the bed then, and I decided to waste no time saying what I had to say.

"Olivia, last night, I had a dream," I said, because who was to say it hadn't been a dream? "And I . . . in the dream, I spoke to Hector. He said he understood, that he forgives you. He said he loves you and wants you to live."

She smirked.

"Did you even know Hector? He would never say that."

"Well, he did. He said, asked me to tell you that, that you were his Olivia. That you'd always be his olive tree, that he wants—"

"What did you say?"

I knew what had made her eyes widen, what she needed me to repeat.

"That you are his olive tree."

"Shut up! Stop it!" she said, seizing me by the shoulders and shaking me.

I assumed she meant talking, so I did, and after a few minutes of looking at every inch of my face, she let go of me.

"I'm telling you the truth," I ventured.

Her eyes still trained on me, she sat on the chair again.

"Then tell me. The dream," she said then.

So I told her, combining the good bits of Hector I'd been lucky to receive over the past two weeks into one dream, editing it in my mind, trying to give her a gift.

Because if Hector had given me gifts of passion, excitement, and culture while we'd been together, Olivia had given me a mirror in which to see myself and my life. And maybe she'd never be my friend. But she was, I decided that day, my sister. She had not intended his death. She'd made a mistake that she'd have to work her whole life to forgive herself for. But Hector was gone, while I could still save her.

In fact, the more I looked at her face alternately cry and light up as I told her some of the funny details of my weeks-long "dream," the sharing of memory a reprieve for how desperately she must have been missing him all those weeks, I knew that she was worth saving. That I'd convince her, somehow, not to turn herself in, and that I would keep her secret.

Chapter 30

The black-and-white sign commissioned for placement at the entrance to Jorge's new restaurant almost got made spelling **MARIELA'S** in big bold letters, and beneath that, in smaller, cursive letters, *a bohemian community eatery*. Instead, high above the cement portico with the wooden beams rests a more appropriate sign, reading simply, **Sí**, which means "yes" in Spanish, but sounds like the word *see* in English. I didn't come up with it. Jorge did, and I love it. I love that it's about seeing, about saying yes to seeing, about seeing all that's around you and being aware, the awareness making you happier than you ever thought possible. I love how clearly he must see me to have come up with it. Lately, I've begun to see how much we really do love each other.

I look at the big plate in front of me. The small, round, dark gray cement tabletop has old tile pieces embedded here and there. The plate is made of white porcelain, but of an irregular round shape, somewhere between stone and glass.

There are seven thinly sliced pieces of cheese on one side of it: sheep's and goat's milk cheese, Jarlsberg, others I don't recognize. The other side of the plate is lined with quarter-moon avocado slices drizzled with olive oil and sprinkled with smoked salt so coarse, I can see it without straining my eyes, its color the color of brown sugar. A small hand-painted bowl full of quince marmalade sits in the center of the plate, the delicate handle of a small silver spoon sticking out of it like a tongue about to lick its lips. This plate, the rustic baguette positioned nearby on a piece of wood, and the tall, clear glass bottle with lemon slices floating in water seem, at the moment, all I need to feel the most blessed of women.

The place has come to life, but as beautiful as each detail of it is to me, the most amazing thing about it is still the statue, the one Gustavo had begun with the intention of entering the East Little Havana Development Agency contest, but decided to give to Jorge as a "restaurant-warming" gift. The piece that had Gustavo's heartbreak embedded all over, and was even more beautiful for it. It is huge and has many curves and swirls of different sizes . . . the oxidized metal goes from the darkest chocolate browns in some places to mustard yellow, turquoise, and deep azure blue in others. For the occasion of today's opening, he has placed a thin piece of gauze the color of wet sand and the shape of a summer dress over it, and from a few feet away you can see it is a woman hugging a bundle to her breasts. It is a mother, the long curlicues of her rusty silver hair floating in the wind. Rather than positioned to welcome visitors as they come in, she appears to be walking in with them, as if coming home to someone. I long to touch and pray to her, if only as a symbol of us, women.

But not now. Now I sit, enjoying the cheese and the quince, watching Jorge beam as he welcomes the guests, searching for me with his eyes every once in a while and smiling, Gustavo at his side, everyone oohing and marveling at the simple, sophisticated beauty of everything.

And then I see her, as if the statue had made Gustavo's dream come true. Abril and Henry are crossing the street toward them, and I can't help thinking of Hector, waiting for her in the park, doubling over in pain, dying alone, the three women in his life mere yards away, all three furious at him.

But I shake the thought. His death wasn't Abril's fault, and I'm glad she came. I thought I wouldn't get a chance to say good-bye to Henry after the cleansing cyclone of events that had descended on our lives since that day I'd spent with Olivia. I couldn't believe almost a whole month had gone by since that morning that had turned into afternoon and then evening, the last leg of my scavenger hunt for the last of the missing pieces to the puzzle of Hector's life and marriage, his affairs, and his death.

First, Olivia had made me tell her my "dream" again, as if gathering strength from it. Then we'd gone over the details of what had really happened.

Hector had been trying to pick a fight with her that night, we decided, to intimidate her into not questioning where he was going at that late hour. That's why he had acted particularly obnoxious. After swigging back a mouthful of the belladonna mixture and pronouncing it a waste of money and time like all her "macrobiotic nonsense," he'd left so quickly, she'd barely had a chance to react. She remembered thinking there was no point to anything: He would never change.

She'd woken around six in the morning and grown desperate when she realized Hector hadn't returned. She'd called his cell phone over and over, then called the police, and then began to call the hospitals after police told her he hadn't been gone long enough to file a report, her due diligence making her innocence more plausible in the eyes of the detectives investigating the case. Sometime around seven that morning, she'd heard the screaming and the rumble of people, and known, even before the officers knocked on her door.

"How come they didn't find the belladonna? Did you throw it away?"

"There was none to find. I discarded the bag it came in when I bought it and had been drying it in brown paper bags from the flower market. And whatever Hector didn't take, I rinsed away when cleaning the kitchen that night, knowing my remedy would never reach the boy, to judge from his mother's attitude that day. There was nothing left by the time they asked if they could look around."

As she spoke, I remembered waking up early that morning, my birthday, cutting my hair, walking to Tinta in search of coffee, without a clue that the insistent thoughts of Hector popping into my head were more about his death than about our breakup.

"For a while they believed he'd been robbed, and I felt relieved that it had been a mugging, that I hadn't hurt him or failed to save him from himself, from me," she said.

As we talked, she'd kept insisting that the only way to atone, to live with herself was to turn herself in.

"Wouldn't it be better if you did something worthwhile instead?"

"Like what?"

"How about you work things out with Abril? Make sure Henry is provided for, dedicate your life to coming up with new remedies that will help people, I don't know. What good would it do Hector for you to end up in jail, if that's even a possibility? You yourself said he left almost immediately after he took the belladonna. Had you not been so distraught, you would have warned him, wouldn't you?"

Which made her cry again, saying, "I really would have, Mariela. I was angry, but I could never really hurt him."

Of course we both knew she *had* hurt him, that she'd wanted to, even if just for that one minute. All her life loving him despite everything, and in one moment, hate had overtaken her, defeating her.

I kept talking, figuring I had a good chance she'd listen. The fact that she hadn't turned herself in when they told her the results of the autopsy could only mean that she had been too scared or weak to do it. All I needed to do now was to give her a good reason not to do what, to her, was "the right thing."

Instead, I had to give her something else to do that would also be a right thing, a better thing than turn herself in that she could do to atone.

That's how papers were filed that would soon give Henry a new last name: Ferro, and some treasury bonds to go with it, as well as his father's entire rare book collection, and more money coming to him when the bookstore sold and Hector's estate was executed.

Olivia decided to move back to Argentina to be with her family, and Abril decided to move back to New York and do the same. At some point, she, and the rest of Coffee Park, had apparently decided to stop hating and fearing me, even though no one ever really found out exactly how and why Hector died.

Now Abril was going to start over in New York, away from this place that no longer held any real sway for her. She'd come over to tell me herself a few days ago and to thank me, refusing to answer my "For what?" or to get into details, as if all were understood and she trusted I too would forgive her, that I'd understand the spell of resentment and confusion she'd lived in all the time she'd known me.

"I'm going to New York!" said Henry now, trying to jump into my arms, orthopedic shoes and all, before I could make it all the way from my out-of-the-way table to the entrance where they stood.

"Yes, I know, darling. Are you excited?"

Henry smiled wide and nodded as if he were trying to get his head to come off.

"Remember what I told you."

It was Gustavo, who had walked over, followed by Abril.

"To take good care of my mom?" said Henry.

"Yes. Take care of your mom and study hard," said Gustavo.

"I always study hard. I study so hard that—"

He didn't get to finish the sentence—Gustavo was hugging him so hard.

"Hey, you're squashing me. Let go!"

"Sorry, little man," said Gustavo.

"Not cool," said Henry, smoothing his little guayabera.

"You're right, not cool. I'm sorry."

"It's okay. Better than crying."

"A man can cry and be a man, you know?"

"I know. I cry sometimes too," said Henry. Then he whispered, "But not in front of *them,*" using his chin to gesture toward Abril and me.

Which made everyone smile.

Iris made her appearance just then, in a fabulous hot pink wraparound jersey dress and silver sequin high heels.

Soon, we'd sat to eat together, with Jorge coming over every few minutes with more food for us or a kiss for me, which made it impossible for anyone at the table to believe me when I said we were taking it slow, seeing how it went.

Looking at him, I remembered how he'd been sitting on my stoop a few days after that night in the park. Jorge had been waiting for me, he said, and heard noises in the empty apartment that had been Ellie's. The one I'd been avoiding and hadn't gotten around to renting, despite needing the money.

"Maybe we should check the apartment," he'd said.

"You think Ellie could have sneaked in? To do what?"

"I don't know, but maybe we should check it out," he insisted.

"All right, let me get my keys."

And then I'd walked into some other landlord's rental apartment. Because every inch of *apartamento tres* was now clean.

"What happened here?" I said, looking at the half-used cleaning supplies I'd bought the morning of Hector's death, neatly arranged on the counter.

"You like? Iris said it just needed a little cleaning. Cool, huh?"

"Are you kidding? It's beyond cool. I can't believe you and Iris did all this by yourselves. I don't know what to say."

"Gustavo helped."

"This is amazing! I love you! And Gustavo and Iris," I'd said, meaning it, feeling loved and grateful, and laughing when Jorge said, he'd prefer it if I loved just him, but would share with Gustavo and Iris for now.

It was the same feeling I had now, surrounded by these people I loved, letting myself almost float out of my body to look at the scene, to see myself being happy so that I'd never forget what it was like or that it was possible.

I also felt my mother close to me that night, a feeling that had become more frequent over the past month, and that I can only describe to you as a deep, all-encompassing well-being. It was so complete, this feeling, I didn't even need to call her to me or to speak to her to know her essence would always be with me, her adored child. And even though I didn't see myself making a career out of clairvoyance that night, I could see it being a part of my life again, could see helping people do what they didn't yet know how to do for themselves or were afraid to do, loving and being proud of what husband number one had once accused me of as if it were a bad thing, this "making nice with the tenants." It was called community, and I loved being part of one.

And there we all were: Gustavo, Abril, Henry, Iris, and I, celebrating Jorge's restaurant, his dream come true, saying good-bye to Henry and Abril with love and warm hearts, eating, drinking, reminiscing, and laughing, feeling the bittersweet excitement of new beginnings, hoping and dreaming about the turns our lives would soon take, all of us enjoying this last chance to be together under the moonlit skies of Coffee Park.

The Clairvoyant of Calle Ocho

Anjanette Delgado

ABOUT THIS GUIDE

The suggested questions are included
to enhance your group's reading
of Anjanette Delgado's
The Clairvoyant of Calle Ocho.

Discussion Questions

1. What specific themes are emphasized in *The Clairvoyant of Calle Ocho*? What do you think was the author's purpose in emphasizing those themes?

2. What kind of character is the heroine, Mariela Estevez? Would you say she is an antiheroine? If so, does she remain so throughout the novel?

3. What is the view that the book presents of "other women" or mistresses?

4. What is the view the book presents of clairvoyants? And, after reading the book, would you say the book demystifies clairvoyance and psychic abilities in general?

5. What was unique about the setting of *The Clairvoyant of Calle Ocho,* and how did it enhance or distract from the main story?

6. Speaking of which, what was the main story? Is this novel about clairvoyance? Is it about infidelity? Is it about the sisterhood among women, in spite of men? Or is it about all of the above, and, if so, how are those themes woven into Mariela's story?

7. Did you think the book's portrayal of Latinos is accurate? Or did you find the portrayal specific to Caribbean immigrants living in South Florida, and therefore, distinctive?

8. Were you aware that Coffee Park is a creation of the author's mind and does not exist as described within the confines of Little Havana? What made it real for you?

9. Could Mariela have solved the mystery of Hector's death without his ghost?

10. In the novel, the relationships between women are as important as, if not more important than, male-female relationships. Was this realistic for you as a reader? Did you believe the relationship that develops between Mariela and her lover's wife, Olivia? Do you know of such relationships in real life? If not, what made this one believable for you?

11. Under what genre would you catalogue this novel: women's literary fiction, chick lit, or mystery?

12. Did *The Clairvoyant of Calle Ocho* remind you of other books you've read? If so, which ones and in what way?

13. What characters did you feel changed or evolved the most in the novel, and how?

14. Did you feel that the events of the novel reveal the author's point of view?

15. And finally, did any part of the book make you uncomfortable? If so, why do you think you felt that way? Did this lead you to a new understanding or awareness of some aspect of life or society that you had not thought about before reading it?